'It made me smile . . . and the last chapter or two had me laughing out loud several times'
mac-adventureswithbooks.blogspot.co.uk

'This is a wonderful, heart-warming book with a great big dollop of humour, guaranteed to draw in the reader and hold their interest until the very last page'
thecuriousgingercat.blogspot.co.uk

'A touching story of friendship and growing up. *A Robot in the Garden* is a very unique and quirky read'
lynseysbooks.blogspot.co.uk

'*A Robot in the Garden* WILL make you laugh, it WILL make you shed a tear, it WILL make you stay up reading way past your bedtime'
bookaholicconfessions.wordpress.com

'IT REALLY HIT ME RIGHT IN THE FEELS OKAY. I found myself hugging this book after I finished.'
realitysabore.blogspot.co.uk

'I absolutely loved *A Robot in the Garden*. It's good fun, it's got a lot of heart but it also has some serious points to make . . .'
thewritesofwoman.wordpress.com

'*A Robot in the Garden* is such a brilliantly plotted novel which left me gripped and wishing my morning commute was longer!'
gymkhanaclub.me

'This book of unconditional friendship is so unique that I have a feeling it is destined for great things.'
sincerelybookangels.blogspot.co.uk

D0240734

'If you're going to read one story this year
then I suggest this one!'
wordsfromareader.weebly.com

'This is a beautiful, humorously written book about
relationships . . . loss, discovering who you are, what's
important to you (and having a really fun road
trip along the way) . . .'
the-bookshelf-reviews.blogspot.co.uk

'. . . a magical story . . . It will have you smiling and you
might even end up having to get a robot for yourself'
aloverofbooks.wordpress.com

'It is a great summer read . . . pick it up
and get lost in the story'
trishbsblog.tumblr.com

'. . . a quick, engrossing read, with some really
cute and funny moments.'
magazine.100percentrock.com

'. . . an original story . . . It shows humanity at its best and
its worst, but does so with the lightest of touches. I have no
reservations about recommending this book to all.'
neverimitate.wordpress.com

A ROBOT IN THE GARDEN

Deborah Install

BLACK SWAN

TRANSWORLD PUBLISHERS
61–63 Uxbridge Road, London W5 5SA
www.transworldbooks.co.uk

Transworld is part of the Penguin Random House group of companies
whose addresses can be found at global.penguinrandomhouse.com

Penguin
Random House
UK

First published in Great Britain in 2015 by Doubleday
an imprint of Transworld Publishers
Black Swan edition published 2016

Copyright © Deborah Install 2015

Deborah Install has asserted her right under the Copyright,
Designs and Patents Act 1988 to be identified as the author of this work.

This book is a work of fiction and, except in the case of historical fact,
any resemblance to actual persons, living or dead, is purely coincidental.

Every effort has been made to obtain the necessary permissions with
reference to copyright material, both illustrative and quoted. We apologize
for any omissions in this respect and will be pleased to make the
appropriate acknowledgements in any future edition.

A CIP catalogue record for this book
is available from the British Library.

ISBN 9781784160524

Typeset in 10½/14pt Scala by Kestrel Data, Exeter, Devon
Printed and bound by Clays Ltd, Bungay, Suffolk

Penguin Random House is committed to a sustainable future
for our business, our readers and our planet. This book is made
from Forest Stewardship Council® certified paper.

MIX
Paper from
responsible sources
FSC® C018179
www.fsc.org

1 3 5 7 9 10 8 6 4 2

For Stef and Toby,
my inspiration

1

Underdog

'THERE'S A ROBOT IN THE GARDEN,' MY WIFE INFORMED ME.

I heard her footsteps a few seconds later, then her head appeared round the bedroom door. I glanced up from the newspaper I was reading in bed to see that look of hers – the one that says *'you are a continual source of frustration to me'*.

I looked blank.

'I said, there's a robot in the garden.'

With a little sigh, I threw back the duvet and went over to the window that overlooked our unruly back garden.

'Why would there be a robot in the garden? Have you left that bloody gate open again, Amy?'

'If you fixed it, as I keep asking you to,' she replied, 'then it wouldn't be a problem. Old houses need maintenance, Ben, and so do gardens. If we could just get someone in . . .'

I ignored this.

Drawing the curtain back properly, I stared out of the window. Sure enough, there was a robot in the garden.

It was half past seven in the morning when the robot entered our lives. I didn't need to be up at that time, but since my parents died six years ago – just before I met Amy – I had found it difficult to sleep in in the morning. My house had been their house, my childhood home, and in my head my mother's voice called me from downstairs to 'get up and make use of the day' the second I woke up.

I stumbled downstairs after Amy, eyes half-closed and still hoping for a gentle introduction to the day by way of reading the paper. In the kitchen, I found Amy had already staked her claim to it by setting a mug of tea and a cream-cheese bagel down upon the society pages. She was wearing her most severe work clothes – a navy pinstripe trouser suit and bright-white, wide-lapelled shirt paired with vicious heels. Her naturally blonde hair was scraped into a perfect roll at the back of her head, and she was wearing full make-up – all of which indicated she had a serious day in court ahead of her. She didn't seem in the mood to converse, so I made myself a strong black coffee and retreated to my study. Not *my* study . . . my father's, I suppose. I had no need for a study as such, but when Amy worked from home in the evenings she preferred to be in the sitting room, and it suited her if I was out of the way.

As I sipped my coffee, I could hear her stacking the dishwasher from the night before, while I turned aimlessly around on my old desk chair – my father's old desk chair – which creaked and protested with every spin. I saw my father's books that lined the study walls rotate around me, the early-morning sun highlighting the dust that lived on top of their pages and which emerged every day for a wander around.

I put the radio on to listen to the breakfast show. The sound of hi-ball glasses and dinnerware clinking carried over the top of it and across the hallway, every so often punctuated by the click of high heels stalking across the kitchen, then followed by a short silence as Amy ate and drank her breakfast. It was all done briskly, and I frowned as I tried to remember what she'd told me about today – whether she was expecting a difficult court case to close or another to open.

After a long pause, she called to me, and when I didn't reply she sought me out.

'I said, there's a robot in the garden . . .'

The robot was about four feet and two inches tall, by my reckoning, and about half of that wide, with a boxy metal head and body, and rivets that seemed like shoddy workmanship, not that I knew what they should look like. He had squat little legs that looked like spray-painted tumble-dryer venting tubes and arms to match, with flat plates for feet and hands that were like the ends of those grabber things that old people have. All in all, he looked the very picture of a school project.

'Do you think it's alive?' Amy asked, as we stood peering through the kitchen window.

'Alive? You mean as in sentient? Or alive as in functioning?'

'Just go and have a look.'

I told her she should go first, as she had been the first to see it. My suggestion drew from my wife the same look she gives me when I propose she buy herself some flowers if she wants some.

'I haven't time for this, Ben. You go.' She strode into the sitting room to gather up her papers and briefcase from the coffee table. I went round to the back door, and as I turned the handle I heard the front door slam.

*

The robot was sitting under the willow with his back to our window and his legs sticking straight out in front of him. There were droplets of water on his metal casing from the autumn dew, and he looked a fusion of some sort of Japanese fine art and materials from a scrapyard. He did not seem to be moving, but as I drew closer I saw he was looking towards a field of horses beyond our garden. It became clear from the slight side-to-side turns of his head that he was watching them.

I stopped a little way from him and paused. I was unsure how to begin a conversation with a robot. Though we'd never had one in the house while we were growing up, I'd known friends who did, and it was generally reckoned that they weren't too bothered about things like greetings as long as they had a job to do. They were mostly domestic servants – shiny chrome and white-plastic artists' dummies who pottered round your house doing the vacuuming and making breakfast, and now and then maybe picking up your children from school. My sister had one and my wife wanted one, but I'd never seen the need with only the two of us in the house. Cheaper ones were available, too, which were not as shiny and had less functionality. These might only iron your shirts and take your recycling out. But I'd never seen one like this. Even the cheap robots weren't this shabby.

'Er . . . hello?'

The robot gave a jolt, startled. He squealed and tried to scramble to his feet but fell with a thud on to his side, exposing a flattened square of grass. As he lay there, soles of his feet towards me, his legs kicked wildly like an upset ladybird. I felt compelled to help him.

'Are you OK?' I asked, pushing him back up into his former sitting position. He swivelled his head towards me and blinked a few times, his domed metal eyelids whirring. Under his eyelids, two shiny spheres flicked up and down as the robot studied me, pupils like camera shutters widening and narrowing according to what he was looking at. Below his eyes sat a nose the size and shape of a Lego brick, which seemed to me to serve no purpose other than aesthetics. His mouth was a dark rectangular gap that looked to be an old CD drive; the maker had obviously had one spare and gathering dust somewhere, and so put it to good use.

There were little dinks and dents all over him, and if he moved suddenly, his rattling chest-panel swung open to reveal a mixture of brass clockwork and intricate computer chips bound up together in a way I couldn't begin to under-stand. Evidently his creator was an artisan of both the high-tech and the old school. At the centre of this mechanical mess radiated a light that pulsed rhythmically and which I assumed must be his robot heart. I peered more closely and saw that next to it was a glass cylinder containing a yellow liquid, the function of which was not apparent. On closer examination, I saw a tiny crack in the glass, but I thought no more of it.

As I stood contemplating him in the breeze, I saw just how filthy his bodywork was. From the detritus that was sticking to him, it appeared as though the journey he'd been through to get here had included crossing a desert, a farmyard and then a city. Since I had no idea where he came from, this could very well have been the case.

I crouched down next to him on the grass.

'What's your name?'

He made no response, so I pointed a finger at my chest. 'Ben. You are?' Then I pointed to him.

'Tang.' His voice was jangly and electronic.

'Tang?'

'Tang. Tang. Ac-rid Tang. Tang!'

'OK, OK . . . I get it. Why are you in my garden, Tang?'

'August.'

'It's not August, Tang,' I said gently. 'It's the middle of September.'

'August.'

'September.'

'August! August! August!'

I paused for a moment and then tried a different line of enquiry. 'Where do you come from, Tang?'

He blinked at me but said nothing.

'Is there anyone I can call to come and get you?'

'No.'

'Excellent, we're getting somewhere. How long are you planning to stay in my garden, Tang?'

'Acrid Tang . . . Tang . . . Tang . . . Tang . . .'

I repeated my questions gently.

'Tang! Acrid Tang . . . August . . . no . . . no . . . no!'

I folded my arms with a sigh.

When Amy arrived home from work twelve hours later, she opened the back door and waved me in.

'Stay here,' I told Tang, though there seemed to be no need. For most of the morning I'd sat in my study and ignored him in case he went away of his own accord, but he hadn't budged. The rest of the day I'd spent going back and forth between the house and the robot, trying to think of ways to get through to him. By the time Amy got back, his obstinacy alone had piqued my interest.

'What's happening?' she asked, then raised an eyebrow as she noted my bottle-green pyjama bottoms and old blue dressing gown – the same clothes I'd been wearing when she left the house that morning. She hated that dressing gown; it always smelled musty no matter how many times it was washed.

'Well, it's a boy robot,' I said, 'or at least it sounds like one, anyway.'

'Do they have a gender?'

'Generally, I'm not sure. This one does, though. He's a bit different.'

'It certainly is. It's not even a basic model.'

'No, I mean he's different as in special.'

Amy wrinkled her nose at this and said, 'How do you know?'

'I don't know. I just think he is.'

'Has it said anything?'

'He said his name was "Acrid Tang" and something about it being August.'

'But it's not August, it's the middle of September.'

'I know that. He's really beaten up – he's covered in dents and he's got a cylinder on his insides with a crack in it.'

'Oh great, so it's a broken robot, too. That's just perfect.'

I didn't react.

Amy softened slightly. 'What else did it say?'

'Not much.'

'Well, why is it here?'

'I don't know; he wouldn't say.'

'Well, how long is it—'

'Look, I don't know that either, all right? We didn't get that far.'

Amy narrowed her eyes.

'We can't just let it sit in the garden for ever, until it rusts. Go and talk to it again.'

'I've been trying to get through to him all day. You talk to him if you think you can do better.'

That look again – like a slapped kitten. I hated it when she ordered me around, but I also valued a quiet life, so finally, despite my frustration, I muttered, 'OK' and opened the back door.

After a week of this, Amy decided that having a second-rate robot in the garden was unsightly, and that she didn't want to see him every time she looked out of the kitchen window. I'd managed to get him to talk to me a little, but I hadn't managed to get him to move. Nor had I got very far in finding out where he came from.

'Can't you get rid of it?'

'Why me?'

'Because you're the one who's been talking to it.'

'But I can't get anything out of him . . .'

'Well, it can't stay in the garden.'

'How many times are we going to have this argument? If you want to get rid of him, then you find a way.'

'I think you like it. I think it's something else to concentrate on rather than finding a job.'

'Seriously, Amy, why does every single argument have to be about me being unemployed?'

'If you had a job, then we'd never have to have this argument . . .'

'We don't *have* to have it at all. I don't need a job, you know that.'

'Yes, yes, your parents left us plenty enough to live on

16

in their will, but a job isn't just about the money, don't you see?'

'No, I don't. And Tang's a "him", anyway, not an "it".'

Amy changed tack. 'The point is I'm not having a robot in the garden any more. Especially one like that.'

'What do you mean "one like that"?'

She gestured at him with her bare, goose-pimpled arm. 'You know . . . one like that. An old one. A broken one.'

'Oh, I see. It would be OK if it were a shiny, top-of-the-range robot, with fingers and toes and a proper face.'

'It might be.'

At least she was honest.

'Look, you've been insisting we get a robot for ages, and now we've got one. I don't see what the problem is.'

'That's like buying an old wreck of a car and asking what the problem is. I wanted an *android*. What can it do? It doesn't want to do anything but sit and stare at horses. What's all that about? What good is a robot if it's not useful? And if it's broken, then it'll need fixing. Why should we do it?'

'He's not *that* broken. Don't be so dramatic. And if he does need fixing, then we'll get him fixed.'

'By whom?'

I told her I didn't know but that I was sure someone out there could do the repair.

Amy threw up her hands in despair, turning away from me to clean the kitchen worktops with extra force. There was silence for a moment, then she mumbled, 'Anyway, like I say, I've been asking that we get an *android*, not a robot.'

'What's the difference?'

'There's a world of difference! Like you say: fingers and toes and a proper face, for a start. I want a new one like

Bryony's. She showed me the article about it in *What 'Bot?* It has the latest technology and everything.'

Bryony is my sister. She and Amy have been best friends for about five and a half years. Amy and I have been together for five and a quarter years.

'What could it do that this one can't?'

'Well, it could do some work around here, like clean and dust and do the gardening and things. If it could cook, too, that would be nice. I can't see this short little box being able to reach the cooker, let alone make a meal.'

'But you do the cooking.'

'Yes, exactly! I spend all day at work, trying to untangle some really difficult legal problems for some very difficult people. The last thing I want when I come home is to have to cook.'

'But I've offered to cook for you and you say you don't like anything I make – that it's experimental and unappetizing.'

'OK, the second to last thing I want when I come home is to cook. The very last thing I want is to face a plate of your partially cooked bacon.'

'I thought you liked bacon.'

'I do, but, Ben, you're missing the point! If we had an android, then I wouldn't have to prepare an evening meal and neither would you. I've seen them at friends' houses. You give them a recipe and point them in the direction of the fridge. Reliably good food every time.'

'You sound like an advert.'

'Oh, don't be so childish.'

Her words riled me, and I felt a prickle of irritation up the back of my neck. I knew I should leave the argument alone, but I couldn't.

'Just because all your friends have got one you want to

have one. I suppose you want one of those bloody Cybervalet things, too.'

'Of course I don't. Just a normal house android.'

'Where would we put it anyway?' I persisted. 'They need to go somewhere when they're not working. Don't they need to charge up or something?'

'Yes, and we've got space.'

'Where? The dock for Bryony's android takes up a huge amount of space in her utility room, and ours is tiny by comparison. And it needs an expert to plumb it in, or whatever it is they do with it. I just don't see the point.'

'No, you don't . . . and that in itself *is* the point. I would like an android not because all my friends have one but because it means I wouldn't have to do everything around the house as well as working in a full-time job.'

I just couldn't let this argument go.

'But I don't understand why we need an android for the house. I could do those other things.'

'Yes, yes, you could. But you don't, do you?'

'That's not fair, Amy, I do stuff around the house.'

'Like what?'

'I take the bins out.'

'You took the bins out two weeks ago.'

'Yes, when the rubbish collection was due.'

'Ben, the bins need taking out every few days.'

'That's ridiculous; they don't fill up that quickly.'

'That's because *I* take them out!'

'Do you?'

Amy gave me a long, hard stare. This squabble, like so many others we'd had, was a closed circuit, and the only way to end it was to break out. I returned to the original issue.

'Anyway, what do you suggest I do with this robot . . . the one that isn't good enough for you?'

Amy puckered her mouth then looked slightly uncomfortable. I wasn't going to like her suggestion, and she knew it, but I'd riled her so she didn't really care.

'Well, it's no good for anything, is it? So maybe just take it . . . take it to the tip?'

I paused for a moment at the horror of this suggestion. Admittedly, I was fascinated by our new visitor, and I wanted to find out more about him. I told Amy so.

'Besides, it's exciting, isn't it? A robot turning up out of nowhere?'

Hands on hips, Amy looked unconvinced, so, unusually, I decided to put my foot down before she had a chance to reply. 'This is my house, and I say he can stay as long as he wants.'

Amy glared at me, her eyebrows drawn together with stitches of fury. But she knew I was right. It was my house.

'It's my house, too, Ben,' she said quietly. 'I'm your wife. Don't I get a say?'

I bit my lip. 'Of course you do. But don't make me send him to the tip. At least let me find out where he comes from. Someone might be missing him.'

Amy agreed but asked me to at least move it into the garage and clean it up a bit.

'I can't invite anyone round at the moment with it sitting there.'

This was the point. Amy wanted everything to look perfect if any of her friends came to visit.

I made to put my arm around her, but before I could touch her she gave a little cough and turned away, leaving me alone in the kitchen.

2

Silence

THE NEXT MORNING, I SAT OPPOSITE THE ROBOT ON THE STEP just inside our integral garage; it was the only place to sit unless you counted the floor or the bonnet of the Honda Civic my parents had also bequeathed me. Amy insisted upon the old car staying in the garage, while her gleaming Audi stood proudly on the driveway.

Tang stared straight back at me, as if waiting for me to make some sort of breakthrough, but without his help I didn't see how I could. It was by now apparent that he didn't intend to go anywhere, and I decided that Amy was right: I should at least clean him.

I fetched a bowl of warm soapy water and our de facto car-cleaning sponge, but as I brought it dripping up to Tang's body he didn't seem keen. He stamped from foot to foot, looking agitated, until I put the sponge down. He looked at me like I was a fool.

'I guess you're worried about the water?'

He blinked.

'OK, how about if I use something smaller? Something that holds less water?'

I cast around and found a small rag, and though the robot still wasn't keen, at least he allowed me to get the worst of the dirt off. As I wiped him down gently, he wobbled from foot to foot, making it difficult to see where I'd wiped and what was left to do. Also, it seemed the rivets that joined panel to panel just weren't coming clean with a rag, and I was still only on his front. It was going to be a long task. It might take days. This pleased me. I knew, though, that it would not please Amy. She probably thought I'd throw a bucket of water over him and that would be that. Or perhaps she thought I'd take him to a carwash.

I left the garage to find more suitable cleaning tools.

'Amy? Amy? Where are you?'

'Upstairs. What do you want?'

'Have we got an old toothbrush?'

'An old toothbrush?'

'Yes.'

'Why do you want an old toothbrush?'

I didn't answer her straight away, because I'd had an idea. We had old battery-operated toothbrushes that we kept in our suitcases. They had been relegated for holiday use when we bought new electrosonic plaqueblaster ones, but Amy and I hadn't been away together for a while and so I didn't think they'd be missed.

'Er . . . never mind.'

I went to the spare room where we kept our suitcases and that sort of thing, and fished around for the toothbrushes. As I left the room, it occurred to me that one of the suitcases had recently been placed on the sofabed, not stacked beside it with the others.

*

There was something strange about cleaning a robot with an electric toothbrush. Maybe it was the hum of the brush as it worked away at the dirt on Tang's metal body or the look on the robot's face as he watched it uncover surfaces he'd clearly forgotten existed. Or maybe it was that the vibration of the brush kept popping his flap open, making the whole process longer, because I had to stop to shut it every few minutes. Eventually, I moved on to his underside. I got Tang to lie on his back while I carried out this uncomfortable part of the task. It was then that I made the discovery.

Sitting equidistant from each corner of Tang's under-carriage was a plate. Secured by four more slapdash rivets, it was battered and scratched, but clearly at one time some words had been inscribed. The light from the single overhead bulb was dim and it was too late in the day, and indeed the year, to sit with the door up, so I used the light from my phone to help me read the plate. There was barely anything left that was legible, save for a few half-words – 'PAL—' and 'Micron—'. A little way above these was an entire half-sentence: 'Property of B—'.

'Tang, who's "B"?'

Tang lifted his head as best he could and looked unblinkingly at me but made no answer.

Just then the door leading from the garage to the house opened, and I heard Amy's voice.

'So, why do you need a tooth . . . what the HELL are you doing?'

I can understand why she was alarmed. When she came downstairs, she probably didn't expect to see Tang lying flat on his back while I peered at his gusset like a gynaecologist, with a camera phone and an electric toothbrush in full oscillation.

'Amy, I know this looks bad, but I promise you I'm just cleaning him, as you asked.'

She looked unsure.

'Look, I found a clue about him.' I gestured to the plate, but she did not move.

'Ben, listen to yourself! You're asking me to look for clues UP A ROBOT'S ARSE.'

'But if you'd just look I can explain . . .'

'I'm going out.'

I winced as the door slammed. Tang started, too, making his flap jump.

I pulled him to his feet and asked again, 'Tang, who is "B"?'

He cast his eyes downward and didn't respond. I thought he must miss this B, whoever he was, and it didn't look as though he was coming to find Tang. I felt sorry for the little broken box.

Amy came back for dinner that night a lot calmer and in the mood to talk to me, unusually. I sat on a high stool in the kitchen as she cooked, and listened to her talk about her barrister work, keeping half an eye on Tang as he sat in the garden watching the horses. Amy had by now given up the fight to keep him concealed in the garage. We found we couldn't keep Tang anywhere he didn't want to be. At least he was clean, though.

As I watched her chop shallots, I decided she was amenable to hearing about the plate.

'So, Tang's plate . . . it says "Property of B—"'

Amy stiffened but tried to feign interest. 'Who's "B"?'

'I don't know. I asked Tang, but he wouldn't tell me.'

'*Quelle surprise.*'

It was almost a joke. I was pleased.

'The rest of the word has been scratched off over time. There were two other half-words on there as well: "Micron—" and "PAL—".'

Amy stopped chopping to consider this for a few moments. 'Maybe "Micron-something" is the name of the company that made him?'

'I thought so, too. I thought maybe they'd be able to fix him. I had a look online and narrowed the search down based on how old he must be. He doesn't have a serial number, so I think he's a one-off. I found only one company: "Micronsystems". It's in San Francisco, California.' I paused for a moment and then continued, 'It's supposed to be nice over there at this time of year.'

Amy put down her knife again. 'Ben, don't you dare.'

'What? It's just a simple statement about California, somewhere I've never been.'

'Yes, exactly – somewhere you've never been, somewhere you'd like to go. Somewhere you'd have a bloody good excuse to go to if you thought they'd have a magic robot crack-fixing device. I know you. You're already spending far too much time with that thing; it's not a sensible way for a grown man to behave.'

I ignored the last accusation and dealt with the first.

'It's worth a try, though, isn't it? I want to keep him, and if I could get him fixed, then . . . well, then maybe I could teach him to do some of the stuff that an android can do. Besides, he looks pretty sad and bashed-up. It'd be a nice thing to do.'

Amy curled her lip. 'Ben, it's a robot, it doesn't have feelings. It doesn't care where it is or how broken it is. And this talk about you teaching it . . . you can't even get it to talk properly. Wouldn't you be better off doing something more productive?'

'What's not productive about taking a broken robot to California and bringing home a fixed one? Amy, think about it – it would be an achievement.'

'You said yourself it's not even that broken, so why bother?'

'There's more to him than meets the eye, I just know it.'

'So, rather than taking a damaged robot to be recycled and buying a brand-new android, you'd rather go halfway across the world on a hunch that this one company in America just might be able to repair it? *Then* you're going to work out if it's any use?'

I paused before replying, 'It's not *such* a bad idea, is it?'

Amy ate dinner in silence and then went out. She didn't tell me where she was going or when she'd be back. When I awoke on my own in the early hours of the morning, I felt angry that she always made me feel like I'd caused yet another argument, so I didn't have any inclination to message and ask where she was. Besides, it was highly likely she'd be at Bryony's – her usual bolthole when she wanted to be away from me.

When she came back the next morning, she still wasn't speaking to me.

'Where did you get to last night?'

She looked at me pointedly for a moment, and I knew she was hiding something, but she said nothing. Instead, she went upstairs, showered, changed and went back out again for work.

'Oh, well done, Amy, very mature,' I shouted at the closed front door. Then, 'Tang? Where are you? Let's go and look at the horses.'

Amy didn't speak to me for a whole week. It stung, but it wasn't the first time. Then, one night, after going to bed, she turned to me.

'Ben?'

'Yes?'

'I'm sorry I've been angry with you. I don't want things between us to be awkward. Do you want to . . . how about we . . . ?'

Stunned as I was, I was prepared to be the bigger man and pretend that nothing had happened.

'Erm . . . yes, of course I want to. Always.'

Sex had become like that between Amy and me: a Question, the Agreement, the Act. Afterwards, she lay looking at the ceiling. Then, out of nowhere . . .

'Ben, did you take the bins out?'

I looked blank.

'The bins – did you take them out?'

'Yes, of course I did. For the second time in as many days.'

She looked over at me and ignored my last comment.

'Did you lock the back door?'

'Yes.'

'Where's the robot?'

'In my study.'

Amy still wasn't happy about Tang being in the house, but she didn't protest.

'Is the door shut?'

'Yes. Unless he works out how to turn the handle, he's safely stowed away. He's not going to jump out on you in the middle of the night.' This was childish, I'll admit. Twenty minutes after we'd started speaking to each other again, we'd both already managed to irritate each other.

Amy glared at me, rolled over and went to sleep.

Three hours later, we were woken by a clanking sound.

'What's that?' Amy sounded frightened. 'Go and have a look.'

I swung my legs out of bed, but as it turned out I didn't need to. From the bottom of the stairs came the unmistakable sound of a robot's voice.

'Ben . . . Ben . . . Ben . . . Ben . . . Ben . . .'

There was a pause.

'BEN . . . BEN . . . BEN . . . BEN . . .'

I didn't even glance at Amy as I left the bedroom. I didn't need to.

A week later and things between me and Amy were no better. Nor did I push the notion of a visit to California. Wherever I went, Tang followed. I didn't seem to be able to shake him off, but I didn't mind. It became more of a problem when he followed Amy, which he also did, though not as often. She usually scared him off by calling for me to come and take him away. I began to spend more and more time with Tang in my study, trying to get him to talk, and to be fair to him he did learn a few new words, 'No' being an example.

'Tang, how about you go outside and look at the horses while I have some lunch?'

'No.'

'It wasn't really a question, Tang, it was a suggestion.'

'No.'

'But I need to do some stuff. I need you to go outside for a bit, OK?'

'No.'

And so it continued.

28

One afternoon, after a particularly long and frustrating vocabulary lesson for Tang, I left him in front of the window in my study from where he could see the horses. As I made my way to the kitchen for a large drink, I heard Amy talking on the phone. Not wishing to intrude, I paused, wondering if I should step back into my study. Then I caught part of the conversation.

'When it first came, I thought, "Great, Ben's finally taking some responsibility for something," but the longer it's stayed here the more I've realized he's just not going to change. He spends all his time with the bloody thing . . . it follows him around, and me too; it's nauseating. And the other week it woke us up at four in the morning shouting, "Ben . . . Ben . . . Ben . . . Ben . . ." over and over in that stupid little monotone voice, until Ben got out of bed and went downstairs. Next thing I knew it was in our bedroom. It'll be in our bed next! And Ben's talking about flying off to California to get it fixed. It's a robot gap year, that's what it is, but he's thirty-four years old. He shouldn't be backpacking, he should be getting a career and having a child, surely?'

There was a pause while the person at the end of the line gave their verdict. Whatever they said, Amy both agreed and disagreed.

'Well, yeah, I get that it's exactly the sort of crazy idea your parents would have had, but the difference is they'd have actually done it, wouldn't they?' Pause. 'I don't know if I'm more angry with him for even thinking of going or because that's all he is going to do about it.' Pause. 'But that's not the point. The point is, why couldn't Ben have lavished some attention on a baby? Why a robot? It's not even useful.'

I heard Amy's voice crack, then there was another pause.

'Yes, of course he knows. I've talked about it hundreds

of times.' Pause. 'Well, no, I don't think I've ever actually said to him, "Ben, I want a baby now, how about it?" but I've dropped enough hints.' Pause. 'I suppose you're right. Perhaps I should have spelt it out.' Pause. 'No, Bryony, it's too late now. There are too many other problems, the amount of time he's sinking into the robot is just the last straw.' Pause. 'Well, like the fact that he's never actually achieved anything. When I met him, I thought, "He's training to be a vet, he must be clever and kind," but what happened to that? Nothing. And he still hasn't fixed the gate. This stupid idea of taking the robot to the States will fall by the wayside, just like everything else he does.' Pause. 'Yes, I know, but I've been cutting him slack for that since I met him. At some point he's got to move on . . . You've moved on, haven't you? Why can't he?'

Amy was laying out my flaws to my sister and dissecting them. I felt ashamed and inadequate, but also confused. Since when did Amy want a baby? When we met, she was only concerned with her career . . . she'd just got a promotion and joked that she had no time for children 'ever'. I thought she meant it. I didn't even know if I wanted children; it just wasn't on my radar. Supposing I was a terrible father?

But one thing she had said hurt more than anything else: 'He's never actually achieved anything.' She was right. I hadn't. It was about time I did.

30

3

Gaffer Tape

AMY LEFT ME ON A SATURDAY MORNING. I WAS IN MY STUDY, unusually without Tang, when the phone rang. Minutes later, Amy appeared in the doorway.

'Bryony rang,' she said.

'Oh, yes, what did she say?'

'She said any time was fine to come over as long as it's after eleven, because she and Annabel won't be back from the stables before then. Georgie's at his tennis lesson and Dave's flight doesn't land till three.'

My sister Bryony is an overachiever. A barrister like Amy, the two of them seem to enjoy discussing my shortcomings. I am a failed veterinary surgeon. I have been working to qualify for twelve years and was sacked from my last placement over a problem involving dog anaesthetic and rabbit antibiotics. Bryony also rides horses for Berkshire, has two children – a boy and a girl, of course – and has been happily married to an airline pilot for years. Bryony is the son my parents never had.

'I didn't realize we were going over today,' I replied eventually.

31

'We're not. I am.'

'Good, well, give her my love.'

'She also asked if you'd got a job yet. I said you were too wrapped up in trying to be a robot whisperer.'

There was silence for a moment.

'There's something else . . .' she began.

I raised my eyebrows.

'Bryony and I both think you should keep the house. Your parents left it to you, after all, and it's not like she or I really need it. Not like you do.'

'What do you mean, "keep the house"? I've got the house. We've got the house!'

'In the divorce, Ben. It would be unfair of me to take it. I could, but I won't.'

'The divorce? Whose divorce? I don't understand.'

'Ours,' she said quietly. 'I'm leaving you, Ben. I'm going to stay with Bryony for a while until I find a place to buy.'

I breathed out slowly. 'Of course you are.'

At that point her pity and calm demeanour vanished, and her face clouded over.

'See? That's exactly why this is happening. You don't take anything seriously. Nothing's important to you except that damn robot.'

'It's not Tang's fault we don't know where he comes from or what to do with him.'

Amy left the room, slamming the door behind her. As I got up to follow, I heard her swearing. Out in the hallway, Tang was sitting on the parquet floor with Amy's smart luggage beside him. At his feet was a puddle of oil.

'And now Tang's upset,' I informed her.

With a wordless scream, Amy flung her raincoat round

her shoulders and wheeled her suitcase out of the door. It slammed behind her, too. So that was it. She was gone.

That night I sat at the breakfast bar in the dark, drinking my way through the fanciest bottle of champagne in our drinks cabinet from Amy's favourite mug. The bottle had been a fourth anniversary present from Bryony and Dave. They'd bought us one every anniversary. We'd drunk the others, but this one had been gathering dust for over a year.

'If she ever comes back,' I said to Tang, 'she's going to be furious about this.' I lifted the mug into the moonlight coming through the window and took another swig.

Tang sat at the end of the bar, slumped forward with his head resting on it. He looked downcast again, his arms hanging pathetically by his sides. Mine were stretched in front of me on the bar, though I too was resting my head. I wondered if Tang understood what was happening. Did he understand anything at all?

After a while, he drew himself up and pointed one of his grabbers at himself. The movement made his flap swing open, and he closed it again before asking, 'Me?'

'You?'

'Amy . . . me?' He pointed to himself again.

'Oh no, Tang, don't worry, it's not you at all. Things have been wrong for a long time. It's all my fault.'

Tang offered no opinion but looked reassured, as much as he could do.

'Actually, no, it's not all my fault. It can't be. It's not my fault I'm a crap vet. It *is* my fault I haven't applied myself properly, but I can't help being crap.

'It all comes so bloody easily to Amy. She never had to

33

deal with being useless at anything. I'd always just been the second child who'd never live up to the first. Then, when they died in the accident, it was too late to prove them wrong . . . so now what am I supposed to do?

'Maybe I could've been a better husband. Maybe she could've been a better wife – did she ever think of that? I bet she'll be all like, "Oh, Ben, I still love you, let's be friends." Well, fuck that. I don't need her. Or Bryony, or the rest of them. I've got you, haven't I?'

Tang blinked at me more rapidly than usual, then reached up and enclosed my sleeve in his little grabber fist.

'You know what, Tang? Fuck it!' I said, getting unsteadily to my feet. The bar stool toppled over behind me, landing with a clatter on the oak floor. I stared at my left hand for a second or two, then cried out 'Fuck it' once more and threw my wedding ring into the cutlery drawer.

'You know what else, Tang? Let's go to California. Let's go tomorrow.'

Whilst drunk on a vintage bottle of champagne, I decided to show them all and go on a road trip with a broken robot.

It was a couple of days before I got round to packing. One day was lost to a hangover, the next staring at guidebooks in my father's study, trying to decide if I should take any with me. I confess I was probably a little reluctant to fly, too. I had been ever since my parents' accident. In general, I avoided it if I could.

Tang spent most of the interlude going in and out of the garden, looking at the horses.

I stood in our . . . my . . . bedroom looking at the exploded suitcase laid out on the bed, and it occurred to me that a suitcase was a stupid idea for the kind of trip I had in mind. I might be in my thirties, but there was nothing wrong at all in backpacking, I decided. The problem was I didn't have a backpack, and I ended up with a bad case of online-shopping time slippage as I tried to choose and order one. More hours passed in this venture than I intended, and Tang was so bored with me pushing him away while I scrolled through image after image of rucksacks that he took himself off to look at the horses again.

While I waited for my new backpack to arrive, I decided to work out a daily budget and an itinerary. The former fell by the wayside because it felt tedious, and the latter . . . well, the latter was a gamble since I had no proof that Micron-systems was the place we were looking for. I decided to have another go at getting some information out of Tang. I was going to have to start from the very beginning.

'Tang, are you listening to me?'

'Yes.'

'Good. How did you come to be in my garden?'

Tang gave me an Amy-ish look and shrugged.

'Yes, I know I've asked this before, dozens of times, but this time I mean it literally.'

We were in our sitting room. I got up, grabbed an old grey cardigan from the back of the sofa and opened the French windows that led to the garden, stepping out on to the terrace that Amy had insisted on having built – 'for entertaining'. Tang clanked out to join me, and I crouched down next to him, placing my hands on his little metal shoulders. 'You were right over there by the willow tree, not five weeks ago. Do you remember?'

Tang bobbed his boxy head up and down.

'How did you get there?'

He still didn't seem to understand the question, so I

strode towards the side gate. 'Did you come through this gate?'

He nodded again.

'So, did you open the gate or was it open already?'

'O-pen?' He turned the word over . . . It seemed to be a new one to him, though it shouldn't have been. I knew he knew the word. I was starting to wonder whether he was deliberately obtuse at times.

I opened the gate by way of demonstration, its hinges creaking and groaning with the effort of moving in the chilly October air. 'Like this?'

'Yes.'

So it was Amy's fault after all.

'Come with me, Tang,' I said, walking purposefully through the gate and round the house to the front garden, a large expanse of neatly trimmed lawn with a small rosebed in the centre. A few minutes later, a whirring, clanking noise signalled that Tang was making his way round to join me.

'Where were you before you got here?'

Mercifully, it seemed Tang had got the hang of this game, and he raised a grabber to point at the bus stop over the road.

'You came on a bus? Why?'

He looked at me in wide-eyed panic and shifted from foot to foot. Then a pool of oil appeared at his feet.

'Oh, Tang, I'm sorry.'

He tilted his eyes down. I rummaged in my trouser pockets and found a lint-covered handkerchief I'd rarely used, indelibly scored with dirty folds from the years it had languished in my pocket. I wiped Tang's leg where the stream of oil had taken a diagonal path. Then I heard a cough. I looked up to find my neighbour, Mr Parkes, in his own front garden, looking worried about what I might do to the robot next and attempting to stop me before it happened, so he wouldn't be the one to see it.

'Mr Parkes, how lovely to see you. Fine weather we're having for the season.' My words clouded in front of my face as I spoke, but the irony was lost on Mr Parkes, who sniffed and shifted in his rhombus-padded gardening gilet, looking under his eyelids at the still clouds: the kind that only come in autumn, the kind that signal mist and gloves. He adjusted his dogtooth-tweed old-man fedora and hoisted a pair of Felco secateurs from one hand to the other. I knew they were Felco because Amy made me buy some for her when she had a gardening phase. She didn't want to be seen in the front garden with the rusty old pair we had inherited from my parents with the house, the same pair my grandparents had probably used before them.

I smiled at my neighbour and, with a small wave, resumed my task of cleaning Tang up. Mr Parkes coughed again.

'He came on the number thirty,' he called. 'I saw him get off. He looked both ways before he crossed the road and everything. Then he went straight into your garden. I thought you must have been expecting him. I gather now that you weren't.'

Mr Parkes! I could have kissed him. Harley Wintnam, or more specifically the stop over the road, was one of the few that broke the number thirty bus journey between Basingstoke and Heathrow.

My new backpack arrived the next day, smelling of warehouse and containing an excessive amount of little packets of silica gel. As fast as I bundled things into the bag, Tang pulled them out again, each item of curious interest to him for about ten seconds, then discarded. Until he found my sunglasses.

'Tang, be careful, they're breakable.'

He took no notice, continuing to wave them around and pass them from grabber to grabber.

I tried to take them from him, but he moved his arm out of my reach, his body making rapid jerky movements. The more irritated I became, the funnier the game seemed to him.

'Tang, stop it, will you?' I snatched the glasses from him and put them back in their case. I hadn't meant to shout, and I immediately felt guilty as he plopped himself down on the carpet with a sulky thud that popped his flap open. By way of apology, I reached over and shut it for him. It popped open again.

'We're going to have to do something about that flap. It can't be good for your innards – they'll get dirty – and I don't think anyone else wants to see your workings, either.'

Tang's body heaved up a little, then down again. At the same time, a slight hissing noise came out of his mouth, like an old kettle or a pressure cooker – definitely a sigh.

I had an idea. 'Stay here, I'll be back in a minute.'

I headed as fast as I could down to the garage and rooted through my poor excuse for a toolbox. I spotted a sealed plastic packet containing a pair of shiny new gate hinges. I frowned and tossed them aside, picked up a roll of gaffer tape and skipped back upstairs to the bedroom. I found Tang on the landing and making his way towards the stairs.

'I told you to stay where you were, Tang.'

Tang looked at me as though he didn't understand.

Hmm. I knelt down and bit off a strip of gaffer tape.

'We'd better take this with us,' I told him.

I was just about to shut his flap and seal it when I noticed that the cylinder next to his heart, which when I first saw him had been full, now had liquid only two-thirds of the way up. The crack in the glass seemed to have got bigger, too.

'Tang, what does this fluid do?'

Tang couldn't see over the edge of his body, so I held up a hand mirror for him and pointed to the cylinder. He lifted his grabbers, indicating that he didn't know, though from the way his eyes darted about nervously I wasn't sure I believed him.

'Is it important?' I pressed.

He blinked a few times. 'Yes,' he said, then shut the flap and kept his grabber across it.

'What will happen if there's no fluid left?'

He shifted from one foot to the other.

'Stops.'

I took stock of this.

'You mean to say that if the cylinder runs empty, then you stop working entirely?'

'Yes.'

I panicked. All this time I'd been faffing about with backpacks. 'God, Tang, we need to find someone to fix you.'

But with no further information about his origin, the best and only course of action was to stick to my original plan: we'd go to Micronsystems. I'd man up and we'd fly to San Francisco on the next flight we could get.

4

Premium

I'D BE LYING IF I SAID WE DIDN'T GET SOME CURIOUS LOOKS as we headed for the check-in desks. While there were of course other people with androids, there was no one like me, trailing through the airport with a gaffer-taped science project in tow. I caught a ripple of comments as we passed – 'Wow, he really needs to upgrade' from a young student, and 'Ah, bless' from a granny. I even heard 'Maybe he's doing it for TV?'

I moved with faux dignity, head high, striding through in my blue boating shoes to the check-in queue. Tang shambled mechanically after me and came to a whirring halt at my side. He picked at the gaffer tape.

'It's for your own good, mate,' I told him.

Tang blinked at me and turned his eyes downward, his arm falling to his side.

'And don't bother sighing at me, it doesn't work.'

Whilst in the queue, we passed a shelf carrying forms to be filled in by passengers with oversized baggage for the hold. While Tang's attention was drawn to a shiny luggage cart nearby, I hastily filled one in. As I was doing so, I felt my phone vibrate in my pocket. I ignored it.

When we reached the desk, I slid the form across to the clerk and waited while she cast her eyes over it. I fiddled with the space where, until a few days previously, my wedding ring had been.

'So, the robot's going in the hold?' The clerk peered over the counter at Tang with an expression of distaste, then nodded.

I heard the loud, clear whirr of a robot shaking his head vigorously.

'Yes,' I said, ignoring Tang, 'I also have a bag. It's new.' I felt a tug on my shirt sleeve.

'Bro-ken.'

'What is?'

'Tang is.'

In the excitement of going on a journey, I'd almost forgotten its purpose. Tang gazed at me with his eyelids slanted diagonally, looking like a wounded puppy. I felt my resolve slipping. Nevertheless, I persisted.

'Look, mate, you can't sit in the plane with me, there's a special bit for humans and a special bit for . . . for robots. It'll be better for you in there.' I didn't even believe it myself, and when I looked at the clerk it was clear she'd been won over.

'There's a section of the plane where the seats convert so they're bigger. They'd be perfect for him. They're in Premium.'

At this, Tang's eyes opened as wide as he could make them, and he began hopping from foot to foot. I glared at the clerk, but she just smiled back, inscrutable.

'I can't justify two seats in Premium, Tang. You'll have to go in the hold with the other lugg—'

'Actually, I'm taking my Cybervalet in the cabin with me,' a chap chirped behind me. 'It's a long flight to San Francisco; I think it's inhumane to put him in the hold all alone.'

'Inhumane? Don't they have to be living to be the victim of inhumanity?'

A businessman and a young family in the queue began to protest and shake their heads. I heard tutting.

'Tang, listen, mate . . .'

Suddenly, Tang released his grip on my checked shirt and stretched both arms round my thighs, clamping on to me as if his life depended upon it. He hopped from foot to foot and let out a piercing cry.

'Tang . . . Tang . . . Tang . . . Ben . . . Tang . . . seat . . . Tang . . . Tang . . . Ben . . . Tang . . . seat . . . Ben . . .'

Tang loved it in Premium. When I tried to sit by the window, he brewed up another tantrum, the like of which had got him there in the first place, until I let him take the seat. I realized that by caving in at the check-in desk I hadn't averted an embarrassing scene, I had merely taught him a valuable way to play me instead. So I decided to do the sensible thing and ordered a number of complimentary gin and tonics in perhaps a shorter amount of time than was strictly necessary. As I drifted off to sleep, I left Tang staring out of the window.

I woke, several hours later, to Tang's cool metal grabber poking me in the cheek.

'Ben . . . Ben . . . Ben . . . Ben . . . Ben . . . Ben . . . Ben . . .'

'What?'

'Ben . . . Ben . . . Ben . . . Ben . . .'

'Stop poking me, Tang, what do you want?' I said, keeping my eyes closed.

Tang made no response.

I opened my left eye and looked in his direction. The hand that wasn't poking me in the cheek was gesturing toward the seat-back screen in front of him.

'It's a telly, mate, let me sleep.' I closed my one open eye again and shuffled my flight blanket higher up round my neck. Tang removed his hand from my cheek, and for a split second I thought he was going to obey me. Then the hand came back, harder this time, smacking my jaw with more force than I think even he intended to give it.

'Ow, Tang, what the f—?'

He glared at me unblinking, then swivelled his head and stared at the screen, then turned back to me.

Ah, the touchscreen.

I spent the next hour cycling through the vast array of shit that was the in-flight entertainment before Tang found something he wanted to watch for more than thirty seconds. There was an animated film about a world inhabited by robots that looked like him, and unsurprisingly he settled on this. There were androids in this film, too, but they were considered weird and different, and Tang thought this wonderful. I guess the moral of the story was about being true to oneself and that being different is not a bad thing, or something like that, but the point was lost on Tang and I chose not to enlighten him. The point, for me, was that he would be quiet for the next ninety minutes or so, underneath the extra-wide foamy headphones specially sourced for him by the stewardess. I closed my eyes gratefully.

Ninety minutes later, I woke with a sense of déjà vu.

'What now?'

'Again!' He pointed to his seat-back screen.

43

'Are you sure? You've just watched it. Don't you want something else?'

Tang's eyelids lowered a little in confusion, then one eye started to blink. It was as if the very suggestion was beyond comprehension.

'Again.'

I lined up the film again for him. 'You enjoyed it, then?'

He made no answer.

I lifted an earphone. 'I said, you enjoyed it, then? The film?'

'Yes,' he said, removing my hand from the earphone, which he then clamped back to the mesh-covered hole that made up one half of his aural apparatus.

'What's so special about it?'

He lifted the earphone again.

'Good robots fight bad robots,' he said. This had to have been the longest sentence I'd ever heard him speak.

'What makes them bad?'

'Bad robots bad to good robots.' He pointed at himself, then at the screen. 'Good robots bad to bad robots.'

So that was it: he liked the film because it showed him a world where his kind were the masters and appeared to be exacting revenge upon androids for former mistreatment. I couldn't decide whether it was my place to deal with it. One thing was certain – I was either too drunk or too sober to try to explain why two wrongs don't make a right. I patted Tang's metal shoulder and left him to it.

5

Pedantry

IT WAS THE MIDDLE OF THE NIGHT WHEN WE LANDED IN SAN
Francisco. When I booked the flight, I hadn't considered
the time difference, nor that autumn nights could be chilly
in California even if the days were still warm. Shuffling
through the arrivals hall I wished I'd worn a jumper, jeans
and some thick socks, not canvas shoes and a cotton shirt
and slacks.

We stood at the carousel waiting for my shiny new backpack to appear through the rubber curtains and glide
its way towards me. I suddenly remembered the missed
call – from Bryony. I frowned then set the phone to 'do
not disturb' and shoved it back in my pocket. I considered
switching it off altogether, but at least this way I could still
use the Internet.

Tang sat on the carousel ledge, despite my protestations,
and trailed his grabber along the conveyor belt. He had to
pick it up and move every few seconds before he got swept
along.

Eventually, I went and hauled him back to a safe distance
away from the carousel. I did not want to have to go to lost

property at 3 a.m. after a long-haul flight and explain that I'd lost my robot because he wouldn't be told 'no'.

When at last it circled towards my feet, my backpack was heavier than I remembered. The tiredness had dulled my initial exuberance about the trip somewhat, and the best thing we could do was hire a car and get to a hotel. Incredibly, all the car-hire places were closed. An international airport and one couldn't hire a car in the middle of the night? I didn't consider getting in a cab. Instead: 'Come on, Tang, we're catching the bus.'

'Bus?'

'Yes. This way.' I strode off in the direction of the sign, leaving Tang to clank after me as fast as his tumble-dryer hoses would carry him.

Formless shadows shuffled around in the dim artificial light of the bus station, and every now and again a broken door on one of the tall lockers that lined the wall banged open and slammed closed again. A tramp in a stained overcoat sat in a corner eyeing my new backpack.

One solitary android ticket attendant sat behind bullet-proof glass in a tiny booth. He was wearing a flak jacket. You know it's a bad place if an android needs protection. They often get assigned jobs like this – somewhere a human doesn't really want to work but which needs something a bit more than a straightforward machine.

For some reason, it was important to me not to lose face in front of Tang, so I attempted to maintain a breezy composure and walked straight up to the booth, leaving Tang to follow in his own time.

'Excuse me, do you know of this corporation?' I held up my phone upon which I'd stored the name of the company I

46

thought I'd found on Tang's underside.

'Sir, please keep your cell out of view,' the android said flatly.

I glanced about me and understood. Even the sound of my voice had drawn attention to us from one or two of the nearest shadows, and holding up a shiny phone was just an invitation. I put it away in an inside pocket.

By this point, Tang had caught up with me. He grasped my shirt sleeve and held on tightly. I told the droid the name of the company again, and this time he was more responsive.

'Yes, sir. It is in my databanks. Micronsystems: makers of the latest in humanoid home-assistance technology. A Fortune 500 company, winners of the Technology in Action Award for three consecutive years. Chief Executive Mr . . .'

'OK, OK, I get it,' I said, then tried a different tack. 'Thank you for the information, but what I really need to know is how to get there.'

'I am programmed with a variety of local knowledge, ready to serve your needs.' He shot me a smile.

'Well?'

'I'm afraid I don't understand, sir. Can you tell me what you mean by "Well?"'

'I'm waiting for you to answer my question. About Micronsystems.'

'Which question, sir?'

'About how to get there.'

'Sir, an assessment of our conversation suggests that you have not asked a question about the location of Micronsystems.'

'Oh, for goodness' sake!' Bloody android. This was exactly the kind of pedantic shit that made me not want to bother with one at home. Tang could be literal, but at least he was amusing. I asked him if he could tell me the whereabouts of Micronsystems.

'Yes.'

I sighed. 'Then where is it? Actually, no, don't answer that. Tell me this instead: is there a hotel nearby?'

'Yes, sir. There are a number of hotels in the area. There is one just across the street.' He pointed.

'No, I mean near Micronsystems.'

'Yes, sir. There is a hotel one mile from Micronsystems that fits your requirements.'

'My requirements?'

'Yes, sir. I calculate that you are in need of a room because you are low on energy. You need a hotel that is open at this hour of the clock, and you would prefer one with a food outlet so you may purchase some fuel. There is one hotel in the area of Micronsystems that matches those parameters. Here is some printed information for you, sir.' The android turned one hundred and eighty degrees at the waist and pulled out a leaflet for me.

I thanked him. Tang eyed him from below the booth. He released my sleeve and grabbed at the leaflet.

'Tang, get off. I need that.'

Tang just squeezed the leaflet tighter and began slapping it repeatedly against the side of the ticket booth.

'Tang, I told you – give it back.'

He glared at me and wandered off, leaflet in hand. I turned to the droid to ask for another copy.

'Which hotel is it?' I asked, looking at the list on the leaflet.

'The Hotel California, sir.'

'Are there any buses that run near there?'

'The number twenty-two, sir. You can board it from right outside this station, there,' he gestured, 'and alight outside the hotel itself.'

I asked him when the next number twenty-two was due.

'In twenty minutes, sir. The journey will take exactly fifty minutes. Unfortunately, for a journey of this duration there are no toilet or catering facilities on board. However, in the unlikely event of a road-traffic incident there are fire extinguishers and first-aid kits located at the front and back of the cabin.'

I thanked the android and requested two bus tickets.

'Yes, sir. Two adult tickets?'

'Yes, one adult and a . . . and a . . .' I waved a hand in Tang's direction. He was heading for the lockers. 'Tang, don't go far.'

'No,' he called, without turning round.

I resumed dialogue with the android.

'You don't have a special rate for robots, by any chance?'

'We have special rates for children, the elderly, persons with mobility restrictions and registered Cybervalets and capability-assistance droids. Robots, no.'

'Seriously?' No wonder Tang didn't like androids.

'I'm sorry, sir, I don't understand your question. Please repeat.'

I asked him again for two adult tickets. Then I looked around for Tang. He was reaching up to try one of the locker doors. 'Tang, leave the lockers alone! Come back, will you?'

'Yes,' he told me, but remained exactly where he was.

I wasn't sold on the idea of spending another minute in the bus station, let alone twenty, but at this point there were no quicker options. We'd just have to sit tight and hope that a skinny Englishman and a bored robot didn't attract any attention. With a heavy heart, I took a seat on a fixed plastic chair and looked around again for Tang. He was now jabbing at the locker door with a grabber, making a loud 'donk, donk, donk' noise.

Suddenly, a door next to us burst open and a grey, pale-looking man in a grey tracksuit emerged, shoving Tang out of the way as he left the bus station at a run. Tang wobbled, regained his balance and stared wide-eyed. Then he shuffled back to me and picked at his gaffer tape.

I watched the station clock tick down the minutes. Like an exam clock, every second that passed sounded louder than the last. I slumped down in my seat as best I could and ran my hands through my hair. I hadn't done a great job of taking care of Tang and myself so far. I imagined Amy raising an eyebrow and making some comment about how if I'd had more common sense then this wouldn't have happened. And she'd be right.

Amy used to plan our holidays, so we never got stuck in a bus station in the middle of the night. The closest we ever came to it was when our car broke down next to a bus stop in the Dordogne one driving holiday, but Amy just phoned the local recovery service and asked them – in French – to come and get us. An hour later, we were in a lovely rural guesthouse drinking hot chocolate.

There was a call from a door behind the ticket attendant.

'Downtown San Jose bus leaving in five. Have your tickets ready.'

Oh, thank God. Before the bus driver had even finished his announcement, I was on my feet.

'Come on, Tang. Let's go.'

*

Tang struggled to make it up the bus steps, and I had to push him from behind with my palms flat on the plates of his back. The bus he'd travelled in when he turned up in my back garden was a low rise, disability-friendly bus, but there was no such luck here. The steps were one challenge, but then there was the narrow aisle of the bus itself. Tang scraped and squeezed his way along, banging the elbows of sleeping passengers, which didn't endear us to anyone.

Fortunately, the back seats of the bus were free. It meant that Tang could heave himself up into the middle of them and have plenty of room. We bounced along over the bus's suspension, Tang with his round eyes fixed straight ahead while I lay my head against the window pretending to doze, but all the time keeping a keen eye on Tang. I didn't want to worry him by unpeeling his flap all the time to look at his cylinder, but on the other hand I had no idea how much time we had. Maybe I should have tried to find someone closer to home that could fix him. Maybe this was a stupid idea. Or maybe . . . maybe it would all work out in the end. I had no way of knowing.

6

Room Service

THE BUS DROPPED US OFF OUTSIDE THE HOTEL CALIFORNIA, just as the droid had said. The faintest rays of morning light were beginning to show behind the run-down hotel as we stood in front of it, our backs to the shoreline. The pinks and greys and blues of dawn made the area look a lot more appealing than I feared it actually was. Despite being a gnat's fart from the beach, the road in front of the hotel was not any sort of Santa Monica hipster hotspot. Quite the contrary in fact. In my eyeline was a dilapidated bus shelter. Looking around more closely, I saw used condoms blocking a number of the drains and more than one spent syringe dropped carelessly underneath the benches that lined the pavement . . . sidewalk. The prospect of daylight did a lot to cheer me – that and the thought of a coffee and a flat soft surface upon which I could sleep. Even the worst sort of hotel could manage the latter, I decided. And so they did. They could not, however, accommodate Tang, as the hotel proprietor made clear.

As soon as we'd crossed the threshold, I heard, 'Hey, you . . . yeah, you, with the floppy hair.'

He looked like one of the minor characters in a gangster movie who always gets in the way: an off-duty pawnshop owner in a string vest and a peaked green cap with a gun under the counter.

As I approached, he said, 'We don't serve their kind in here.' He waved a fat finger at Tang.

I tried to respond, but he interrupted me, 'Androids only. Can't you read the sign?' He pointed at a sign on the wooden box that passed for a check-in desk. It said: 'Strictly no robots. And payment up front.'

Tang made a low noise like a dog growling and stamped from foot to foot.

'Look, it's just for a few hours while I get some sleep . . . We've just got off a plane.'

'Is you deaf? I said, no robots.'

'But he's broken. He needs to rest, too.'

'Especially no broken robots.'

'Fine. We'll go somewhere else.' I turned on my heel and made a move towards the door.

Then he said, 'Hey, listen, you say you just wanna sleep?'

I took a deep breath. 'Yes. I've been on a long-haul flight. My wife's left me, I'm tired, I'm on an expedition to who knows where, and we nearly got attacked in the bus station on several occasions. I'm not in the mood to argue with anyone, so we'll just be on our way.'

'Ain't no place open at this time except us. And no place that's gonna charge you for only a few hours, pal. No place except us. Look see, I can give you a ground-floor room, but you gotta be quiet about it. I run a well-respected establishment here, and I can't be seen to be takin' robots in, y'hear?'

As I'd told him, I was too tired to argue. I was also too tired to carry out my threat of leaving.

It didn't occur to me at the time to ask what the deal was with robots as opposed to androids. I simply handed over some dollars for the room, and he selected a key from the bank of hooks hanging behind him. He laid the key flat on the counter and said we could have breakfast, for an extra charge, if we wanted, and that it was served 'seven through ten'. The thought of coffee piqued my interest, but I needed to sleep first. It was all I could do to thank the man and head towards our room.

My power nap turned out to be a twelve-hour affair. I awoke just before 5 p.m. still in my clothes and lying like a starfish on top of a patchy pink waffle bedspread that was covering a manky mattress. What Tang did in the intervening time I have no idea, and I was relieved to see him lying in more or less the same position as me on the floor with his eyes closed, apparently asleep, on standby, or whatever it was. I say 'more or less', because while most of him was on the floor, one of his arms was in the air with his grabber apparently resting on the side of the bed. As I looked more closely, I realized that the 'wrist' of his tumble-dryer hose arm had got caught on a dangling thread of the bedspread, rendering him unable to move. If he'd asked for help, then I'd clearly been too deeply asleep to hear him. I unhooked his arm and laid it gently down by his side.

My sleep had not been without disruption. Strange knocking noises had permeated my brain during the lighter phases of my sleep cycle. I attributed them to old plumbing, but I couldn't be sure. The knocking noises were one thing, but I also heard squeals and clanks – like a boiler arguing with a kettle. At one point, I swear I even heard the sound of a spring snapping, followed by something that resembled a Slinky going downstairs.

I heaved myself up to a sitting position, rubbed my face with grubby hands and looked around me. In the half-light of our arrival I hadn't noticed any details about our room. Now, in the waning but adequate light of an autumn afternoon, the price I'd paid for a power nap, even a long one, seemed very large indeed.

The curtains were made of a thin gauze and hung very low where hooks were missing, rendering them almost useless for their purpose. The wallpaper was a dark-olive flocked effort, with wet patches at the corners and smudges here and there of an unnatural-looking dark patina. Damp seemed to permeate the air in the room, too, making it smell like a neglected basement.

There was no carpet. The floorboards upon which Tang lay were covered with small rugs almost like bath mats. They curled up at the edges, as though they were trying to get as much of themselves off the floor as possible. I suddenly felt very sorry for Tang. I hadn't tried very hard to find him a bed. Admittedly, I was still unsure if his metal body appreciated soft things.

I'd been awake enough to take my watch off before going to sleep, and as I leaned over to the bedside cabinet to retrieve it, my hand lighted on a damp patch. I jerked it back, sharply.

'Yuck. What the hell is that?' I sniffed my fingertips. Oil. Weird. Really weird. Especially for a hotel that didn't take robots. I reached for my watch again, and then for no reason at all I decided to look in the bedside drawer. I expected, or rather hoped, to see a Gideon Bible – something that would lend a sense of normality to this place. But as I pulled out the drawer I saw a selection of batteries ranging from triple A through double A to nine volt and beyond. I caught sight of something half-hidden underneath the bed, and so I leaned further over to see what it was. A car battery. And some jump leads.

Choosing not to speculate, I pushed them back under the bed and shut the bedside drawer. I got up from the sagging, dusty bed and padded as quietly as I could to a door that I figured must lead to the bathroom. The owner had told us that all rooms came with an en suite because his clients found they needed one. Then, inexplicably, he had winked at me.

Standing in the bathroom to pee, I had a good look around. On the top of the toilet cistern was a chamois leather and a pair of heavy-duty suede gardening-type gloves – rather extreme for use in the lavatory, I considered. Then I peered behind the drawn shower curtain. In the corner of the bath, where one might expect to keep bottles of shampoo and other sanitizers, there sat a can of WD-40. Next to it sat a bottle of all-over hair and body wash. The whole bath area looked filmy, and I decided I didn't need a shower that badly.

By the time I'd finished washing my hands in the bathroom, with what seemed to be a bar of soap made of wax, Tang had heaved himself up off the floor. When I opened the bathroom door, he greeted me by clapping his grabbers together.

'Go now?'

'We can't, Tang. I'm really sorry. We came to talk to somebody just down the road, but I slept longer than I wanted to, so I think we'll have missed him. We'll have to wait till tomorrow.'

Tang pouted at this by pushing out his lower metal jaw, and picked at his gaffer tape.

'Hard floor.'

I suddenly felt very guilty that the broken robot had not had a bed to sleep on and that my oversleeping had delayed the possibility of him being fixed.

'I know, I'm sorry. I'll do better next time. I was just tired is all.'

'Ben not tired now?'

I thanked him for his concern and said, 'Maybe we can see if there's another place we can stay nearby. Come on, let's take a look.'

The late-afternoon sun fought hard to find its way through the fog and largely failed. As we walked up and down the street looking for an alternative to the eccentric place we'd stayed in that day, both my feet and Tang's echoed mutedly on the sidewalk, and the further we walked the duller they sounded. The hotel proprietor had been right: there seemed absolutely no other place at all to stay. An entire parade of shops and businesses were nailed shut with aluminium plates, and litter seemed to be the only thing visiting. The Hotel California was the single building open in either direction that I could make out in the cool mist.

I turned to my friend. 'Tang, look, I think we're going to have to go back to that hotel. There's nothing else around here, and it's too foggy to go far.'

To give Tang his due, he didn't make a fuss, although he looked a bit crushed. He could be a real pain sometimes, but he understood when a situation was hopeless.

*

We returned to our room in the Hotel California. At least I'd kept the key – a poor victory. In reality, all I'd done was screw up again.

Tang dropped himself down in a rickety chair by the window and pulled aside the gauze curtain thing to peer out at the gloom. I searched for the obligatory hotel information binder and found it in the drawer of the other bedside cabinet.

The binder informed me that the restaurant that served breakfast also catered for 'intimate dinners'. The sample menu consisted of set meals with comedic names such as 'nuts and bolts' and 'oily fish'. I pondered over the thematic effort for a hotel with an aversion to robots. Then it occurred to me I hadn't eaten since the flight, and the realization made me wolfish. I also still hadn't had a coffee; the withdrawal was giving me a headache.

I wasn't sure I wanted to leave the room and brave the dining area, or any other of the public areas of the hotel in fact, so I ordered one of the room-service specials. I asked for a coffee, too, but was informed that the machine was broken.

'Can't you just do me an instant?'

'Sir, we don't serve that sort of coffee here . . . We're a high-quality establishment.'

I paused.

'OK, could you just bring me a beer with it, then?'

An android in a French maid's outfit delivered the meal. I'm not sure who found this more tasteless – me or Tang. The maid stood with one hand on hip and cocked to the side, balancing my dinner tray in the other.

'Shall I come in to serve, sir?' she said, and gave me a wink.

I declined her services and said I could serve myself.

She gave me another wink. 'Yes, sir, I understand, sir. Just call the desk if you want me, and I'll be right back.' Then she sauntered off.

'What the hell was all that about?' I asked myself, but Tang looked at me and his little metal shoulders gave a small but discernible shrug.

Tang and I kept a morose silence while I ate, then killed some time trying to coax a watchable picture from the seriously old television. After a while we gave up, and I decided the best thing to do was to get an early night. I moved to the edge of the bed so that Tang could have the other half. It was a smallish double, so Tang's bulk meant I spent the whole night on the verge of falling off.

The next morning, the hotel hallways and lobby were suddenly busy with people coming and going, all with an android in tow. Having slept poorly and still under-caffeinated, I was in no mood for anything challenging, but one look at Tang – who walked very close to me while spinning his head round nervously – suggested he felt even more ill at ease. As we made our way to the lobby, it became obvious that both humans and androids were turning their heads to stare at us in amusement.

I'd brought my backpack with me from the room, having spent enough time in the hotel and the area in general to be too anxious to leave it unattended while we went for breakfast. I placed it by the counter and pressed the desk bell in front of me. The clerk on the morning shift was a thin, elderly woman with too much make-up and nails far longer than was at all practical.

I asked politely for the way to the dining room.

'That way,' she told me, pointing a crone-ish arm to the other side of the lobby.

I paid the balance of our bill and started to walk off in the direction of breakfast – and coffee – when I thought of something. 'Excuse me again, but do you happen to know why people are staring at us?'

Her thin rouged lips twisted into a smirk. 'Because you got a robot with you. They think it's . . . well, it's quaint. And if I may say so, a little bit perverse.'

'*Perverse?*'

'Look around you. You see anyone else in here with a little guy like yours?'

By now, I was used to being the only one with a robot like Tang, but as I looked around an alarming fact dawned on me. All the androids were female-oid, each costumed, like the room-service waitress, in coquettish outfits entirely unsuited to the outside world.

So the penny dropped: Tang was, in their assumption, my 'companion'. I picked up my rucksack.

'Come on, Tang, we're leaving.'

7

Glass

AFTER THROWING THE KEYS AT THE CLERK, I MARCHED OUT of the hotel as fast as I could. Tang clanked after me but struggled to keep up.

'Ben . . . Ben . . . Ben . . . Ben . . . Ben . . . stop . . . Ben!'

When I reached the bus stop where we had disembarked the previous day, I halted. A minute later Tang arrived, glaring at me, his eyes pushing out of their sockets.

'I'm sorry, Tang, but I just wanted to get as far away from the hotel as possible.'

Tang nodded. 'But . . . Ben . . . coffee?'

'I'll get it somewhere else.'

'Oh.'

'You were right, Tang, we should have left yesterday. We're going right now,' I said, but when I peered at the timetable – obscured by layers of graffiti – I found there wasn't a bus due for another forty minutes. At least, not in the direction in which I thought we were going. 'Sod it, we'll get a taxi.'

Five minutes later I managed to hail a cab, and I more or less shoved Tang into the back seat, piling in after him.

'Where to?' asked the cabbie.

'Erm . . . Microsystems, do you know it?' I held up my phone to show him the address.

He gave me a look like I was a dead rodent he'd found in his engine.

'Yeah, I know it. Shoulda figured.'

'What's that supposed to mean?' I asked, as the cabbie sped off.

'You're just the type to be at the Hotel California but wanna go to work in a shiny big building the very next day.'

'The type?'

'Yeah – clean and tidy but kinda compensating for something you ain't getting at home. There's a lot of your kind at that hotel, although I gotta say I ain't ever seen an escort like yours before. They're usually . . . well, they usually look more human.'

'Yes, so I gathered,' I answered. 'But you're wrong about me. About us.'

I caught sight of him raising an eyebrow in the rear-view mirror. 'If you say so, pal.'

'I do,' I said, trying to make it clear the conversation was over. I was beginning to get fed up with hearing what people round here thought of Tang and me.

The cab drove through the fog and dropped us outside a large glass building in the shape of a skatepark, with two high sides sloping down to a trough in the middle. There was a paved area in front of it, and lovingly manicured miniature trees lined the path to the entrance like emergency gangway lights. Tang and I clanked and walked respectively up the symmetrical avenue, never seeming to get any closer until we were actually there. The cold fog that enveloped the building gave the impression it was up in the clouds.

The foyer inside was exactly as the exterior promised it would be, with similar potted trees dotted around and some hard-wearing leather sofas near the front doors. At the back of the foyer stood a high reception desk. The distance from doors to desk was so immense it meant that both the receptionist and the visitor were made to suffer an awkward interlude before the latter arrived at the former. We were lucky, as the petite blonde girl sitting behind the desk was on the telephone and so was otherwise distracted as we made our way up to the desk. Other than the two of us, the entire foyer was empty of visitors.

I found myself almost tiptoeing through the hushed space, but Tang's feet made such a racket as the metal hit the marble that our arrival would never have gone unnoticed. I looked closely at Tang for any sign in his compact little body that he might recognize where he was.

'Do you know this place, Tang?'

'No.'

'Are you sure?'

'Yes.'

'It's not where you come from, then?'

'No.'

Just as the receptionist's pleasant voice sounded the end of her phone call, Tang and I reached the desk.

'Can I help you, sir?' she smiled.

'Yes, hopefully. I found the name of this company online and wondered if there was anyone available who might be able to talk to me about a robot.'

The receptionist wound her fingers around the oversized bow on her stylish blouse.

'A robot?'

'Yes, this one.' I gestured to Tang.

She stood up from behind the desk and peered over the counter top at him.

'Do you have an appointment?'

'I'm afraid I just came on spec. I'm trying to find out who made him, and there's a metal plate on his underside that says "Micron—" and I thought that might be something to do with your company . . . you making robots and all.'

'We make androids, sir.'

'Oh.'

'I don't think this is likely to be one of ours.'

I paused.

'Can I help you with anything else, sir?'

I hadn't been prepared to fall at the first hurdle.

'Is there anyone who might know about old robots, or ones like this anyway, even if you didn't make him?'

She creased up her brows and tapped her teeth with her French-manicured nails.

'I guess you could speak to Cory. He's in the games division, but I know he's got a thing for robots – a hobby.'

'That sounds marvellous.'

'If you'd just like to take a seat in the waiting area, I'll see if I can buzz him.'

Tang and I looked at each other, then back at the sofas that sat across the expanse of the marbled foyer.

'Thanks, but by the time we get down there it'll be time to walk back again.' I chuckled, but the receptionist didn't share my amusement. I scratched my head a while to cover the awkward pause and felt my dark mop already curling at the ends. When we first met, Amy said she liked it that way.

She thought it was cute. By the time she left it grated on her. She said I looked like a student.

The receptionist typed something into the shiny thin laptop in front of her, then she smiled. Then she typed again, finishing her input with a short bounce on the carriage-return key.

'He's on his way down.'

Cory kept us waiting for a long time. I fretted about Tang's boredom levels and the glass walls around us. When Tang's patience eventually cracked, he chose to bother the floor, not the windows. Seeing his muted reflection in the marble, he stooped down for a closer look and his feet slid away from under him.

I told him not to hurt himself.

'No.'

He moved one foot tentatively forward, his eyes widening with the sensation of sliding on the marble. Then he turned away and clanked off at speed. I realized with horror what was about to happen. Tang squealed at the top of his voice as he skated over the smooth surface.

'Tang, come back.' I tried to hiss quietly, but there was no possibility of silence in that aircraft hangar of a foyer. Tang's squeal and my rebuke bounced off all the windows. The receptionist got to her feet.

'Sir, please can you get your robot to stay with you. We don't want him to cause any damage.'

I gave her a frown and called Tang over. He skated back to me. 'I need some sort of reins for you,' I said.

'Rains?' Tang asked, pointing a grabber to the sky out-side.

'*Reins*. Like on horses.'

65

Tang's eyes lit up.

'Ben's horses?'

'They're not my horses, Tang, but, yes, like on those horses.'

'Tang likes Ben's horses.'

'Yes, so do I. Now can you please just stay where you are?'

Tang sighed, dropped himself on the floor and picked at his gaffer tape.

Ten long minutes later, the piercing sound of a glass door turning on its hinges made us look to our right. A tall man was approaching; the kind of man who made me feel inadequate – broad shouldered and tanned, but not too orange, with a designer shirt and fashionable shorts that shouldn't have been suitable for the office but on him were absolutely appropriate. He seemed an unlikely candidate to be a robot hobbyist. He held out his hand to me, showing a smile of perfect teeth and peachy dimples on both cheeks.

'Cory Fields, good to meetcha.'

'Ben Chambers.'

'Kaila says you got a robot for me to look at. You thinking of selling?'

Tang wrapped his grabbers round my leg.

'Not at all. He's broken, you see. He needs help. I need to find someone who can fix him.' I tried to be cool, but listening to myself speak I knew I wasn't.

'Come this way and I'll take a look,' said Cory, with another smile.

He led us back through the door and down a sunny glass corridor that had been shielded from view from the foyer by clever use of prisms, or something. A short distance down the corridor, Cory suddenly turned left and walked through a wall. As I drew level, I saw he was holding open another glass door for me.

It was a meeting room, with an environmental-charity water cooler plumbed in and a selection of funky and uncomfortable-looking chairs surrounding a large conference table, which was also made of glass. Cory sat down and invited me to do the same before beckoning Tang over to him.

'Come here, lil' fella, I won't hurt you.'

Tang looked at me for approval, and I nodded. He clanked over to stand in front of Cory. Then, to my surprise, the man pulled out a pair of glasses. From what I'd heard of California, I'd thought eye defects were illegal.

'The wife,' he said, waving his specs around. 'I wanted to get laser, but she thinks the glasses look "distinguished". Like I'm some sort of egghead or something, God love her.' He looked at Tang. 'He's certainly unusual, ain't he? For this day and age, anyway.'

'Agreed. It's his cylinder that's broken. It's in his flap.' Then, to explain what I meant, I peeled back Tang's gaffer tape.

Cory nodded when he saw the crack in the glass, then puffed out his cheeks and said, 'Kaila's right, though, he's not one of ours, not even from back when we started up. It's just not our style. I have no idea where you'd get a part like that, or even how you'd fit the cylinder if you did get one. I guess you could get one made, but I don't know who by or how long it'd take.'

'Oh,' I said, growing worried. Cory's next comment went some way to soothe me, however.

'I wouldn't worry too much, though. I'd say he had some

67

miles left on him. Get the cylinder replaced when you can, but he ain't about to drop dead, if that's your fear.'

I felt my shoulders drop, and I huffed out a breath I hadn't realized I'd been holding.

'Can you tell me what the fluid in the cylinder is for?' I asked, but Cory shook his head.

'Sorry, I honestly couldn't say. It could be a number of things: lubricant, coolant, fuel. Could even just be a balance thing, y'know, like you got fluid in your ear?' He shrugged. 'What I think you have here is a robot made by someone who needed to do it in a hurry, but who knows a lot more about AI than you'd think. See here.' He pointed to where Tang's arm met his body. 'This may look like just a tube, but the creator's done this for a reason. I'm guessing he didn't have everything he'd normally like to use at his disposal, so he used whatever he had. Using a tube like this means your robot's got a good range of motion. If he'd used fixed pieces of metal an' welded them together, he wouldn't be able to do half the things he can. The robot's body's a fixed box, as you see, but the range of arm movement compensates for it. The legs, too. He knew what he was doing, whoever put him together. Your best bet would be to find the guy who made him.'

I glanced at Tang, whose eyes were wide but whose feelings were impossible to discern. At the time it seemed he neither agreed nor disagreed with Cory's suggestion.

Cory rubbed his chin. 'I'm gonna go so far as to say I think it's almost deliberate what he's done.'

'Deliberate?'

'Yeah, the creator. You know, a bit like when they made the Eiffel Tower and it wasn't supposed to stay up very long, but it's still going.'

'I don't follow . . .'

'I don't think this little guy's body was ever supposed to last. I think it was meant to be temporary, including the cylinder.'

'Why would someone do that?'

Cory shrugged again. 'As I say, maybe he was in a rush. Maybe he didn't have the parts he needed. Maybe he intended to upgrade him when he got the chance.'

'Do you mean upgrade as in get a new one, or upgrade as in rebuild him?'

'Either.'

I nodded and then paused a moment.

'I have another question.'

'Shoot.'

'Why are you so sure it's a man that made him?'

Cory smiled and sat back in his chair, waving a finger at me. 'That's a good question. The answer is I'm not completely sure, more like 90 per cent sure. I've seen a lot of AI, and after a while you get to recognize types of work. It's a case of experience. You know how you can often tell whether handwriting belongs to a man or a woman? Well, it's the same sort of thing. I can't put my finger on it, he just seems . . . man-made. Literally. He's very masculine.'

I agreed with him. 'I knew when I first met him he was a boy robot. I mean, I know his voice is male, but it's more than that.'

'Funny, ain't it, the way we apply human qualities to these machines? People can get real attached to them. We have a cemetery just down the road for folks who've lost their androids.'

'You're kidding?'

Cory shook his head. 'Nope. They're like useful pets to

some people. I know what you're thinking, though – only in California, right?'

I made a gesture of protestation, but he was right – it was more or less what I was thinking.

'Anyway, about your trip, mission, whatever. I may not be able to help you, but I have a friend who might. Well, she's an online buddy, really, called Kittycat9835, real name Dr Lizzie Katz.'

'Does she make robots?'

He shook his head again and took off his glasses to rub his eyes with his clean fingers. 'Nope, she works in a museum in Houston, Texas. She's a robot historian, and I kinda figure that's what you need, Ben.' He paused and looked directly into my eyes. 'You should upgrade, y'know. I could give you a deal on one of our new models. You'll find they can do a lot more. And they don't come broken, obviously.' He gave a hearty laugh and slapped me on the upper arm.

Tang, who had been very patient until that point, rocked violently from foot to foot and clutched my arm so tightly I felt pain. My heart contracted with guilt that Tang had to hear that. I knew I cut a strange figure, hanging out with Tang, but I was so used to him that I kept forgetting how badly he stacked up against androids. He wasn't *that* old, probably not even six – but then, that probably *was* old in AI terms.

'Er, no, thank you. I'll stick with this one.'

Cory shrugged. 'Suit yourself. Here's my card, in case you change your mind.' Then he leaned in to me and hissed loudly into my ear, 'I wouldn't worry about offending your robot, Ben. Everyone upgrades eventually, and since he's already broken, well . . . he'll understand.'

He sounded like Amy. I didn't think Tang would under-stand, but I didn't say so. I thanked him for his time and his advice about my next move. Before leaving, I had one more question for him.

'You don't have a coffee machine around here, do you?'

8

Born to be Wild

AS I ORDERED A TAXI TO TAKE US TO THE NEAREST REPUTABLE car-hire firm, I began to feel more human. This was entirely due to the glorious taste of a hot mug of coffee, furnished me by Cory Fields, my new best friend.

Tang and I argued on the way.

'No, Tang. Can't you just leave it?'

Tang pointed to the sky. 'Preeeeeemeee-um.'

'No, Tang, I told you: it's too expensive.' Even as I said it, I knew I was lying. The truth was that Cory's comment about Tang having 'some miles' left in him had given me an excuse to take the slow option . . . to avoid flying.

I should have just said this to Tang when he started to argue again, but I was too proud.

'Pre—'

I held up a firm index finger in Tang's general direction. He gave me a Look and picked at his gaffer tape. I had put my foot down successfully. At least this time I wasn't being emotionally blackmailed by the product of a junkyard guesstimate.

I was back in charge for about twenty minutes – the time

that passed until a car-hire rep asked me, 'So, what kind of car did you have in mind?'

Tang hung on to my leg, pinching me with his grabbers and insisting that the car should be low-slung, so that he could get into it – a muscle car, in short, preferably a Mustang. I refused to hire a Mustang. Tang would not make a cliché out of me. The attendant, who took my side, offered us a mobility car instead, with a hoist that we could use to winch Tang in. Tang was unimpressed.

We hired a muscle car.

The attendant, who looked too young even to have a driving licence, managed to muster the professionalism required to ignore the beat-up demeanour of my robot. I tipped him handsomely for telling us they were all out of Mustangs, and he put some extra fuel in the car – a Dodge Charger – enough to just about get us off the forecourt, but I appreciated the thought.

Tang half-whirred, half-heaved himself into the passenger seat and proceeded to fiddle and push every button he could find. As he cycled through the radio stations with mounting glee, Californian rock was followed by Canadian ballads and a God channel.

'Tang, turn it off.'

He withdrew his arm and slumped back into his seat, picking at his gaffer tape.

'I'm sorry. Look, we can listen to whatever you want when we get going, OK?'

His little legs kicked up and down in front of him, a gesture I chose to see as agreement.

We set off. As we left San Jose behind us, the hilly terrain began to flatten, leaving us with expansive pale-blue vapour-trailed skies hanging over a sandy earth sparingly stippled with hardy green bushes but not much else. There were shadows of mountains in the distance, but the road never seemed to reach them, like they were part of a painted landscape being forever moved just beyond our reach.

Tang lost no time in rifling through the radio stations, just as I'd said he could. It took a while for him to settle. By the time he finally found something he liked, we were in the middle of a vast expanse of nothingness heading down Highway 5. I heard the song on his choice of station and my heart sank.

Not so very long ago I'd been in my comfortable, mortgage-free home, happily doing whatever I liked, and I had a wife who loved me. Well, maybe not the last, as it turned out, but I'm sure she was fond of me at least. At one time, perhaps. Now I was driving a Dodge Charger through California past dust-blown succulents and tumbleweeds, with no wife, no job and no idea where in hell I was heading. I also had a retro robot who'd decided, of all the stations, to pick the one playing 'Born To Be Wild'.

Scowling at the windscreen, I reached for the radio controls, but Tang brought his metal fist down with a painful thump on top of my outstretched hand and I withdrew it, wincing. He gave me a hard stare. It was obvious that Tang took pleasure in the song. He rolled his window down, slumped as best he could in his seat and laid one of his little metal arms on the car door, giving a whirring squeal of delight at the rush of air that came through the open window and tickled his eyeballs. He leaned as much of his head then upper body out of the car as possible, and his gaffer tape flapped at high frequency in the wind, making a buzzing noise like a fly in a beer bottle.

'Tang, close the window . . . It's too noisy!' I shouted, with no result. 'Tang,' I clonked him on the side, 'shut the window . . . you're missing the song!' I pointed to the car stereo, and he sat back in his seat and rolled the window up.

He sat for a while, fidgeting one of his feet vaguely in time. The fidget became a definite move, then his other foot joined in, then his arms, and before long he was expressing his love for the driving song with his own brand of jerky dancing, which made me laugh. Tang noticed me chuckling and began to kick his legs up and down with happiness. But as the tune continued to ring out, my mood began to dip. Tang had such a lot of personality, and it was growing all the time. Yet he was not 'born to be wild'. He was . . . 'made to be servile'. And with the thought of his leaking cylinder that meant his time would be up sooner or later, it all made me sad.

The monotony of Highway 5 eventually skirted past the urban sprawl of Los Angeles, which in turn popped back out into flatness and end-of-the-rainbow mountains again. We did see a wind farm, though, upon which Tang kept his eyes fixed as we drew nearer, his head making tiny circular movements in an attempt to keep up with the motion of the turbines. After we had driven past them, he turned as best he could and watched out of the back of the car as they faded into the landscape behind us.

For hours on end I drove. The car was on cruise control, which was fortunate because I found it difficult to concentrate with so little change in visual stimulus. My mind wandered to Amy. I wondered what she was doing at that moment and what she would say if she were with us. She'd probably tell me to concentrate on my driving and stop drifting around in my own head.

Without noticing, we'd passed into Arizona and were well on our way towards New Mexico when a tug of Tang's grabber on my rolled-up shirt sleeve dragged me back from my thoughts. I'd slowed down, without realizing, to go through a town – such as it was – and Tang was gesturing at something behind us.

I looked in the rear-view mirror and saw nothing.

'Oof . . . w-oof,' said Tang, 'woof.' He frowned when I looked confused.

'What're you saying, mate? You sound like a dog.'

He sat back down, squealed and kicked his legs.

'You're being a dog? Why?'

'Yes. Dog.'

I asked him why a dog.

'Dog. Dog. Dog. Dog . . .' he said, gesturing behind us again.

This time I rolled my own window down and peered out to see behind the car. Near the boot, too close to be seen in the rear-view mirror but just visible as he legged it behind us, was a sausage dog.

I turned back round to face the front. What I wanted to do was to completely ignore this tiny dog chasing us down the road. I wanted to look straight ahead and drive through this apparently deserted town without incident. But fate intervened as my bladder called for attention. I sighed and looked in my wing mirror in time to see the dachshund pop into view from behind the car and pop back out of sight again. He weaved from side to side behind us, following the car, somehow able to keep up.

'Dog . . . dog . . . dog . . .' said Tang at intervals, every time the dachshund popped into view on his side of the car.

'Shut up, Tang, I know it's a dog.' But even as I said it

I knew I was going to have to stop to find out what the dachshund wanted.

'So, I need the loo anyway.' I pulled off the road and drew up alongside a sidewalk in front of a small parade of hardware, liquor and grocery stores, all of which were closed. As I looked up and down the street, it seemed that everything was closed: doors, windows, shutters.

'What's going on here?' I thought out loud. 'Bank holiday? Zombie invasion?' I felt a nudge on my leg and looked down to see the dog's narrow face staring up at me. He was ginger all over, with glazed green eyes and half an ear missing, and he sported – as dachshunds must – a red spotted neckerchief. I bent down to pat his head and squinted at the tag on his collar.

'He's called Kyle, Tang. Kyle – that's hilarious!'

Tang heaved himself out of the car and clanked round to join me. He poked the dog in its side. The dachshund responded with a sniff of Tang's legs and undercarriage. Then he picked up one short leg and urinated on the robot. Tang shrieked and tried to bat the dog away, but the dog was persistent. He gazed up unblinkingly into the robot's face. Understandably, Tang looked angry, and I didn't help matters by finding it funny.

'Aw, come on, Tang, he's just being friendly.'

'Friend,' he said, considering the word. 'Ben friend. Dog not friend.'

I shooed the dachshund away with my foot and looked around for something with which to wipe Tang. All I could find was a shammy leather from the boot of the car.

'Go now,' requested Tang.

'You've changed your tune. A few minutes ago you wanted me to stop.'

77

'No people in town, only dog,' he explained. 'And dog faulty . . . leaks. So town faulty.'

I couldn't argue with his logic, but I still needed to relieve myself. The dog himself was trotting round and round the car on his little legs, sniffing the wheels and radiator grill.

I wandered up and down the main drag looking for a café or bar – anywhere that might have a bathroom I could use – but there was nothing open. In the end, I peed behind a dumpster in an alleyway. Out of the corner of my eye, I could see Tang watching me. When I finished, I strolled quickly back to the main street to resume exploring.

'What a weird place,' I thought out loud again. It was not much more than just the one street, but not a single shop was open, nor was there a house or apartment without its windows shuttered. We must have taken a wrong turn somewhere, though on the big, wide American highways I wasn't sure that was possible.

A veneer of desert dust covered every surface, and as I looked around I came across a sign tacked to the inside of a shop window. It read 'CLOSED until we're allowed back again'. I walked down to the end of the parade. At the very last house there was a fence post on which a length of broken plastic tape flapped. Across the yellow tape, in big black capitals, were the words 'CAUTION' and 'RADIATION'.

With horror, I legged it back to the Dodge as fast as I could. Tang was looking at me, confused. 'Tang! Get back in the car – we're leaving!'

Kyle was still nosing around the wheels. I grabbed him around his soft tummy and tossed him on to the back seat.

Tang looked even more confused now. His little eyes began to turn inward.

'Don't worry, Tang, we just have to leave. Now. And Kyle has to come, too – it's not safe for him.'

I saw Tang's face cloud over, the same way that Amy's used to. He swivelled his head to look at Kyle, who lunged over and licked his face. This caused a screech and some panicked flailing. Tang glared at me, eyes blazing, and slumped back in his seat.

Now, I have to admit that the idea of travelling across the desert in a Dodge Charger with a retro robot and a radio-active sausage dog is not something I would have imagined myself doing. But life takes us in peculiar directions sometimes, and on those occasions the only thing to do is give it a high-five and roll with it. There are also worse ways to spend an autumn. Tiptoeing round a house in the middle of a failing marriage, for example. Yes, this was infinitely more pleasurable.

I'd been driving for a long time and had even slept in the car by the side of the road. But we were only just arriving in Texas and still nowhere near Houston. The road we travelled on seemed endless and unchanging, and it felt like the only other vehicles to pass us were huge oil tankers and pick-up trucks, one of which had a dead horse in the back.

I felt hungry and fed up, so pulled in at the first gas station I could see, filled the car up and wandered into the shop to pay and find something to eat. I selected a microwave hotdog, some cheese slices and a variety of other gastronomic treats. The attendant behind the counter was a fat man who looked like he kept grenades in his basement, so I wasn't keen to stop too long. However, as I handed over some cash it turned out I couldn't avoid conversation.

'Are you lost, friend?'

'Er, no, I don't think so.'

'Yeah, y'are.'

'Why do you say that?'

'Because you're here. And you came from *that* direction. Everyone knows what's in *that* direction.'

'The town? The one with no people?'

'Yup, nobody except one dog, and he just keeps goin' back 'n' forth.'

'Back and forth?'

'Yup,' he said with finality. It was clear there was no more to be had on the subject of Kyle, but he continued along a different path. 'You ain't the first to get lost down here and not know it.' The attendant spread a map across the counter and pointed a pudgy finger to where we were. 'This here is where y'are,' he said, then moved his finger to a different spot. 'And I'm guessin' that's where you need to be. I never know how you people get here, but if you carry on up this road you'll get to a crossroads, and you need to take a right. That'll get you back on track.'

I looked to where he was pointing. Sure enough, the road led right to Houston. When I say 'led right to', it was still several hundred miles away, but this was Texas.

'If you don't mind me asking,' I said, 'what happened to the town?'

'Radiation leak,' he offered helpfully, slinging my hotdog into the microwave behind the counter. 'That town was built entirely to support the workers in a facility nearby. And that's why I'm here, too. But I'm not stupid. I didn't want to be sitting on top of a nuclear reactor, so I parked myself just that little bit further away.'

'Very wise,' I said, 'in hindsight.'

'Yup. Anyways, whatever they were doing there went

wrong, and they came and shipped everyone out and closed the place down.'

The attendant picked up on my discomfort.

'Don't worry – it was a long, long time ago. You'll be fine. I'm still here, ain't I?'

I think that was supposed to make me feel better, and I suppose it sort of did. I was on the verge of asking how long was a 'long, long time' but decided I didn't really want to know.

I thanked the attendant again and took my now steaming, floppy hotdog back to the car.

'O-kay?' asked Tang.

'Yep, don't worry about it, mate,' I said, more confidently than I felt, but I was determined not to alarm him, if for no other reason than I had a deposit down on the car that would almost certainly be compromised by an oil stain on the seat. I also felt the pressing matter of Tang's broken cylinder, which was worrying me more and more.

A snuffling sound at my ear made me jump, and I glanced to find Kyle trying to wrap his chops around my hotdog. I'd got so used to not having to feed Tang I'd not considered whether the dog might be hungry. I ripped off the top of my hotdog and gave it to him. He didn't look malnourished, but he was still a dog and dispatched the food like he'd never eaten anything so good. So I opened a packet of crisps and offered him a few from the palm of my hand.

As soon as I'd eaten, I drove off swiftly, because despite what the attendant had said I still wanted to get as far away from OneDog as possible. The fact remained, however, that we now had a dog in the car, and I wasn't sure what to do about him.

'Tang, we might need to spend a bit more time around here. We're going to need to find Kyle's owners.'

We found out pretty quickly that Kyle didn't need – or want – owners. Whether it was the terrible junk food I'd given him, or the fact that Tang kept turning round to poke Kyle in the ear with a grabber, or pinch his paws, when I stopped at the next town for another loo break and some dinner the dog hopped out of the car of his own accord. I expected him to follow me to the bathroom, but he just sat with his small bottom on the hot tarmac. I walked a few paces away before turning round and calling him over to me.

'Leave him,' Tang said from the car.

'That's not kind, Tang.'

I walked back up to Kyle, crouched down with my cramped knees and put my hand out for him. He licked it and nuzzled under my fingers for me to stroke his head.

'Hey! Kyle, my main man,' came a voice from behind me.

I turned to see a good-looking bloke in a checked shirt and pale jeans swaggering towards us. He bent down next to Kyle and raised his hand in front of the dog's face. The dog high-fived him.

'You know him?' I asked.

'Yup, everyone knows him. He's a regular around here.'

'Who does he belong to?'

The man laughed, showing a couple of unexpectedly dazzling teeth. 'He don't belong to no one. There's not one family in this town that ain't tried to adopt him, but he just won't be doing with the restriction. He gets fed everywhere he goes, but he don't ever stay more than a few hours. He likes to go home.'

I asked him where that might be.

'Small town back that way,' he gestured. 'It ain't got no people in it, just the dawg. I figure it's the way he likes it. Don't get me wrong, he ain't a loner, he just likes his freedom is all. He don't wanna be no pet.'

'But he has a collar . . .'

'Yup, that he does. No one knows who put that on him, must have been the folks that did own him once upon a time, back when that town had a life.'

'Oh. I just brought him from that town. I thought he was lost. He chased our car.'

'Yup, he does that. Crazy lil' bastard.'

Kyle gave a short yap and leapt into the air, as if to second the man's statement.

'Should I have left him? I didn't mean to take him away from home.'

The man waved away my question. 'Naw, don't worry 'bout it, he likes to hitch a lift from people. You'd be surprised how many folks get lost along this way. He just comes along for the ride with them sometimes. Anyways, I gotta get goin'.' He shook my hand and high-fived the dog again. 'Catch ya later, Kyle. Don't do anything I wouldn't do.'

As he walked off, I remembered the conversation with the gas-station attendant.

'Goes back and forth,' he'd said. It seemed that Kyle had just used us as a shuttle, and apparently it wasn't the first time.

A door opened behind me, and Tang appeared at my side.

'Leave him?' he suggested.

83

'Erm . . . yeah, I guess we can do.'

Tang hopped from foot to foot and squealed before wrapping his grabber around my legs.

'Ben and Tang,' he said. 'Ben and Tang.'

'OK, Tang, I get the message.' I detached him, and we set off to look for a diner.

9

All God's Creatures

IT WAS GETTING LATE IN THE DAY WHEN WE PULLED UP AT our motel of choice – a single-storey, horseshoe-shaped establishment somewhere near Fort Stockton on Highway 10, a signpost said. The motel choice was based entirely upon the fact that it appeared to be clean, reasonably well maintained and most importantly not like it was run by a murderer. The last assumption was based entirely upon my assessment of the two former, although I suppose if you were a psychopath trying to lure motorists to your establishment you might make it clean and appealing. But I didn't think of that at the time.

We pulled off the road and crossed the parking lot; the sandy micro-gravel with which it was covered crackled and creaked under our wheels. With his whole head locked on it like an owl, Tang kept his eyes fixed on the motel's flashing neon 'Stay Here!' sign as we drove slowly by. The yellow and blue light seemed to delight him, and every time it blinked off then on again he squealed like it was the best thing he'd ever seen.

Tang's squealing announced our presence, and a tall,

broad man stomped heavily out of a prefabricated office set to one side of the motel complex. He was a stereotypical Texan, from his country-rock Stetson and his beard/ moustache combo to his checked shirt and the shotgun perched like a parrot on his shoulder. But when the eye reached his knees, it met one faded-denim real leg and one metal one gleaming in the sunset like a Cadillac.

Tang's eyes widened when he saw it. To him, this man was not the victim of an unfortunate accident or, more likely, a war vet. To him, he was a bionic man, a crossbreed, the stuff of robot fairy stories.

'Lookin' fer a room, friend?'

'Yes, please. Both of us . . . twin beds.'

The man raised an eyebrow but nodded. He cocked his head towards his office and began to walk off, so we followed.

'Fine little critter you got there. A classic. Yup.'

I glanced at Tang, and if there had been bubbles in the shape of hearts coming out of his head I would not have been surprised. To this man, Tang was not a rusty robot or a throwback. He was a classic. What's more, the Texan was the first person we'd come across, bar Kyle the dachshund, who hadn't done a double take at me and my old model. Hell, I was beginning to fall in love with him myself.

'He is, thank you. Most people only see him as an obsolete specimen.'

'Nope. What you got there is solid-gold ingineerin'.'

I flicked my eyes across Tang's gaffer tape.

'Yup. They sure don't make 'em like that any more.'

'Well, that's certainly true.'

We'd reached the office by this time, and the Texan was running his finger over a bank of room keys along a wall.

'Here y'are. Room 8. Got twin beds and one of them's broke, so it's lower down than the other . . . Might be easier for the lil' fella to git up on to it.'

I thanked him.

'Don't mention it. There's a TV set in the room and hot and cold runnin' water and shower an' all. Laundrybot comes by every evening. Give me a holler if y'all need anything else. Have a good night.'

I don't know if it was the broken bed or if he just took a shine to Tang and decided to do us a deal, but he quoted us a very reasonable rate.

As I headed back to the car for our things, I caught sight of my reflection in the car window. I needed a shower. Getting a few items cleaned via a Laundrybot wasn't a bad idea, either. They were mostly used in hotels and motels as the most efficient way of offering a cleaning service to guests. In general, I didn't see the point of an android, but Laundrybots were a bit different. They were very handy. And polite, usually. Easy too, since all a person had to do was to chuck washing inside its body, feed it a few coins and away it went. Well, off it went chuntering to itself in a corner while it cleaned your pants . . . it didn't literally go off with your clothes, not unless it malfunctioned. But that was very rare. Newer models almost never did.

I have had only one notably bad experience with a Laundrybot. Amy had to go on a business trip to Geneva a few years ago – back in the days when we still enjoyed each other's company. I went with her, and we stayed in a lovely hotel overlooking the lake. Amy's firm was paying, and they didn't spare any expense – I could have quite easily amused myself for the duration of the trip without even leaving the hotel, such were the amenities. I got to spend the first evening with Amy, as her conference didn't start until the next day and her colleagues had not yet arrived. We went for dinner in one of the hotel restaurants, and in the middle of the meat course I managed to knock a full glass of wine across the table and into Amy's lap. It soaked through her floaty cream dress – her favourite, naturally – in milliseconds and soured the evening. We didn't stay for dessert.

'I'm really sorry, Amy, I'll get a Laundrybot to look at it tomorrow.'

'That's no good now, though, is it? By then it'll be ruined. It needs to be dealt with quickly. I'll have to soak it overnight.'

'Well, let me take it to reception to see if there's still a 'bot active in the hotel at this time.'

Back in the room, she changed into her pyjamas and handed over the precious dress for me to make right again.

At reception I was informed that all Laundrybots were either in use or docked for the night.

'Please, please help me. It's my wife's favourite dress, she's really angry with me and I don't want to spend our entire stay in Geneva being given the silent treatment.'

'*Pardon, Monsieur,* but we have no Laundrybots available at this time. I can book one to come to you first thing in the morning?'

I gave the receptionist my best, floppy-haired, English puppy-dog eyes.

'Please . . . is there really nothing you can do?'

She pouted as she thought for a moment. 'Well, we have just upgraded all our Laundrybots, and we do have several of the old ones left in storage in the basement. They have not been used in a while and only speak French, but I can see if there is one charged enough to come and see you.'

'Thank you,' I said, heaving a sigh of relief. 'Thank you so much.'

A maintenance man appeared a while later with a Laundrybot shuffling behind him. It looked a little dusty and confused.

'*Monsieur*,' the maintenance man said gruffly. He gestured to the 'bot, which blinked at me. Then the man excused himself, and I was left alone with the droid.

'*Parlez-vous Français?*' asked the Laundrybot.

'*Non*,' I told him. I could just about ask for two beers, but that would not be helpful here. The android and I stared at each other. Late though it was, there were still some people in reception, so I decided to take the Laundrybot elsewhere to avoid embarrassing myself. I found a corridor down near the spa and sat down on a chair. Perfect. The Laundrybot squatted down opposite me, waiting for my washing. I sighed and pointed to the dress.

'This. Delicate. Gentle wash. Yes?'

The droid blinked at me and started to make a ticking sound. I leaned forward in my chair to read a plate on the front of it. It was also in French, but there was a brief English translation underneath which read:

1 – normal
2 – fast
3 – full
4 – natural fibres
5 – linen

I wasn't sure what 'full' meant, but it probably wasn't what I wanted for the dress. I also didn't know what the dress was made of, though a look at the label told me it was half silk and half something else that I had never heard of. Then there was 'fast', which seemed like a good idea because Amy had said it was a matter of urgency. I held up two fingers to the Laundrybot.

'*Deux?*'

'*Oui.*'

Then the droid said something else in French, which I took to be an instruction to insert the dress and the appropriate money. I did so. Then all that was left was for me to sit, wait and hope for the best.

About twenty minutes into the cycle, the Laundrybot suddenly got up and walked off.

'Er . . . excuse me? Um . . . where are you going? . . . Oh, bloody hell.'

I chased after it and tried to block its way, but it pushed passed me unstoppably and carried on, leaving me to follow helplessly like the ignorant Englishman I was. To my great relief, the Laundrybot headed back to reception. At least there I could plead with the clerk to intervene.

The android was surprisingly fast, stalking straight through reception and making a beeline for the elevators. As I flew after it, I called out to the receptionist.

'It's going off with my wife's dress! Help me, please. Stop it!'

The receptionist gasped, then shouted something in French to the droid, which stopped instantly and turned its head to face her. There followed an argument between woman and Laundrybot that the android seemed at first to be winning. In the end, the receptionist clonked it on the head with a pumped fist, then there was a click and the door to its washing cavity opened. Soapy water flowed on to the floor, along with Amy's dress, which was now a scary shade of blackish green.

'*Merde*,' the receptionist said.

The laundry droid came by that evening, just as the motel man had said it would. Tang was spread out like a star on his broken bed and I was in the shower when I caught the sound of a faint knocking at the door.

'Tang, can you get that, please?'

Silence.

'The door, Tang, the door.'

'Get . . . the door?'

'I mean open it; see who's there. Please.' There was a pause, then a faint draught drifted into the bathroom, causing the shower curtain to swish. 'Who's there?'

'Android,' said Tang, disapprovingly.

'Oh, is it the Laundrybot?'

'Yes.'

'Can you tell him to wait?'

'Wait?'

'Yes, I have some things to clean.'

'Android is leaving,' Tang informed me.

'Tang! I told you to tell him to wait!'

I turned off the shower in a hurry and flung a towel around my waist. I stepped back into the room in time to see Tang about to close the door on the Laundrybot.

'Tang, what did you say to him?'

'Go away now.'

'So, the exact opposite of what I told you to say.'

'Yes.'

'Why?'

'Ben does not need and-roid. Ben has Tang.'

'Oh look, Tang, yes, I've got you, but I also need clean clothes. Understand?'

Tang turned his eyes downward and picked at his gaffer tape.

'Look, sometimes androids are necessary. And he hasn't done anything to you, has he?'

'No.'

'Well, good then.'

I ran out into the mild Texas night after the Laundrybot, still wrapped only in my towel, and brought him back to the room. I noted with relief that the android was a new model. The motel might have broken beds, but when it came to AI the owner knew what he was doing. I fed the droid's chest cavity some shorts, underwear and a few shirts, and put some coins in. It settled down where it was and stared into the middle distance as its innards worked on my washing.

Tang sat on his bed and stared the android down. The difference between the two was marked. Tang was two square boxes stacked on top of each other, scratched, battered and rusting a little. The Laundrybot was a sleek, curved and shiny piece of kit that operated silently and carried out its business with no fuss.

Occasionally, when the laundry cycle moved on a stage, the android woke up a bit. When this happened, it stared back at Tang with equal force, as though they were on the main drag in the Wild West.

The washing done, the droid thanked me for my custom, picked itself up and left. Tang looked at me from under his eyelids in a grump, but he was instantly more comfortable.

'So, tell me again why you don't like androids.'

'No.'

'Is it because you're jealous?'

It was a moment before Tang replied, 'No.'

'Then what?'

Tang was silent.

'Tang, don't be obstinate. Talk to me.'

'Sleep now.'

I sat down with a sigh on a wobbly wooden chair in the corner and folded my arms. 'OK, fine, be like that.'

Sleep didn't come easily to me that night. I lay on my bed, fully dressed, watching the neon sign blink on and off through a small gap in the curtains. Light spots seeped on to the wall like the mash-up of aurora borealis and a digital watch.

My mind was churning about Amy. What was she doing now? Where was she staying? Was she with anyone? Was she happy? I had thought her irrational and reactionary during our relationship, but something in the back of my mind was racing to the fore now that told me I was partly to blame. Perhaps she could have loved me if I'd only been less . . . frustrating.

At around midnight, I decided to go and find a late-night bar. Tang was sparked out with his arms flopped over his head. He made a soft tick-tick-tick noise when he slept, which was cute but was stopping me from drifting off. It did indicate that he was on standby for the night, so it felt safe to leave him.

I drove through the warm, thick evening to the nearest town, similar in size to OneDog but more lively, where I found an open bar.

There was a boxing match playing on a mounted screen in

a top corner, the clientele occasionally offering their advice to the fighters. As I pushed through the wooden door, the barman, who was cleaning a glass, nodded to me and turned back to the match. I settled myself on a bar stool.

'What can I get ye?' he asked, his eyes fixed on the screen.

I perused the shelves and opted for beer. He popped the top off a Bud and set it down in front of me. Then he returned to the match, which suited me fine.

I sat quietly for a long time, drinking my cool beer. The first bottle went down easily, the pleasure of it offsetting the grimy feeling of sweat and dust that had coated my skin in the short time since I left the motel. I ordered another beer. A few large swigs of the second bottle and I realized it too would be gone in a moment if I wasn't careful. I wanted to get the Dodge back to the motel if I could. I didn't plan to go weaving down the highway to get stopped by a brown-hatted depudee. Besides, I had a robot to take care of, and what would happen to him if I were banged up?

After a while, I felt myself being watched. I ventured a tentative glance to either side and spotted a grey-moustachioed old man peering at me from the end of the bar, the only patron other than me not to be watching the match. Glancing had been a bad idea. It was an invitation. The second he caught my eye, he slid along the bar in a way that told me he'd done this before and that he was half-cut already, shuffling the bar stools out of the way like skittles. As he drew alongside me, I got a better look at him. He had two yellow forefingers on his left hand that spoke of tobacco, and a shirt that'd been dyed the colour of Jim Beam.

'The name's Sandy.' He offered his hand to me. It felt clammy and full of bone.

'Ben.'

'Y'know what they say about folks that pull the labels off their beer?' (Something I'd been doing just a moment earlier.) He nodded to my bottle.

I said I didn't.

'They reckon it means you need a girl.'

'I have a girl. Well, had.'

'Aha.'

'Now I have a robot.'

Pause. Sandy raised a bushy white eyebrow.

'I mean, I'm looking after a robot . . . I don't have any time for a girl. I'm trying to get him fixed . . . the robot.'

Sandy creased up his eyebrows and wrinkled his long nose, stumped for words.

'Well, I . . . that there's a good profession.'

'Not as good as being a vet,' I continued.

Now he had a glimmer of hope in his eye (glazed as it was). 'Ah now, there's a lot to be said for being a vet, but don't forget there's a lotta pain that goes along with it.' He sank down on the stool and looked fixedly ahead of him as if reading some small writing on the wall. 'Yup, you don't ever forget the things you seen.'

'Oh . . . no, I mean a veterinary surgeon.'

'Say, what's that you say?'

'I said I meant . . . Never mind.'

But Sandy wouldn't give up.

'So where is your lil' . . . rowbaht?' He rolled the word around his wide mouth with its varyingly cemented teeth, and it was pleasing to hear in his deep Texan accent.

'He's back at the motel, sleeping. Well, on standby.'

'Is he safe?'

'What do you mean, "safe"?'

95

'Without you there . . . is he gonna be OK?'

'Why not?'

'Well, you said you was takin' care of him, but here y'are drinkin' with me. So, I gotta ask myself, is he safe?'

I wanted to tell him I wouldn't go so far as to say we were 'drinking together', but I didn't. Instead, I said, 'He's a robot, what's he going to do?'

'Suppose he wakes up and you're not there. Won't he get scared? Let me tell you a story. This one time I was working on my ranch, back when my hands worked properly and when my darlin' Ginny was still alive. Anyways, I had a little rowbaht, humanoid-type thing, 'bout five feet,' (he gestured with a hand up to his chest) 'and I used to take him with me when I went pannin' fer gold.'

As he continued his story, I started to wonder whether he was making it all up – was he a soldier, or a rancher or a miner? It seemed he couldn't decide.

'. . . So this one sunny day I thought I'd have myself a little sleep under this tree, and when I woke up my little guy was gone. I looked all over fer him, that day and into the night, and the next day, too. I figured he couldn't ha' gone far. After a few days I found him. I went downstream and there he was, round a bend in the river.'

'Was he OK?'

'Nup, not a bit. I found him face down in the stream. He'd just gone.' At this point he indicated with his hand and a whistle the robot falling face down into the stream, ending with a slap of his palm on the bar. 'I tried to dry him out, but, y'know, once they're wet no amount of hairdryers or ovens or bags o' rice are gonna get 'em right.'

'That's really sad,' I told him.

'Yes, yes, it is. So I say agin, is your robot gonna be OK without you there?'

I paused, my chest suddenly contracting with a tremor of fear. I had my doubts about the validity of his story, but what he said had touched me unexpectedly and made me anxious. Suppose Tang did wake up while I was gone. What would he think? Would he get out of the room somehow and go wandering off looking for me? And what about his broken cylinder? I realized I hadn't checked his gauge in a while.

'I have to go,' I said suddenly, picking myself off my stool.

'Yeah, y'do,' agreed Sandy.

I shook his hand for the second time. 'It was a pleasure to meet you, Sandy.' I unfolded some notes from my wallet and laid them on the bar, calling for the barman as I did so. 'That's to close my tab, and some more for whatever this gentleman is having next.' Sandy tipped his hat to me and I all but ran out of the bar, my legs trying to keep pace with my heart.

So I hurried out to the Dodge and back to the motel as quickly as I could safely go, given that I'd had a few. As I pulled into the parking lot, it was clear that something was wrong. Blue lights lit up the motel buildings, and a small crowd was gathered around the entrance to my room – probably the entire staff and guest complement. I felt tight in my stomach and my palms had begun to sweat. I parked awkwardly, threw myself out of the car and ran the last few feet. The owner with the metal leg spotted me and stared me down. He held his hands on his hips.

'It's you. You ain't got no right. What kind of monster are you?'

'Can someone please tell me what's happened? And can I get into my room? Tang? Are you OK, mate?'

I couldn't see him. The small crowd were surprisingly solid as I tried to push my way past them.

'You should be ashamed of yourself,' continued Metal-Leg.

I found Tang sitting on his low broken bed wrapped in a blanket, with a police officer crouched next to him, patting him on his small metal shoulder. As I came hurrying through the door, they all turned to stare.

'This your robot?'

'Yes. Tang, are you OK?'

'Yes,' he replied dully.

I crouched down and put my arms around him as tightly as I could, making the blanket fall to the floor. He reached for it.

'Blanket. Blanket. Blanket. Blanket.'

'OK, OK. Here you go.' I tucked the blanket back around his shoulders, and he gripped it with his grabbers like it was going to fall again.

'What happened, Tang? Tell me.'

But before he could speak, the cop offered his account.

'I got called here by the proprietor around twelve thirty, saying he heard screaming coming from this room . . .'

Metal-Leg took up the tale.

'I brought my shotgun and kicked the door down . . . Saw here yer lil' friend screamin' and carryin' on like the end of the world was coming. He wus marchin' round the room, shoutin', "Ben! Ben! Ben! Ben! Ben!" So I called the cops.'

I began to breathe more calmly now.

'So, nothing had happened to him? I saw the blanket and thought he'd fallen in a river somewhere.'

'Nup. Just scared on his own. You oughta be ashamed of yourself, leavin' him like that. Supposing he'd wandered off?'

I thought about telling him he wouldn't have gone off from a locked room unless the door had been kicked in, but I took his point.

'Scared,' said Tang.

'I know you were, mate, I'm so sorry.' And to everyone's surprise, mine included, I leaned forward and kissed his cool head.

'Mr . . .'

'Chambers.'

'. . . Mr Chambers,' the cop said as he got up from the floor on creaky knees, 'we take robot cruelty very seriously around here. I don't know what you do or where you come from, but here they's workers, and you gotta care for them.'

An old guy standing at the back of the crowd that had filled my motel room piped up, 'Yessum. Otherwise they breaks on ya. Then the harvest don't come in.'

'He may not be one of those fancy-ass *aaaanndroiid* types,' the cop continued, brushing down his uniform, 'but he's God's creature. And don't you ferget it.'

'Yup,' chorused the old guy, nods of agreements coming from what seemed like his wife and a couple of other late-comers to the scene.

'Be that as it may, I don't think there's anything I can arrest you for here, so I'm leaving now. But I'm warning you . . .'

I was almost down on my knees with shame and self-disgust. I told the cop it wouldn't happen again.

'You're damn right it won't,' chimed in Metal-Leg. He

bent down to Tang's level. 'Why don't you stay here with me, buddy?'

A sudden cold tremor shot through me, and I found myself a little shaky. But Tang swivelled his head to look at him and then twisted it right and left, giving a clear 'No' signal.

'Ben,' he said quietly, and reached out his grabber to take my hand.

'So be it,' Metal-Leg turned back to me, 'but I want you off my property first thing, y'hear? I can't have people thinkin' that screamin' is what goes on in this motel; it's bad fer business.'

The police officer disappeared out of the door and the onlookers followed him out of my room. I was surprised by the strength of feeling around here and aggrieved that they didn't know how much I had begun to care for Tang. Perhaps I hadn't demonstrated it, though, and my feelings had taken me by surprise. When the last of the spectators had left, I checked Tang's cylinder. Cory had been optimistic – though there was still a decent amount of fluid in there, the level was noticeably lower than it had been in California.

Early in the morning, we waved goodbye to the motel – Tang very much with the moral high ground and me suitably chastened.

10

Museum Piece

WE DROVE THE LAST DISTANCE FROM THE MOTEL TO HOUSTON – a mere seven hours – in companionable silence. Tang seemed to have forgiven me, although I still felt ashamed of myself. I put his favourite radio station on, and he stared out of the window at cactus after cactus, swinging his foot along to the beat.

It was well after lunch when we reached the suburbs of the city, and the sun was hot in the sky. I decided to pick up some food from a convenience store, then head straight to the museum.

The Houston Space Museum was an old NASA facility with an industrial feel to it, an old brick-and-metal warehouse where school parties went on trips to learn about the twentieth century's Final Frontier. Few people seemed to care about space travel these days, and I thought the entrance hall was grander than the museum warranted, with miniature rockets and a model solar system suspended from the ceiling. Several doorways on each wall of the hallway marked the entry to various exhibitions, and a metal staircase swept up the middle to a mezzanine with a similar set-up of doors. Arrowed signs stood sentry outside each doorway to orientate the visitor, though from the entrance I couldn't see what they said. Since we weren't tourists but were rather looking for a member of their staff, I marched confidently to the information desk and asked for a Dr Lizzie Katz.

'She's expecting me . . . us.' (I'd had a brief conversation with her by email on our way from California, each interaction taking place when we stopped for me to eat.)

'One moment, please.' There was a pause while she called Dr Katz. 'She'll be right down. Take a seat, please; help yourself to water.'

I looked around for the seats and, finding none, stuck my hands in my pockets and waited. When Dr Katz wasn't 'right down', I poured myself a cone of water from the nearby drinking fountain. It was then I noticed Tang had wandered off. I looked around but couldn't see him, and a glance at the clerk filing her nails and flicking through her magazine told me she probably couldn't see him, either.

'When Dr Katz comes down, can you tell her . . . tell her I'll be right back. Please don't let her cancel my appointment.'

Not waiting for a reply, I decided to go through one of the doors leading to an exhibition. I didn't bother with the grand staircase. Just as I stepped through one of the doorways, I heard a crash coming from another room. I skidded over to the sound of the noise – in an adjoining room – and there was Tang standing with one of his grabbers stretched out in front of him, on the other side of a rope barrier, and what looked to be a model of an android dismantled on the floor in front of him.

Tang froze when he saw me.

'Tang, what on earth are you doing? Did you break this?'

'No . . .'

'Tang, I think what you just said is a lie.'

'A lie?'

'Yes, it means you say something that you know is wrong, something that isn't true. Is it true that you touched the model and it fell over?'

Tang considered this. He withdrew his grabber slowly and carefully, then I noticed he was holding a plastic finger. Tang spotted me looking and dropped it on the floor, where it rolled a little before coming to a rest by my bare toe.

'Tang, is it true?'

'Yes.' He cast his eyes downward.

'Well, I'm glad you were honest . . . eventually. Why were you touching the model in the first place?'

Tang didn't get a chance to answer, for through the doorway behind me stepped Dr Lizzie Katz.

The robotics historian was surprisingly friendly, considering we'd been here only ten minutes and had smashed one of her exhibits. Tang sat on a cracked old green-leather chair in Dr Katz's office while she peered inside at his cylinder. To my relief, I saw that the fluid level was not much lower than the last time I'd checked. She shut Tang's flap and smoothed the gaffer tape back with long delicate fingers, then set about looking Tang over in great detail. She raised one of his arms, then the other, wiggling his feet around until he shook with what I took to be his giggling again. She had unruly blonde hair, artfully tamed in a ponytail, and wore a purple cotton blouse and coordinating wide-leg trousers. She didn't look at all how I imagined a curator to look . . . a bit like Amy, in fact.

I looked down at myself, in camel-coloured ripstop shorts, Birkenstocks and a white shirt, feeling every inch the tourist. Though it was autumn – Halloween, to be exact – it was still warm. In Texas, they may have been used to the heat, but I wasn't. I raised a hand self-consciously to the crown of my head. My hair was wavy and thick, and still black like my mother's but starting to run to grey like my father's.

But if Dr Katz noticed what I was wearing she gave no sign. She was absorbed by the vintage article I'd brought to see her. I explained that although I was primarily looking for someone who could fix Tang's cylinder, I was also looking for any information at all she could give me about him. I told her I'd found him in the garden. For some reason, I didn't mention Amy.

'He's amazing,' she said.

I said, yes, he was.

'And you said he just turned up? My God, how did you ever find where to bring him?'

'Process of elimination. And a lot of luck. And Cory.'

She nodded. 'I know Cory through a chat room. AI hobbyists. And before you give me a look, I'll admit I'm a nerd. Cory designs supposedly realistic games for teenagers in a company that makes androids, and I make sure those kids don't forget how we got there . . . sorta.' I detected a note of envy in her voice. She sat down behind her desk, her eyes lingering on Tang for quite some time.

Tang and I looked sidelong at each other.

'I'm thinking,' she said eventually.

From his chair, Tang wiggled his feet absently but didn't interject. Out of nowhere she smiled then stood up suddenly.

'I'm sorry, I can't tell you anything about him . . . and I can't fix him. I don't recognize any of the parts he's got inside him. He's one of a kind.' She caught sight of my worried face and quickly added, 'But I think I know someone who might be able to help you. His name's Kato Aubergine. I knew him at college. He went home to Tokyo a few years back.'

'Aubergine?'

'It's a weird name, right? His name means eggplant in Japanese. When he came over here, no one could pronounce it, so he translated it to a word we understood. I guess he thought "eggplant" sounded too stupid. I haven't seen him for a long time, but he's awesome. He'll be able to help you.'

'What makes you think so?' I felt despondent at being sent to yet another place and afraid that time might be running out on us with Tang's cylinder. But at least there was a next step.

'Because after college he went on to be one of the best brains in AI and worked with some of the top people; he got the kinds of jobs every robot enthusiast dreams of. If there's anything he doesn't know about robots, it isn't worth knowing. He had a big break with some top-secret android project, but it didn't last. He lost his position. That must've been about . . . eight years ago maybe? That's all I know.'

I felt hopeful. 'Do you have any contact details for him by any chance?'

'I sorta lost contact with him,' she said, looking down and twisting her fingers. Her voice was tinged with regret. Then, seemingly out of nowhere, she brightened. 'But I have an email address, if that's any good?' She scribbled something on a sticky note and handed it to me. It was a street address.

'What's this?'

'It's where I live. You'll need it so you know where to come for dinner tonight. I don't have Kato's email on me. I'll have to dig it out at home.'

I must have looked blank for a few seconds, but she stared back at me with a half-smile on her face. Then I blushed and she smiled.

'Well, y'know, I was going to ask you out to dinner, but I figured it'd be difficult for you with the robot, so I thought why not invite you over?'

'But you don't know me, I could be dangerous.'

'Let's hope so.' She gave me a broad, mysterious smile.

Tang and I got back into the car, but it was a few minutes before I could handle the idea of driving.

'What just happened to me?' I said to myself.

'We saw museum lady.'

'Thanks, Tang. I mean . . . never mind.'

I switched the engine on and pulled away from the museum car park, still baffled. 'Must be the accent,' I thought out loud. I had a good solid newsreader accent. It was one of my few virtues. Amy had always liked the way I spoke.

The next flight to Tokyo didn't leave till the morning, so I found us a motel to stay in for the night. We collected our keys from the reception desk and settled ourselves into the room. I switched the TV on and gave Tang the remote so he had something to do while I showered and got myself ready to go out again. I'd just come out of the bathroom when there was a knock at the door.

'See who that is, will you, please, Tang?'

After the Laundrybot incident, I'd felt compelled to explain to Tang what I meant by 'getting the door', but he still

106

didn't seem sure, so I moderated my language. He heaved himself off his bed and clanked towards the door.

Upon opening it, he let out the most piercing screech I'd heard in a long while and clanked away as fast as he could into the wardrobe, then tried to shut the doors on himself.

'What the hell? Tang, what's the matter?' I bolted over to the half-open door.

A four-foot witch stood there, complete with broomstick and stuffed cat. She carried a silver bucket, which she held out to me, cocking her head to one side.

'Trick or treat!'

Bloody Halloween. 'You scared my robot,' I said. 'Bugger off!'

'Trick or treat!' repeated the witch.

'I heard you the first time, now go away. Go on, piss off!' I made what I hoped was a commanding pointing gesture and it seemed to work. She turned on her heel and ran away. As I shut the door, I heard giggling and a series of small thuds. When I opened the door again, I saw the witch and a few of her chums throwing eggs at the Dodge.

'Oi, you little monsters, clear off, that's my property! See, this is why we never wanted any of you!' I shouted after them.

It was true, I thought, fifteen minutes later as I wiped a soapy sponge vigorously over the Dodge. Amy and I had discussed kids – and Halloween – early on in our relationship. We'd agreed that freedom from the need to find them an outfit less crap than their mates' and to accompany them while they harassed the neighbours for sweets was a very good reason for not having kids. At some point, though, Amy had changed her mind – last Halloween she'd told me I was mean for refusing to open the door to trick-or-treaters.

'They're just being kids, Ben.'

'You've changed your tune. I thought you hated all this Halloween shit, too?'

'I do . . . I just . . . I think it's . . .'

'OK, each to their own.' I didn't understand the change of heart, and I hadn't thought to ask what had brought it about.

It took me a long while to clean the egg off the Dodge, even though I'd caught it before it dried. By the time I got back to the room, I was already running late for my date, but the bigger problem was that Tang was still in the wardrobe and refusing to come out. Though he'd managed to climb in among the drawers and hangers, it was too shallow to fully accommodate his boxy body, so the doors hadn't shut all the way. A sliver of Tang showed through the gap between the doors, revealing a miserable and frightened robot. I tried to heave the doors open, but Tang's grabbers appeared from inside and held them shut.

'Come on, Tang, it's OK. It was only a kid messing around. She wasn't really a witch. Come out, mate.'

'No.'

'Please, Tang. We have to go now otherwise we'll be late for Lizzie. Remember Lizzie, the lady from earlier?'

'Yes.'

'Come on, Tang, please. The witch is gone now, they're all gone. Long gone. They're probably at home feeling sick from all the sweets they've eaten.'

'Ben is sure?'

Not really.

'Yep. Totally. I promise. Anyway, we won't be here this evening, and they're not likely to come back later – they'll be in bed.'

Tang pushed the doors open and clanked out, his head swivelling round and round like I'd hidden a zombie or an axe murderer in the bathroom. When he was satisfied, he pulled himself up on to his bed and sat back against his pillow.

'Film now?'

'No, Tang, we can't. I told you: we're late for Lizzie. We have to go.'

'I can stay here and watch film?'

'Not a chance. There's no way I'm leaving you alone again. Besides, Dr Katz – the museum lady – invited you, too, didn't she? It'd be rude if you didn't come,' I told him, though I secretly wished I could leave him behind. I toyed with the idea but pushed it away.

'Come on, Tang,' I said again, 'you'll get to ride in the Dodge . . . That'll be fun, won't it?'

Tang considered my words, then half-heaved, half-rolled himself off his bed, making a weird grunting, snuffling noise as he did so.

'OK, Ben. We go. Come on. Ben is late.'

11

Diesel

'HI . . . HI . . . OH . . . HIYA . . . NO, DEFINITELY NOT "HIYA",
what the hell am I thinking? Hi there? Hey, how's it going?
Hi. Yes. Just hi. That'll do.'

We were standing outside Dr Lizzie Katz's building on a
lively street busy with Texan nightlife.

'Why does Ben talk to door?'

'Because I'm working out what to say to her, that's why.'

Before he had a chance to question me further, I reached
up to press the door buzzer. Just as my finger began to
press, a face appeared on the mini screen and a voice rang
out loud and clear.

'I wondered how long you two were going to stand there.
Come in, why don't you?! Second floor.'

Lizzie was waiting when we emerged from the elevator.
She was wearing a cotton blouse and wide-legged trousers,
as she had been during the day, but this time in pale green
and blue, and her hair was down and running in waves that
danced to their own tune when she moved her head. It was
a lot like Amy's hair. Her clothes gave her a vintage look
that showed a feminine side that Amy also used to have

but which had been courtroomed out of her as her career progressed. While I'd been with Amy, I hadn't noticed the transformation, and just then I felt appalled at myself for not seeing it. Standing in front of Lizzie, the changes to Amy seemed obvious.

I hoped I looked more presentable than I had that morning – at least I'd found some smart-ish trousers in my rucksack and ironed a shirt with the tiny motel travel iron. My hair was still a little out of control and greying, but there was nothing I could do about that.

'Hi!' I said. It came out as more of a shout.

Tang jumped a little. Lizzie Katz raised her dark and defined eyebrows.

'HI, YOURSELF!' she shouted back, then laughed. I went to kiss her on the cheek, but she offered me the opposite cheek to the one I'd been aiming for.

She bent down and presented a small pale hand for Tang to shake. He looked at me and I nodded, so he extended a grabber for her, but she then leaned in and kissed him, too. He raised his grabber to his head where she'd kissed him, and I felt pretty sure he'd have flushed red if he could. Still holding Tang's hand, she turned and drew us into her home, gesturing for me to shut the door behind us.

Dr Katz's apartment was bijou, warm and friendly, with a brown-carpeted seating area adjoining a kitchen that had vinyl flooring. It was a corner apartment with dual-aspect windows. Flashing neon from the bars and restaurants outside flooded in and lit up the walls and the floor. On the window ledge sat a small pumpkin with triangle eyes and a rectangular smile carved out on both sides. Light from outside flowed through it and cast long shapes across the carpet.

'Can I get you a drink?' she asked, holding out her hands to me. Then I realized I was clinging on to a bottle of wine we'd picked up on the way over. When I made no move to hand it to her, she gently took it from me. 'Is this for me?'

'Yes,' I said, 'yes, it's for you.'

'Thank you,' she replied, and I caught sight of an expression on her face that suggested she thought I was going to be hard work.

'Sorry,' I said. 'I'm not usually . . . I'm usually more friendly. I'm nervous.'

'I guessed. Why don't you take a seat and I'll bring some wine in?'

There was a sofa and an armchair in the sitting area, both covered with vaguely Aztec-looking chenille throws, and a coffee table upon which there were several mug-ringed magazines, including *Museums Today* and *The Curator*. She also had a copy of *What 'Bot?* I chose the sofa, intending for Tang to sit next to me, but he moved straight for the armchair and clambered up into it, reclined and laid his grabbers along the arms.

'Soft,' he said.

The doctor agreed. 'That's my favourite chair. I use it when I'm watching TV.'

I felt awkward and tried to get Tang to jump down from Dr Katz's favourite chair.

'No, no, it's fine. I'll sit here,' she said, handing me a glass of wine, setting the bottle on the coffee table and placing herself beside me. 'And I think you should call me Lizzie, please.'

She curled up her legs, rested her elbow on the back of the sofa and began to sip her wine. I had to sit back to see both her and Tang at once, but I feared ignoring Tang in case he got bored and wandered off to destroy something. As it was he soon discovered a spider plant spilling over the side of a pot balancing on the edge of a bookcase and had begun to pat at the dangling leaves like a cat after a ball of wool.

I began to agitate, but Dr Katz was calm about it.

'I deal with school parties all the time, so I'm used to being patient. The robot's not so very different.'

After a silence, Lizzie excused herself from the sofa and went to the kitchen.

'The pot roast's in the oven, but I have potatoes to peel,' she explained.

I offered to help, but she wouldn't hear of it.

Watching her prepare spuds made me think of Amy and the first time I'd mentioned to her the idea of my trip with Tang. She'd been so precise with her vegetable chopping, so determined, even fierce. Lizzie made knife-work look like a dance, much more gentle and flowing.

There was a moment of silence during which I felt it was up to me to think of something sparkling to say, but the art of conversation had buggered off somewhere, leaving me in the lurch. Tang kicked his legs up and down on his chair and looked about him, filling the void with pre-nuisance. Sure enough, he heaved himself up on to the floor and picked up Lizzie's pumpkin.

'Ben, what is?'

'It's a pumpkin, Tang.'

This didn't make things any clearer for him.

'What is pump-kin?'

'It's a vegetable, Tang. You eat it.'

Tang stared at me inscrutably. He didn't seem to believe me.

113

'The bit you eat is on the inside, Tang.' Lizzie took over from the kitchen. 'The outside is for decoration. For Halloween.'

At the mention of Halloween, Tang's eyes grew wide. He shrieked 'Witch!', dropped the pumpkin and ran straight into a wall as he tried to leave the room.

'What in the world . . .?' said Lizzie, as she came from the kitchen to help me pick Tang up. As we took him back to his seat, I explained about the children dressed in Halloween costumes back at the motel.

'Scared,' Tang told her.

'Aw, it's OK,' she said, giving him a little hug, 'there are no witches here. Look, even the scary pumpkin's gone now.' She pointed to the mushy blob of orange on the floor.

'I'm so sorry,' I said . . . again.

'It's no bother, really.'

There was another awkward pause while Lizzie cleared up the pumpkin. I offered to help, but once again she wouldn't hear of it. As much to cover the silence as anything else, I said, 'Kato Aubergine, do you have any contact details for him?'

She looked a little bemused that I'd chosen that moment to bring up the subject, and waved the question away.

'Oh, I'll find it for you later,' she told me, then added, 'I promise.'

Lizzie disposed of the pumpkin in a bin under the sink and returned to her potatoes, dropping them efficiently into a saucepan. There was the gentle pop and hiss of a gas flame igniting.

She wiped her hands on a tea towel and came back to sit next to me. There was another silence, then, out of the blue, 'So, how long is it since you split up with your wife?'

The sudden change of tack took me by surprise, and so I couldn't answer.

'Your wife . . . I guess you split up not so long ago, right?' she said again, more gently this time.

Before I could attempt a reply, she reached across my lap and slowly picked up my left hand. The surprise touch of a woman other than Amy sent a tingle all along my arm. I didn't know what to do with the feeling. She smelled nice – of a fresh sort of perfume but also of cooking, seared meat and onions. She made me hungry.

'There's a dent on your finger where you used to have a ring, but it's not faded much so you must have been wearing it recently. And I'm guessing if you'd been widowed you might still have the ring on.' She paused. 'So how long is it?'

'Oh . . . a few weeks . . . or so. You're very perceptive.'

'Well, you know, I'm a single girl . . . I have to be careful. Have to make sure.'

She was way more streetwise and clever than me. I was out of my depth, sitting in a room drinking wine with a robot and an attractive, confident woman not unlike my ex-wife. I was feeling panicked enough to consider leaving, but that would have been rude. Then she said, 'Do you have kids?'

'No,' I said, not intending to elaborate, but under her continued gaze I felt I needed to, so I said, 'My ex . . . I never thought she wanted any, but I found out just before she lef— before we split up that she did after all.'

'Ah,' she said in response. 'I didn't think you seemed like a father.'

I guess I could have been offended by this, but I wasn't. 'No, I can understand that. I always thought I'd be no good at it. But I didn't really get the chance to come round to the idea.'

'No, Ben, you mistake my meaning. I wasn't saying I didn't think you'd be a good father – quite the opposite. I thought you probably weren't a dad because you seem like a really nice guy . . . If you had kids, then you'd be at home with them. Not here with me.'

'Oh.' I fell silent, unsure what to do with her words. Then Lizzie gave a little laugh and seemed to backtrack in the conversation.

'You don't get too many dates, working in a museum. I mean, I don't go around giving my address to every guy I meet.' Now she sounded sad and a little vulnerable.

'I'll take it as a compliment, then.'

She smiled, and I caught sight of her small white teeth. 'You should.'

I felt discomfited by the compliment, so I changed the conversation to something more general.

'So, how is it that you're working in a space museum?' As I asked the question, I noticed Tang wander off into the hallway. I made a move to retrieve him, but Lizzie took my hand and encouraged me to leave him be.

Lizzie's hand lingered in mine for a stretched moment, then she withdrew it and said, 'So, what's wrong with working in a space museum?' She sounded offended, but it was a faux indignation that suggested that she herself thought she shouldn't be in the job.

'Nothing,' I said, with a nervous cough-laugh. 'I didn't mean . . . It's just that Cory said that you were a robot historian.'

'He said that?' She smiled and blushed a bright red that brought out her bright-green eyes suddenly. 'He's being generous. I like to talk about them online, that's all.'

I asked her why she didn't pursue this as a career.

'It's just a hobby, Ben. Kato was the brainy one at college. There's no way I could have followed him, followed his path, I mean. I might be well informed, but I couldn't apply it anywhere. There aren't any robot museums around here. I'd have to move and, well, I've got family nearby.' She got up suddenly and went to the window, where the low sun was shining through so fiercely the room lit up and suddenly it seemed all her books were on fire.

'I understand,' I said, thinking about my sister Bryony, who had settled only as far as the next village from where we'd grown up. 'But what I don't understand is why you don't have an android of your own?'

She turned round and shrugged – her thin shoulders almost reaching her ears. 'Oh, that's easy: I can't afford it, not on my salary. Even the used ones are expensive. Besides, I don't have room.' She gestured around her, where every last space was filled and where books and magazines were stacked on the floor waiting for Lizzie to find a bigger home. 'Where would I dock it in this little apartment? When I marry a millionaire or win the lottery, then I'll have a whole stable of droids, and robots, too, if I can find them. You don't know how lucky you are, Ben, they literally don't make them like that now . . . They never did.'

She paused, as though she regretted what she had said. 'I am sorry I can't fix him, or even tell you anything about him. I could tell you about the history of design from the first mass-produced robots through to the androids we have now, and maybe where they might be going in the future, but I couldn't say where such a beautiful oddball like Tang fits in. Kato should be able to help you, though. He's . . .' she stopped and looked over at Tang, who had at that moment wandered back into the room and seemed to have put some lipstick on his face. 'Anyway, I'm sorry, little robot, we're talking about you when we should be talking to you.' She crouched down to Tang and took hold of his grabber, wiping his face with a tissue from her pocket. 'Are you having a good vacation with Ben?'

Tang tipped from one foot to another in surprise at being addressed directly.

'Y-es.'

'What's been your favourite place so far?'

'Dodge.'

Lizzie looked over at me, eyebrows raised.

'He means he's enjoyed our hire car best. It's a Dodge Charger.'

I began to tell her about our trip thus far – how we came to hire the car, about Kyle and the radioactive town and about the Android Fetishists' Club. She sat back down next to me and just laughed and laughed.

'An android whorehouse?'

'I know! It's fair to say I was a bit out of my depth in the Hotel California.'

'I'll bet! I never heard of anything like it. And they really thought you were there to . . . ?'

'Yep.'

'You make sure you tell Kato about it; he'll be appalled. He always had a real sense of respect for everything, even AI.'

Lizzie looked momentarily sad. Then she seemed to shake the feeling off and smiled at me again with her small and lovely mouth.

'Forgive me, Ben, but you really don't seem the type to be interested in AI.'

'It's true, I'm not. I never wanted an android. My wife . . . ex-wife did, but not me.'

It felt good to talk to Lizzie about Tang and have her amused at his behaviour, not irritated by it. It was so different from the last month with Amy – her treating him like a walking wheelie bin and treating me the same for wanting him there. Maybe Amy leaving *was* for the best.

Lizzie's laid-back attitude didn't preclude her from teasing me, though.

'I'll bet you still have an old phone as well, don't you?' she said, folding her arms.

I denied it and pulled out my phone to show her. 'It's got a camera and a torchlight and everything.'

She fell back, giggling uncontrollably, and even clutched her sides. I put it away to avoid further embarrassment.

'You're right, though, about robots and androids and stuff. Generally, I prefer living things. I was training to be a vet for a while.'

She recovered herself enough to hear me out.

'Was?'

'Yeah. I wasn't doing so well at it, though. In hindsight, my parents were supportive, really patient actually. Then they died in an accident, and . . . I got stuck. A bit lost, I suppose.'

'I'm sorry to hear that. Do you think you'll go back to it?'

'Maybe. I should pull myself together and get some kind of job when I get home.' I took a deep breath in. 'If you're useless at everything, though, eventually you stop trying.'

She paused and then said, 'I don't think you're useless.'

'You don't?'

'Not a bit. Losing your parents is a big deal, Ben. Cut

yourself some slack. Besides, look how far you've come with Tang, that must have taken some doing.'

I couldn't remember the last time anyone had praised me, and I genuinely felt a warm glow grow inside me.

'Thank you,' I said.

Lizzie changed the topic after that, for which I was grateful. We talked easily and the time passed quickly, and before I knew it we'd been there well over an hour. We hadn't yet eaten, but Lizzie had it covered. From the tiny kitchen, she called, 'What would Tang like to do while we eat?'

'Do?'

'Yes. I mean, does he eat? And if not, won't he be bored, watching us?'

'I, er . . . I don't know,' I called back. It had never occurred to me before. Tang had always just peered at me with fascination, or so it appeared anyway, while I ate. Either that or he took himself off to look out of a window or at the telly or something. I'd never asked him what he *wanted* to do.

'Tang, do you eat?' Lizzie asked him directly.

'No,' Tang informed her.

'Well, do you ever need anything to drink, even? How do you run?'

'Run?' Tang looked at me, but I was unable to help him; I was as interested in the answer as she was.

'What makes you work?' She tried rephrasing the question, but it didn't do a lot of good. I knew from experience that she wasn't going to get the kind of answer she was looking for.

'Don't know,' he said. Then, after a minute, he added, 'Diesel.'

'What?' Lizzie and I chimed at the same time.

'Sometimes diesel. Is special. Once a year, or twice. Not

too much. Bad . . . and good.' He glanced around then looked upward at us from under his eyelids. He seemed embarrassed, like we'd wrestled out a deep secret from him. Which I suppose we had.

I sat down next to Tang on the rug and put my hand on his boxy shoulder. 'Tang, why didn't you tell me? I could have got you some,' but Tang waved the suggestion away with his grabber.

'No. Must not have . . . often.'

'Well, have you had any this year?' asked Lizzie.

'No.'

'Well, then, would you like some now?'

Then she said to me, 'I can get some from the can I keep in the back of the car in the garage downstairs . . . It's no bother.'

'Maybe . . .' Tang turned his head to look at me for reassurance.

'If you'd like some, then have some, Tang. Don't worry, we'll make sure you don't have too much.'

Lizzie served Tang a full tumbler, which at first he sipped tentatively but drank more quickly the further down it got. After a few sips, he started giggling, and by the time we'd finished Lizzie's perfectly cooked pot roast he'd slid off the armchair and was staring at the ceiling with one grabber still on the chair.

'Are you OK, Tang?' I asked him.

'Yes.'

'Are you sure?'

'Yes,' he said.

'Let me know when you've had enough diesel, OK?'

There was no answer, and I worried. But then came the

121

soft tick-tick-tick I'd heard him make while he slept.

'Why do you suppose he sleeps?' I asked Lizzie.

She shrugged but said, 'Wouldn't you if you were learning all the time? He's like a child – they need their sleep to process all that's going on around them. Maybe his circuits just need to calm down once in a while.'

Tang shuffled a little, as though in response to us talking about him. His grabber slid off the chair and landed with a clonk on to the floor next to him.

'I think we made my robot drunk.'

'He's in good company.'

She was right, I realized. I'd driven to her apartment, but I'd forgotten all about the car and had drunk every single glass of wine she'd offered me during the evening. Tang and I would have to get a cab back to the motel, then another back to hers in the morning to pick up the car.

'Tell me something,' Lizzie said suddenly, interrupting my thoughts and sitting down beside me so that I began to tingle and my stomach began to flutter. 'If you're not interested in AI, then why did you decide to go on a trip with a robot? What's so special about this one?' She looked over at the now comatose Tang.

I thought for a moment before answering.

'When he turned up in my garden, I felt sorry for him, and I couldn't help wondering how he got there. But the more I've got to know him . . . well, he's not just a retro robot, and he's nothing like an android. He learns things, I'm sure of it. He doesn't just carry out orders; in fact, he rarely carries out orders. He's obstinate and always questions what I do. But he's . . . he's caring. Like you say: he's special.'

I paused for breath, ready to extol more of Tang's virtues. Then Lizzie kissed me.

I woke the next morning in Lizzie's bed. Lying next to me was a note that said:

> *Super to meet you, Ben, and Tang too. Thanks for a great night, sorry I jumped on you – blame the wine, I guess. Stop by for coffee if you're ever in Houston again. Help yourself to breakfast. You guys know your way out. Have a good trip, hope you find what you're looking for. Lx.*
>
> *P.S. Tell Kato I said hi. Would you let me know how he is, please?*

Beside it lay another piece of paper with Kato Aubergine's email address on it. I was relieved. Lizzie had saved us all the crushing embarrassment of the 'morning after' and slipped out to work without waking me.

I lay in bed for a few more moments, thinking things over. I remembered the act of actual sex, so at least I could feel reassured I'd acquitted myself OK. But I was feeling a bit ashamed, wondering what Amy would say if she knew. I fiddled with my finger where my wedding ring had been. Lizzie was right: the dent was still there.

I could feel myself beginning to grow strangely melancholy, so I got up. As I dragged myself out of a virtual stranger's bed, I ran my hand through my hair then fished around for my pants. Then I remembered Tang passed out asleep against the armchair, and I had a moment of panic. When I went into the living room to look for him, he was still there and still sleeping, only now he was covered in a blanket.

'What a lovely person,' I said to no one in particular. 'Amy would never have done that.' The fresh reminder that

Amy wasn't perfect was strangely comforting to me.

Tang didn't seem to be inclined to get up any time soon, groaning and brushing me away when I knocked on him to try to wake him up. So I left him and decided to clean the dishes from the night before.

12

Security

I ROUSED TANG, LEFT A BRIEF 'YEP, CHEERS, I HAD A GREAT time, too' note for Lizzie (not those words exactly) and headed back to the motel to collect our things and officially check out. A hungover Tang stayed in the Dodge, leaning his head against the door and sighing. We took the egg-free and gleaming Dodge back to the hire firm's rental office at the airport in Houston. Or rather I took the Dodge back, and a grumpy Tang sulked when he realized what was going on.

'I told you, we're going to see Dr Lizzie's friend in Tokyo. As much as I'd prefer to drive to Japan rather than fly, we can't. We can't take the car to Tokyo.'

'Why?'

'What do you mean, why? I just told you, we're going on a plane, that's why.'

'Why?'

'Why are we going on a plane, or why can't we take the car on the plane?'

This stumped him. He didn't know himself what he meant. He hadn't quite grasped the meaning of 'why?', and he was still a long way from matching it up with logic. He was easily outmanoeuvred . . . for now, though I knew he'd get the better of me sooner or later.

He sat quietly for the remainder of the journey to the rental office, glowering and stroking the trim on the passenger door. Tang didn't want to let go of the Dodge. Literally. It's surprising how strong a pair of grabbers can be when they're wrapped around a car-door handle. Similarly, it's surprising how many people stare when those grabbers are attached to a snowman-shaped robot and when he's squealing at the top of his metallic lungs. Or maybe neither of these things is surprising. Perhaps 'alarming' is the right word. Alarming and embarrassing.

I didn't even think of trying to put Tang in the hold this time round. As we waited in line at the check-in desks, I considered my options. I wasn't sure I could justify two Premium seats again. We might still have a long way to travel, and I had to make sure I had the funds available. Trying to negotiate with my bank over the telephone from halfway across the world to persuade them to transfer savings from a locked-down account into an instant-access one did not sound easy. Tang was starting to be as expensive a travelling companion as Amy, who'd made me upgrade various holidays at different times. On one occasion it was the change of a hotel room to a suite, another time it was a helicopter ride over the Maldives rather than a boat trip around them (which did not fill me with joy). Actually, Tang was still way cheaper to travel with. If Premium was necessary, then Premium it would have to be.

'How many seats would you like, sir?'

Tang edged closer to me, his little metal foot stepping on top of my exposed Birkenstocked toe.

126

'Two.'

The clerk smiled a big perfect smile at me.

'Wonderful. And where would you like the seats? We have Economy, Business Economy, First Economy, Quality Economy, Business Quality, Quality First and Business First. We also have First.'

I asked him to explain the difference.

'There are a number of differences, sir. If you'd like to study the brochure to one side and rejoin the queue when you're ready . . .'

I declined and asked him for a seat that would suit a robot.

He peered at Tang over the desk. 'You would be better off putting your robot in the hold, sir.'

I felt Tang clutch at my trouser leg.

'I don't want to put him in the hold. I want to know which of your seats will fit him.'

The clerk pushed his glasses up his slippery nose and sighed. 'Any of our top-three seat categories will fit it just fine.'

I stared hard at him. 'And which other ones . . . ?'

'Our seats are designed to fit a range of androids, sir. We pride ourselves on accommodating anyone, but we aren't used to catering for robots. Especially one like yours. Only our top-three seats have a pitch big enough for it.'

'Him,' I corrected. 'It's a him, not an it.'

'It doesn't change anything, sir. He'll still only fit into one of our top-three seats.'

'We'll take the two cheapest of those then, please.'

'Wonderful. May I ask, sir, is he chipped?'

'Chipped?'

'Yes, sir.'

I looked questioningly at him.

'It's a new policy. All robots leaving the US in the cabin as opposed to the hold have to have a microchip. It's a bit like the biometric passports that people have now. Either that or he must be on your passport. Is he?'

'I don't understand. We left the UK and arrived in San Francisco, no questions asked. They just treated him like he was an extra fare.' I tried to recall. At Heathrow I caused a scandal because I'd suggested Tang went into the hold instead of the cabin with me. Here they looked at him like garbage yet still put us through a billion hoops before we could even buy the bloody tickets.

'As I say, sir, it's a new policy. You might find your Heathrow does the same thing now.'

'Supposing he isn't chipped and I don't have him on my passport?'

'Then you can't board the flight, sir. Or you could put him in the hold.'

'Oh, very helpful, thank you.'

'You're welcome, sir. Would you like to put him in the hold?'

'No, I don't want to put him in the hold. I want him to board the flight with me.'

'Is he chipped?'

'I honestly don't think . . .'

Suddenly, I felt a tugging on my trouser pocket and looked down to find Tang smiling up at me. 'What is it, Tang?'

He extended his free grabber, the one not attached to my leg, and reached as far as he could around the top of his body section towards his back. He tapped himself on the back of the shoulder.

'Are you telling me you are chipped?' I asked him.

He nodded.

'Why didn't you tell me earlier?'

'Ben did not need to know.'

I sighed. 'Fair enough.' I looked back at the clerk. 'Apparently he is chipped.'

'Wonderful,' he said, extending a wireless handheld piece of equipment out from behind the desk. Tang turned round to allow him to scan, though he didn't look happy. I could understand why. He didn't approve of being treated like a pet.

The clerk did a double-take at his computer, then frowned.

'Is there a problem?' I asked.

The clerk looked at me, then at Tang, then back at me, then finally at his computer again. He passed a hand across his sweaty forehead and scratched the bridge of his nose. Then he sighed, shook his head and gave us our tickets and boarding passes.

'What was all that about?' I said, as we walked away from the check-in desk, more to myself than Tang, but the robot lifted his boxy shoulders in a shrug. As we walked to the security gates, I knelt down to Tang.

'I'm sorry he treated you like that.'

'OK. Ben did not.'

'I know, but . . .'

Tang took my hand in his grabber. 'Ben?'

'Yes?'

'Thank you.'

'What for?'

He took my other hand.

'Seat.'

*

We made our way up to security in silence. I wondered if we'd fall foul of any other policy quirks threatening to strand us in the US of A.

As we approached the security gates, my heart sank. There in front of us were a number of segregated queues. A notice directed me through a metal detector under the sign 'Humans'. Nearby, a line of humanoid robots waited to pass through another sort of detector labelled 'Androids'. Not so nearby, more or less shoved out of the way in a corner, was a dusty-looking detector, with an equally dusty-looking security official behind it, all under the sign 'Robots'. There was no queue for this one.

Tang saw the situation at the same time as me. Fearing his reaction, I rested my hand on his cool head. But he clanked onwards and headed for his detector without looking back. I watched as he passed by the line of androids. A ripple of synthetic speech followed him. The droids were teasing him. They were laughing at him. I lost it with them.

'Oi, shut up, the lot of you. Bunch of self-satisfied clones. You wouldn't know an original thought if it got rammed through your titanium exoskeletons. Concentrate on your own bloody line and leave my friend alone – he has feelings, you know?'

Tang kept walking.

'Don't worry, mate,' I called, 'I'll be right on the other side; just wait for me there . . . I won't be long!'

I was ages. The human line was endless, and Tang was the only robot in his line. I could only watch as he made his way dutifully through the detector. The elderly security official poked and prodded him, and eventually peeled his

130

flap open and peered inside. Then she said something to him and he pointed over to me. It was all I could do not to scramble over the people and bits and pieces of equipment to reach him.

When I got to the other side, I skidded on the polished floor, racing as fast as I could to find Tang. He was sitting on a bench between his detector and mine, his eyes cast down but looking up every time someone came near, in case it was me. I saw his face light up when I finally made it over to him. He hopped to his feet and wrapped his arms tightly around my leg.

'I'm so sorry it took a long time.'

'Not Ben's fault.'

'Did they say anything to you? The security woman, I mean?'

'Yes.'

'What?'

'Why Tang at airport and who with.'

A thought occurred to me. If Tang had a chip, then maybe it had an address on it.

'Did she say anything about your chip?'

'Yes.'

'What?'

'She said chip broken. Needs fixed.'

'Needs fixing, you mean. That doesn't surprise me. But she let you go anyway?'

'Yes.'

She must've felt sorry for Tang and decided he wasn't a bomb or packed with cocaine. Then I thought of the clerk at the check-in desk and realized he'd probably found the same thing when he scanned Tang and had also chosen not to argue. It seemed Tang had a way of wheedling what he wanted out of people. Like a puppy.

'That was kind,' I said.

'Yes.' He took my hand. 'Fly now?'

'Yes, Tang, we'll leave here soon. We'll fly.'

13

Highs and Lows

THE JOURNEY TO TOKYO WAS AS PLEASANT A FLIGHT AS I could hope for, not least because we'd left behind us the indignity of the George Bush Intercontinental Airport. IAH had been one of the low points of the trip, even considering the frightening experience at San Francisco bus station. For Tang especially, the events at the airport had been very demeaning, and it surprised me to acknowledge that to see him happy made me happy.

Strapped into his seat on our Business Fancy flight, or Quality Fancy, or whatever it was, Tang lost no time in getting me to scroll through the options on his seat-back entertainment screen, as before. This time he spent the entire thirteen-hour journey playing a single game – a punch-'em-up-type affair in which he delighted in controlling the actions of a small, slender Chinese lady with enormous thigh muscles and a kick that reached higher than the heads of all the other players.

I revisited my former trick of downing several gin and tonics, and went to sleep.

*

The dreams one has on a flight are like nothing else. In my gin-soaked haze, I saw a robot dog dressed in a bra top and miniskirt, with one leg missing. The dog morphed into a tramp in an overcoat and miniskirt, who in turn morphed into Amy . . . sadly not in a miniskirt, though. A few times Tang poked me to let me know I was snoring, but I just went back to sleep.

Tang got upset when they switched his game off as the flight attendant announced landing procedures. He banged the armrests with his fists and shrieked, and not for the first time I wished he had an 'off' switch.

There was 'a little bit of rain around' in Tokyo, the pilot informed us over the intercom. But from what I could see through the small oval aeroplane window it looked more like great streams of water, not ordinary rain at all. Tang's eyes grew wide with apprehension, his eyelids coming down diagonally halfway across his eyes.

'It's OK, Tang, we'll find an umbrella for you.'

Within seconds of making our way out into the arrivals hall, we spotted a vending machine filled with clear plastic umbrellas that looked straight out of the 1960s. Tang loved his umbrella and opened it straight away, twirling it around like a metal gymnast. He couldn't understand why I wouldn't let him keep it open.

'Keep it for when we're outside, Tang. That's what it's for.'

'Tang . . . umbrella . . . now.'

'No, Tang, apart from anything else it's at neck height. You're in danger of either stabbing people or smacking them in the face.' Tang frowned and ignored me. 'Tang, close it down or I'll take it off you. It's your choice.'

Tang thought about this for a second or two, then closed

it, tucking it under his arm so his hands were free to fiddle with his gaffer tape.

'Look, Tang, it's this way; there's a sign for the bullet train.' I started walking in its direction.

'Bul-let?'

'Yes, Tang. It's a really, really fast train and it'll get us to the centre of Tokyo in no time. The best thing is it looks like we don't even have to go outside.'

'Oh.' Tang's head dipped downward and his arms fell to his sides in disappointment. He dropped his umbrella. It landed near my sandalled bare toe and I picked it up.

'You can use it when we get off the train, I promise.'

Tang forgot all about the umbrella once we were on the bullet train, speeding through the rain-battered, beautiful countryside that surrounded Tokyo. We enjoyed the scenery together, and I pointed things out to him: houses on the edge of the sea, golden, orange and brown autumn forests that clambered across hills, and flat, square fields covered in rice crops, until eventually we were swallowed up by the urban sprawl of Tokyo. I had emailed Kato Aubergine but had received no response as yet, which left me nervous about our exact destination in Tokyo. The best I could do was pick a friendly-looking hotel and wait for him to get in touch.

I used the last part of our journey wisely and upon arrival at the terminal I had found a hotel on my phone and was fairly confident of our route to it. Tang, on the other hand, spent the entire journey standing on his seat with his face and grabbers pressed against the window, yelling 'wheeeeeeeeeeee' as the landscape blurred past us.

*

It turned out I'd inadvertently misinformed Tang about being able to use his umbrella. When we got off the bullet train, it became clear that we didn't need to step outside the station either but could walk straight into the impressive maze that was the Tokyo Metro. I had to promise that he could use it when we got to the other end. He looked a little pouty and cross, and gave his gaffer tape some more abuse. It needed replacing. I made a mental note to do so when we arrived at our hotel.

Once inside the underground train, Tang was easily distracted. This time it was nothing to do with the speed or the view but entirely down to a uniquely Japanese quirk: the singing subway. At each stop came a little tinkling tune over the intercom, signalling the arrival of the train at the station. At each station it was a different tune, and Tang found this both amusing and delightful, kicking his legs in his seat and squealing. I kept telling him to 'shush', and as usual he ignored me, but contrary to my fears that he would disturb the other passengers it seemed they found him as amusing and delightful as he found their trains. We'd not gone ten minutes before Tang was surrounded by a crowd of uniformed schoolgirls and sharp-suited businessmen alike, all hoping to have their picture taken with him. I too came away from the exchange with dozens of photos of Japanese people making their customary peace sign and Tang trying to copy them but not able to since he had no fingers.

I don't think he really understood what was happening – he didn't seem to get the concept of photography – but he certainly appreciated the attention. He and I had had our fair share of ridicule, so it was nice to arrive in a country where Tang was appreciated for who he was. I decided I liked Japan very much.

The warm, pleasant feeling I had about the country was tempered slightly when bleak raindrops began to fall on us as we made our way to our hotel. Tang wasn't fussed – he finally got to use his umbrella, and as we walked he stared through it at the rain, transfixed by the sight of the drops plop-plopping on the plastic. At one point we were offered a lift from a cheerful, tiny old man in a tiny square car, but there was no way Tang was getting in a car the size of a raisin, so I declined. There was also an element of sheer stubbornness, I'll admit. I got it into my head that it was my decision to come to Tokyo, so it would be me who got us to our hotel, without anyone's help.

The Sunrise was a business hotel, and the counter staff were a little taken aback by the patronage of a wet backpacker and a waist-high robot brandishing an umbrella. Regardless, their manners were exemplary, and within fifteen minutes I was in our beautifully clean, smart room, taking the longest shower of my life.

That evening from the window of our fifty-third-floor corner room I stared at the city below. Streams of cars wound their way along a broad, busy highway, past office blocks and expansive parks, low-fi temples and high-rise hotels.

I swirled an Old Fashioned in a fishbowl-shaped glass, listening to the elaborately carved ice cubes clink together. Tang stood between two windows, a grabber on each, with his face against one pane of glass, then the other. He looked as though he was watching a tennis match, save for the fact that his head clanked against the window every time he switched aspects.

I suspected that, like me, Tang had never been anywhere

like Tokyo before. Part of me wanted to get out and explore, but part of me was too afraid. I was a small man from a small town, and Tang was just small in general. We were quite unsuited to this astonishing city.

'Wow,' I whispered to myself.

'Yes,' replied Tang.

We relapsed into silence for a further hour, letting our minds travel wherever they wanted to go.

I'd only stayed in a hotel like this once before: on honeymoon with Amy. We'd never stayed in hotels when I was a boy. My father had mostly chosen to go on cruises or skiing, or to places that had kids' clubs where he and my mother could leave us during the day. That's why I'd suggested New York to Amy – and we'd stayed in the best hotel we could afford.

'It's nice, isn't it?' she had said.

'The hotel? Yes, it's lovely.'

'No, I mean being able to stay here and not worry about the money.'

'Yes, I guess it must be.'

I'd never been in a situation where I'd had to worry about the money, so I didn't really understand her. But for Amy, it was a big deal. She hadn't had a poor childhood as such, she'd just said she always felt like it was her fault that there was never much money around. She'd been the youngest of four children and grew up hearing she was 'an extra mouth to feed'. Her drive to get to university and become a barrister surprised her whole family, and her success intimidated them. Amy said they felt she was too high and mighty for them after she started working in the City, and with the exception of cursory Christmas and birthday texts they stopped communicating. I always thought it was amazing she's as balanced as she is. It's one of her strengths.

I had been standing at the window, looking out over Manhattan, just as I was doing now in Tokyo. Amy came up and wrapped her arms around me from behind, lightly tanned from a day spent popping in and out of shops.

'Are you OK?' she asked. 'Are you thinking about your parents still?'

'Yes . . . no . . . not so much. The house, really.'

'The house?'

'I suppose I need to decorate it when we get back. It still looks like it did when my parents were there.'

'It's not been that long, Ben. There's no rush. Besides, *you* don't need to do it at all. We'll get a man in.'

I smiled at that but said nothing, shaking off a strange little sense of melancholy. I was in the City That Never Sleeps, with a beautiful, confident, capable young woman who loved me. And she knew I could give her a comfortable life. On balance, I'd gained more than I'd lost.

One memory led to another. Now I was back in Harley Wintnam, in the house where I grew up. The one Amy had walked out of. I wandered around it in my head, peering into rooms, opening cupboards, checking the back door was locked, tapping the barometer in the hallway and winding the plug-ugly retro carriage clock my father had given my mother for their twenty-fifth wedding anniversary. None of us liked it, and yet the damn thing was still on the mantelpiece in the sitting room, forever needing winding up like some irritating toy.

Then I realized something. Despite saying to Amy that I would redecorate my family home, I never had. Maybe I'd never really had any intention of doing so. Though Amy had renovated parts of the house, like the kitchen, in general it remained exactly as it had been when my parents died. Exactly as it was when Amy moved in . . . and exactly as it was when she moved out. Without noticing, I'd made her stay in my childhood, not brought her into a marriage. I hadn't even thought I'd liked my parents that much. When they died, I'd felt nothing – nothing but resentment towards them for leaving Bryony and me, for leaving me with my life half complete and without their guidance to reach maturity, even though I'd been twenty-eight at the time of their accident.

As my mind lingered in the empty house, the telephone in my father's study rang. I recalled the tone perfectly: a shrill, painful ring. My folks didn't have a telephone in the sitting room; they said it wasn't necessary since we all used our mobiles. That said, landlines had been having a renaissance due to the shoddy signal most people received. At least with a landline you could be sure of a whole conversation.

'May I speak with a Mr Ben Chambers or a Ms Bryony Chambers?' Bryony kept her maiden name after she got married.

'This is Ben. Who's calling?'

'I'm from the Oxfordshire Police Family Liaison Team. I'm awfully sorry to have to tell you this, but there's been an accident,' said a woman's voice.

The words didn't register for a few moments. I was trying to recall which of our friends lived in Oxfordshire. Then I remembered. My parents were at a light-aircraft rally in the county, flying their own plane. I couldn't think what to say.

'Oh. Is there a hospital I should come to?'

There was a short silence at the end of the telephone.

'Um . . . y . . . yes, you will need to.'

'What's happened to them?'

'I think it would be better if I gave you directions to the hospital, and I'll meet you there.'

'No, I think I'd rather know what you know now, if you don't mind.' The soft, stalling nature of the conversation had riled me suddenly. I knew what this woman was going to say, because if it had been anything else then she would have said so already.

'Well, it's not the way I like to break this sort of news to the family, but . . . the propellers on your parents' plane failed. We don't know exactly what happened yet, but . . . well, your parents didn't make it. I'm so sorry.'

'That's OK,' I told her, without thinking.

'Mr Chambers, it's natural to respond to news like this in one way, then feel differently later. You or your sister will need to come and identify the bodies, but I want you to know I'm here for you. If you have any questions or need anything, then please let me know.'

She gave me the number of her office, plus extension, along with the mobile number upon which she could be reached. My immediate feeling was that I wouldn't have a use for it. What questions could I possibly have? My parents had gone on one of their 'to hell with it, why not?' expeditions, and this time they wouldn't be coming back. It was simple. If it hadn't been the flying that got them, it would have been a stab wound from a painting elephant in Thailand that took a dislike to them, or a tetanus-filled bite from a penguin in Antarctica or somewhere. I understood what she was saying about feeling differently as time wore on, but I wasn't sure I was ever going to express my grief in the way she was expecting.

Bryony was different. She cried. She threw herself into the funeral arrangements. She cried some more. She moved on.

Amy and I had barely discussed my parents' death, I realized now. Standing at a window in the middle of Tokyo, so very far from home, I realized that I missed them. But I didn't want to linger on this part of my life any more – it was hardly a happy memory. I needed cheering up.

'Right, Tang. Come on, we're going out.'

'Out?'

'Yes, out. We're in one of the most exciting cities in the world; we can't stay here just staring at it through our glass bubble.'

Tang's eyeballs looked upwards, as they did when he was worried. He began to pick at his gaffer tape. It was seriously raggedy now, so I took the opportunity to replace it.

'It'll be OK,' I told him, as I smoothed the new tape over his flap, 'I'll look after you. Don't worry. What's the worst that could happen?'

It turns out the worst that could happen was for me to decide it was an awesome idea to visit a karaoke bar, dragging my poor little robot friend with me. Tang handled himself quite well – much better than I did.

I didn't *mean* to get drunk. I'd decided to stick to Old Fashioneds, since that's what I'd started on, so I'm not sure how I came to be drinking Sapporo, which incidentally is now my favourite Japanese beer. I'd left Tang in a booth, which he liked because there was no seat as such, just a soft area either side of the table on which to sit, where he simply plopped himself down. Meanwhile, I went to the bar to get a drink. In my head I asked for an Old Fashioned, but what the barman heard was 'What's your nicest beer, my good man?' because that's what he gave me. A few beers later, I found myself removing the microphone from the stand on

142

the karaoke stage, drawing a deep breath in, then opening my lungs. I don't think I even knew which song I'd selected until it started. Then, from what seemed like somewhere else entirely, I heard a drunk man with my voice shouting out the words to 'Total Eclipse Of The Heart'.

Within thirty seconds, I had a crowd of Japanese bar patrons surrounding the stage, cheering me on with little sake cups aloft. Each and every one wore a smart shirt and tie with beautifully cut trousers – a stark comparison to my jeans and flowery shirt combo, complete with wet boating shoes. Buoyed by my obvious success, when the song finished and they all cheered, I asked them if they wanted to hear it again. The answer to this was lost in translation, because when the first few lines of the song began again there was a lot of grumbling, and the men all returned to their tables. Undeterred, I carried on until one of the bar staff came to assist me off the platform and back to my seat, which I thought was very kind of them. I found Tang with his face flat on the table and his arms hanging by his sides. I didn't know what his problem was.

I blame the accidental drinking of multiple beers for the singing and for my state at the point Kato entered our lives. He found me cheek-to-table, Tang slumped against the wall absently picking at his gaffer tape, obviously fed up. He was remarkably nice about it all. Kato, that is . . . although I guess the same goes for Tang, too.

'I have been watching you for some time. I very much enjoyed your singing.'

'Thanks. S'fun,' I responded, before I'd been able to lift my head.

'Excuse me, but can I please ask where you got your robot?'

If I'd been a sensible man, what would have happened then would have been along the lines of me raising an eyebrow, taking a delicate sip from a correctly held sake cup, before saying, 'Why would you like to know, sir? Do you have a special interest in robots?' And he would have taken the sake cup I'd offered to him and said (I retrofit, because I know him now), 'Yes, I have an abiding interest in robots. I am something of an . . . expert in artificial intelligence. I have a gift for seeking out unusual robots in karaoke bars.' But on that occasion I was not a sensible man, and that's not what happened.

When a Japanese man asked about my robot, I looked up from the table and squinted at him as he gazed down at me, his face all politeness.

'Well, thash a long story. Achully no snot. Short story. He came to garden.'

'He's . . . he's your gardener?'

'Noooooo . . . he came to my garden. Sat under will tree. Ignore me, I'm jeh . . . jeh . . . jehlagged.'

Then my brain caught up with the conversation. 'Wait . . . wait . . . why?'

He lifted Tang's hose-like arm: 'Because I used to know someone who made limbs like these. A long time ago, and this is not his finest work.' He turned to Tang. 'My apologies,' he offered him for the insult, 'but it's unmistakable. It looks like he made the robot in a hurry.'

'Well, it jus' so happens that I'm looking for someone like you. Something red . . . purple . . . egg . . . eggplant. Somebody Eggplant.'

'Aubergine?'

'Yes, exactly!'

'Kato Aubergine?'

'Correct!' Then I waited again while my brain caught up, which it did, eventually. 'Wait . . . wait . . . how d'you know?'

'Because that is me – Kato Aubergine.'

'Shizt.'

14

Official Secrets

THE NEXT DAY, TANG AND I RODE THE ELEVATOR UP WHAT seemed like a hundred or more floors to Kato's office – another glass building like Cory's place of work in California, apparently de rigueur in the AI industry. That we were even there was some sort of miracle, since in Tokyo of all places it was a million-to-one chance that we'd be in the same bar. But it turned out that his office wasn't far away, and the bar was his local. Like I say, a million-to-one.

I can't remember much of the conversation from the previous night, but Kato tells me I swore at him, then asked why he hadn't replied to my email. Then he told me he had replied to my email, I just hadn't seen it. He said he'd asked me to bring Tang to see him the next day at eleven, so he could take a closer look at him. Then he gave me his card. He told me to keep the appointment because at present my 'mind wasn't on the questions I wanted to ask', and anyway it was 'too dark to see Tang properly' in the bar. This wasn't the last time Kato was so gracious.

The elevator made a 'whoof whoof' noise as it travelled, which was just at the right pitch to make my stomach turn and my hungover head pulsate. One side was glass, too, and Tang took great delight in pressing his cheek to it and calling out 'wheeee' as the heaving street dropped away from us. I, on the other hand, could not bear to look.

'Tang, please be quiet, mate, my head hurts.'

Tang looked at me, swivelled his head back to the view . . . and carried on. I rubbed my forehead and took shallow breaths.

The elevator dinged our arrival at floor fifty-three, and we emerged on to a corridor running to either side. Before we had a chance to wonder which way to go, however, a door opened a little way up to the left and Kato's head appeared.

'Mr Chambers, please come on down.' He gave us a big, warm smile, and I felt even worse about my behaviour the previous night.

'Mr Aubergine . . . san,' I began, attempting Japanese nomenclature etiquette. 'Please let me offer you my humblest apologies for the state in which you found me last night. I'm not usually . . . well, that's not how I am normally.' I put my hands together and bowed, because I'd seen someone in a Japanese film apologizing this way. Then I hoped I wasn't being inadvertently offensive in my manner. But Kato smiled and proffered me his hand to shake.

'Please, I spent a lot of time in America and I have seen a lot of English people come to Tokyo. I have seen . . . jet lag before. And, please, call me Kato.'

'You are very kind.' I was genuinely moved by the honourable way he was treating me. 'Please do call me Ben.'

'Come this way, Ben and Tang-chan. Let's have a look at you.' I later found out that the 'chan' addition to Tang's name was a form of affection, and although it was lost on me at the time it wasn't on Tang, and he gave Kato a wide smile, clanking past him into the office.

The room was absolutely beautiful. Sparsely furnished yet everything in a definite place, with a Perspex box against one wall containing what looked to be a metal arm. There were two holes through one side of the box with a rubber glove over each one. When Kato saw me looking, he gestured towards it.

'I mostly lecture these days and do consulting, but I find it difficult to give up practical robotics. I've found a lot of people who leave my industry never really move on. They always keep some part of it with them, something to work on.'

'Why the gloves?' I asked, bending down to feel them in my clammy hand.

'It's best if the subject remains free from dust.'

'Ah, yes.' That had been a stupid question. In my defence, I wasn't really firing on all cylinders.

'Would you like tea, Ben? I can also do coffee, if you prefer?'

It was tempting to have coffee, very tempting, but I saw a delicately crafted teapot sitting steaming on a lacquered tray with two cups waiting beside it. 'It's Japanese green tea . . . very good for jet lag.'

Now he was just teasing me. He may have been an archetypal Japanese gentleman, but he also had a sense of humour. I had to like him.

Kato handed me a little cup filled with a clear greeny-yellow liquid and moved to crouch in front of Tang. He performed a similar ritual to that of Dr Katz: checking out his cylinder – now just under half full – then shutting the flap and lifting up an arm, getting Tang to waggle a foot, etc.

Kato took a longer look at each limb, however, nodding as he did so.

'There's a plate on his underside with some writing. It's become worn down over time, but you'll probably be able to make sense of it. Tang, would you lie down and let Mr Aubergine look at your plate?'

Tang gave us his little shrug and lay down. Splaying his gusset didn't seem to bother him too much. Kato peered at him, feeling around his little metal joints. In many ways he looked the picture of a stereotypical Japanese man, with short dark hair, dark eyes and a sharp business suit, though in his office he did not wear his jacket but hung it neatly on the back of the door. Something set him apart from other people I'd met in Tokyo, however. Perhaps it was his unusually tall height.

He stood up and helped Tang to his feet. The robot immediately wandered off and started to push his grabbers into the rubber gloves on the Perspex arm-box. Then he opened the door to Kato's office and wandered out. I called him back, but Kato assured me he couldn't get very far.

'Can you fix him?' I asked, feeling optimistic.

'No. I am afraid I do not have the correct part.'

My shoulders sagged. 'Do you know what the cylinder is for?'

Kato shook his head and said more or less the same as Cory had. 'It could be a fuel cell, but I would have expected a more sophisticated system if that were the case. The good news is I can tell you who does know. Or at least might do.'

'You can?'

'Yes,' he said, 'it's Bollinger.'

'Bollinger?'

'"Property of B—". My old colleague, Bollinger. English

eccentric. He was a mentor to me – the most amazing robotics mind I'll ever meet.'

Ahhh. So that's who B is.

'What about those half-words? I thought one or other might've been the company that made him, but so far I've drawn a blank.'

'They aren't company names. They're part of an address. The last I heard of Bollinger he'd retired to a remote island in Micronesia . . . there's your "MICRON". And at a guess I'd say that "PAL" refers to Palau. He must have a postal box there.'

'Sounds like a nice retirement.'

'Doesn't it? But I think it's more of a . . . retreat rather than a retirement.'

I asked him what exactly he meant.

He motioned for me to sit down on a beautifully engineered oak-wood visitors' chair, then sat himself on a coordinating swivel chair behind a neatly arranged desk, also made of oak.

'I met Bollinger when I came to work for the East Asia AI Corporation. It was a bit of a, shall we say, coup for me. I'd followed Bollinger's work, and the company had a lot of money to invest in the project I applied to work on. There were about a dozen of us, all earning very good salaries and all accommodated in special apartments at the facility. This was down near Osaka. We had a good life there, but we worked hard.'

'What were you working on? What was the project?'

Kato gestured towards the teapot and I handed him my cup, which he refilled. He was right: the tea was excellent for hang— jet lag.

'We were there to research and develop sentience in

robots. More specifically, we were there to try to create a prototype who was just "alive" enough to take orders and assess the best method of carrying out those orders, but one that could also make a judgement on whether those orders were right or wrong. Our research would have gone into warfare technology. It usually does.' He was matter-of-fact about this eventuality but sounded sad all the same.

'Did you succeed? In making the prototype, I mean?'

'No. Well, yes and no. We were supposed to create one single humanlike robotic entity that we could teach and protect. Instead, we had nearly two-dozen adult-sized machines with more power than they could handle. They couldn't distinguish between right and wrong, so the main point of our project was lost. This is where Bollinger comes in. I think to this day that we would have been successful were it not for Bollinger's ambition. He reached too far, put too much *life* into the subject . . . subjects. He made more than one, which was not the brief, and they didn't have an "off" switch. Bollinger said that to make them as human as possible meant to have no means to switch them off except to shut them down completely. We should have taught them how to be happy, but we didn't. Instead, they were angry.'

'Wait a minute. You said "shut them down completely"? You mean kill them?'

'Yes, if you like.' He sighed. 'It was a big mistake. There was . . . there was an accident. We all lost our jobs. The project was shut down. Bollinger was "advised" to retire from the industry and go stick his head in the sand somewhere. I guess he took it literally.' He smiled ruefully.

'Kato, what happened? With the accident, I mean.'

'I am sorry, Ben, but I cannot say. Bollinger was very protective of his designs. He didn't like the idea that his ideas

151

might leak outside the project. We were all made to sign a gagging order. I have already said more than the law allows me. I would be putting myself and my former colleagues at risk. All I can say is that in my opinion he is dishonourable, a coward.' He leaned close to me and said in a low voice, 'You have not asked my advice, but I would like to offer you some anyway, my apologies. Take the robot home. Don't go looking for Bollinger. Find another way.'

I understood what he was saying. He'd idolized this Bollinger character, who had somehow gone on to ruin his life. He was worried the same would happen to me. But how bad could this man really be? Surely he could be forgiven after all this time? Besides, if I'd had another way I would have taken it. I had no choice – if this was the man who could fix Tang, then to him we must go.

15

Moving On

AS WE GOT UP TO GO, I HAD A THOUGHT. THOUGH TANG'S cylinder was never very far from my mind, the next flight to Palau wasn't until later in the week, so we still had a few more days in Tokyo. I turned to Kato.

'Kato, you've been very helpful and also very patient with me. I'd like to thank you. I wonder, might I buy you dinner this evening?'

'Thank you, it would be an honour . . . as long as we do not talk about Bollinger.'

'It's a deal.'

Kato recommended a nearby restaurant that he visited often, and we arranged to meet at his office at eight o'clock.

'I look forward to it,' I said. We took our leave and returned to the hotel. We'd made a friend, and with this in mind the city seemed less intimidating.

Back in our room, I lay outstretched on the ridiculous but wonderful oversized bed and closed my eyes to think. Then I felt a movement and found Tang had clambered up next to me. He lay down, too, and rested his head on my extended arm. I didn't have the heart to tell him his head was incredibly heavy and was crushing me, so for a few minutes I just put up with it. Then I noticed Tang's eyes were closed, and a faint tick-tick-tick sound was coming from his head. With my free hand, as gently as I could I slid a pillow under him and removed my arm. I ordered an early room-service lunch of an exquisite noodle bento box and watched endless game shows on Japanese television while I waited for Tang to wake up.

When he awoke, Tang was in good spirits. I was inclined to go out and explore the city before our evening with Kato, and Tang agreed, especially when I promised him we wouldn't be going to a bar.

'Train?' he asked me.

'Yes, Tang, we're going on a train. Is that what you want to do?'

'Yes. Train. Sing-ing train.'

I asked at reception if they could recommend some high-lights for us, and they furnished us with a short guidebook. In addition, they told me that I might appreciate Akihabara, the technology district, since I travelled with a robot.

We took the Yamanote line that runs in a circle around and through the centre of Tokyo. My intention was to get off after a few stops, at Akihabara – the location the hotel receptionist had recommended to us – but Tang was having such a good time on the train that he refused to move and we missed the stop. This being the circle line, the most logical thing to do was to carry on until we'd done a full circuit and make sure we got off the next time. I'm convinced Tang knew what he was doing. By the time we'd gone round the full loop, he had learned all the station tunes and was singing them to himself between stops. It was beginning to get on my nerves, and I worried that it would irritate the other passengers, too, but if it did no one said so.

Reaching Akihabara station for the second time, I grabbed Tang's arm and hauled him off the train before he could begin to resist. I got some concerned looks from other passengers, but they didn't understand what it was like to be at the mercy of a Tang-trum.

We emerged from Akihabara station into pleasantly warm early-evening sunshine; quite different from the rain we'd had over the past few days. The pavement shone and the buildings smelled freshly washed, and although we'd come out into one of the most neon and frenetic parts of Tokyo, the whole scene had a beautiful serenity about it.

'Oooh . . . shin-y,' Tang informed me.

'Very pretty, isn't it?'

It was just the sort of sight Amy would love, so I pulled out my phone and took a picture for her. Shoving the phone back in my pocket, I said, 'So, which way shall we go, Tang?'

Tang elected to go right. We wandered up the street, looking at the vivid and colourful advertising boards just beginning to come into their full resonance against the waning daylight. There was one for a domestic whisky, featuring a log fire and a burgundy Chesterfield armchair – incongruous in the high-tech area. Another ad lit up the delights of a cloudy energy drink through the medium of a Western-looking Japanese model surrounded by cherry blossom. A third was a glittering array of red, orange and gold maple leaves and seemed to offer discounts off winter vacations near Mount Fuji, though without knowing any Japanese it was hard to be sure.

Had Tang not been obstinate about the train, we would

have got here earlier, and we would have missed the moving lights playing in the fading rays of dusk. We could have been in any city. As it was, we couldn't have been anywhere else.

Amongst the technology emporia we passed a cluster of shops that looked quainter and more low-fi. We picked one and wandered in. It sold a range of items aimed at tourists, which were meant to represent Japan. There were fans and kimonos, smiling porcelain cats and paintings of Mount Fuji, green tea and those special socks with two toes. As I looked around, I made a decision.

'Tang, I'm going to buy souvenirs for my family, for Christmas – if we get back in time. I'll order something online for my niece and nephew, but I want to take something home from here for Bryony and Dave . . . and Amy. Help me choose.'

We picked out a set of chopsticks for Bryony and Dave. We took a long time selecting a fan for Amy. I bought Tang a pair of socks because he seemed to find them amusing, but he didn't seem to understand that they were to go on feet. He just wanted to clutch them. The shop assistant offered to mail the items back home for us. I took her up on it, thinking of my full backpack and the unknown duration of the rest of my trip. When she tried to take Tang's socks off him, though, I stopped her.

'They're not going home with the other things, thanks. They need to stay with the robot.'

Excited by our diversion into the souvenir shop, Tang decided he'd like to see one of the famed Akihabara techno-shops that we'd been passing all the way since leaving the station. We chose one that from the street seemed to have wide enough aisles for Tang to clank down, but also because he was attracted to the multitude of bright colours and flickering lights that shone out even from the very back of the store.

I don't know who was more wide-eyed at the sheer extent of electronic goods on offer, Tang or me. I couldn't even begin to describe the purpose of a lot of them, but I guessed if you lived in the technology capital of the world then you would know exactly what was what. I, on the other hand, had Tang in tow, a really old phone in my top pocket that dropped a connection whenever it felt like it, and I had a spluttering Honda Civic waiting for me in the garage at home.

After we'd browsed a few of the shop's six floors, we came across one that contained row upon row of androids all stacked next to each other like washing machines, each sitting in their dock waiting to be taken home and activated. Tang refused to go in, but I was intrigued.

'Come on, Tang, they aren't active. They can't hurt you.'

His eyes narrowed with misgiving, but he let me take his grabber and lead him along the aisles. Signs with yen symbols and bullet points peppered the display area, and although I didn't have the faintest idea what any of them said I could guess that they listed the features of each model. They all looked the same to me. Tang also appeared to be trying to decipher what each of the androids did. He peered closely at one of them, a brushed-steel coloured affair with dull glass eyeballs, standing about six feet tall and holding what may (or may not) have been a garden strimmer.

'Does not understand what they are for.'

'I'm not sure I do either, Tang. Although, look, I think this one's meant to cook. See, it has attachments on its arm – a whisk and a knife. It's like a Swiss Army knife.'

157

'Swiss . . .'

'Never mind. I just mean it's got lots of different bits to help it cook. That's the sort of thing Amy wanted. She wanted something more useful than her husband, I guess.'

Looking at the androids had left a bitter taste in my mouth and had seemed to bum Tang out a bit as well, so I decided to leave. As we walked away, Tang cheered up, and as we approached a wide crossroads I noticed him staring at something. He'd spotted a large, brash-looking store right on the crossroads called 'Condomi!' Mercifully, it seemed to be closed, but that didn't stop Tang pushing his chest forward with great determination, ready to cross the road and head straight for it.

'Tang, let's go this way,' I pleaded. 'Look at the lights down this road, aren't they great?' I took his grabber and pulled him gently in the opposite direction.

'No! Con-dom-ee! Con-dom-ee! Con-dom-ee! Con . . .'

'Ssh, Tang, for heaven's sake.'

He swivelled his head at me. 'What?'

'You don't need to say it over and over; I know which shop you're looking at. But it's closed, see?'

Tang looked at the shop and blinked a few times, then took up his new mantra again. It seemed he liked the sound of the word.

'Con-dom-ee! Con-dom-ee! Con-dom-ee!'

Sometimes the best thing to do in situations like that is just to walk away. I set off, praying that Tang would follow me. I strained to pick up his footsteps behind me over the noise of the traffic, and I hadn't gone far when I heard a familiar clanking coming after me, with the unmissable sound of an old-fashioned robot shrieking, 'Con-dom-ee! Con-dom-ee!' I thought it best to get back to our hotel.

I left Tang in the hotel room, sitting on the floor in front of the television, while I went out to dinner with Kato.

'You're not going to go off on your own, are you?'

'No,' he said, transfixed by a manic game-show host, with his lurid suit and enormous laugh.

I only had Tang's word for it that he'd stay there, since the room locked with a key card and could always be opened from the inside. As a precaution, I informed the concierge that I was going out, and asked that if he saw – and heard – a boxy robot heading for the doors then to please send him back to our room.

I arrived at Kato's office at eight o'clock on the dot, and he was already waiting for me.

'I did not want to put you to the trouble of riding the elevator to my floor,' he explained, adding 'please' as he gestured for us to walk.

'Thank you again for the information you gave me about Tang. It's really helpful.'

'You're welcome. I am sorry I am unable to tell you anything further.'

I waved the apology away. 'I understand you already said more than you should have. I'm sorry I put you in that position.'

'It's quite all right. I do have a question, however. Please – can you tell me how Lizzie is?'

I glanced at him, ducking to the side to avoid a telegraph pole spaghettied with black wires and which was, like the Metro trains, singing. Never thought to ask why they did that.

'You said in your email it was she who suggested you contact me.'

'Yes, it was.' I paused, trying to find the most nonchalant reply. 'She said to say "Hi". She's working in a space museum. I think she'd like to be working with AI, but space is the next best thing.'

Kato nodded at this, apparently unsurprised. We walked in silence for a minute or two, Kato with a distant look in his eye and me not wanting to disturb his thoughts, while pondering whether I might bring up the matter of the 'accident' at any point. I was also beginning to wonder whether there was more to Kato and Lizzie than either of them had let on.

'She spoke very highly of you, said you were brilliant.'

'I'm flattered,' he said. 'It's good to know after all these years she remembers me. I haven't spoken to her in a long time.'

'She said that, too. May I ask why not?'

'We dated in college for a while.'

Aha. I knew it.

'We wanted different things at the time,' Kato began to explain, then said simply, 'It ended.'

'She didn't say you were together. I'm sorry, I shouldn't have asked.' I was tempted to ask what he meant by them wanting different things, but then I thought of Amy and realized I didn't want to know.

To me, Amy's career as a barrister had always seemed an irritant – a job that made her work long hours and appeared only to bring her stress. But talking to Kato I realized I'd only ever seen it from my point of view. Amy's profession was every bit as clever and interesting as Kato's, I just hadn't noticed. Perhaps Lizzie was the architect of her own career disappointments . . . as perhaps I was of mine.

Kato's voice cut across my thoughts.

'It was a long time ago. I don't think either of us meant to lose touch. I am glad to hear that she is well.'

We fell silent again as we passed a cluster of noisy girls dressed as *anime* characters – four of whom wore short skirts and pigtails (which I found very unnerving), and one who was dressed as a wide-eyed green dragon (which I didn't). When their chatter died away behind us, Kato continued.

'Tell me, is Lizzie married?'

I coughed. 'Er, no . . . no, I don't think so.'

'Ah, good.'

'Good?'

'I mean . . .'

'It's OK, Kato, I know what you mean.' Ordinarily I'd have taken this sort of conversation at face value, but just then it occurred to me that it might be possible to thank Kato in a better way than by merely buying him dinner.

'It's a shame, because I don't think she particularly wants to be on her own. I think she's sad to have lost contact with you.'

Kato looked thoughtful, so I carried on. 'Are you married, Kato?'

'No. I have been too busy with work. And . . . I have never met the right person.'

'Are you sure about that?'

He stopped walking. 'Perhaps not.'

'Texas is very nice.'

'It is?'

'Yes. The flight here was direct, too, from Houston.' I caught his eye. 'Kato, maybe you should go and see Lizzie?'

He smiled. 'Perhaps. This is the restaurant, Ben-san.'

*

Kato had brought me to the kind of place you never read about in guidebooks. It was down a side street and very unassuming, a wooden building set right on the street and covered in those hanging fabric panels split down the middle. The building, though apparently squished between two more modern constructions, was detached, and I could see at the side it extended further back than I had first assumed.

Kato held the drapes for me to pass through, then followed me in and slid open a wooden door that brought us into the foyer of the restaurant. A gentleman in a smart suit greeted Kato and ushered us through another wooden door into the main room of the building, seating us at a low table in a booth. The inside of the restaurant was beautiful, but it was the smell that struck me first: warm wood and ocean. The interior was furnished with wooden panels, just as the exterior promised, and I thought from the smell that they must be cedar or sandalwood. The sea smell was coming from two large fishtanks set at the far end of the restaurant, flanking a sort of catwalk stage that jutted out into the room. Booths like the one we were in lined the walls on three sides, with cabaret-style tables forming a horseshoe around the stage. The stage itself was empty, but the restaurant was heaving with customers, suggesting that some entertainment was scheduled.

Over dinner we talked more about Lizzie, during which time I decided it was best to pretend to myself as well as to Kato that I hadn't slept with her. It became clear very quickly that, just as I'd thought, the man was in love with her. Even now, despite having broken up with her roughly a decade before.

'I was always more expressive in my feelings for her,' Kato explained. 'Most unusual for a Japanese man and an

American woman – the wrong way round, I think you could say.'

'Is that why you split up? She thought you were too keen?'

He shook his head. 'It was simply that we had been able to live one life at college, in the same place, but afterwards our individual hopes and dreams lay in different countries. I felt I needed to be in Tokyo, for my career. Lizzie wished to stay home in America, near her family. In the end, the relationship seemed an endless cycle of arguments.'

'Kato, look, I know all about arguments that happen time after time and never get resolved. But I also know life is bigger than a series of regrets. Might it not be a good idea to just go and visit her – see if you still feel the same about each other for a start? Then you can worry about the practicalities of life afterwards.'

As I was giving Kato the benefit of my advice, it occurred to me that this attitude might be one of the very things that had driven Amy away from me. For her, perhaps, feelings and practicalities were indelibly linked. For me, it seemed that if you loved someone then that was all that mattered, but now I could see clearly that it wasn't enough. It hadn't been enough for Amy. I thought I'd tell her that when I got home, whenever that was going to be. I wondered if I would be able to convince her that I'd changed, that I saw things differently now. That I might actually be someone who could make her happy. But part of me still thought she'd done the right thing in leaving.

As I pondered the failure of my marriage, the high-pitched noise of a flute emerged seemingly from under the stage, underscored by a twangy guitar that Kato called a *samisen*. The restaurant patrons at the cabaret tables began to applaud.

I looked up to see a geisha standing in the middle of the stage. Only it wasn't a geisha, it was an android. She wore a red kimono detailed with a cherry-blossom print and embroidered herons, with a pale-pink band around her middle that folded into a large square tie at the back. She even had a black wig and a white face, with dainty rose-red painted lips.

The Cybergeisha held two fans and began to dance, twirling the fans around and looking perfectly human. It was really quite weird, especially when her kimono parted slightly at the bottom, revealing jointed legs with wheels instead of feet.

'It helps them move silently and smoothly, like a true geisha,' Kato explained. Then he added, 'Don't get the wrong idea about me, Ben, this is not why I come here. I like the food. But I also thought you might be interested to see a different sort of AI.'

'Is it your company that makes them?'

'No, Ben, it is not. I cannot help but feel it is an insult to our culture, though I could not say why for certain.'

'When we were in California, we stayed at a place called the Hotel Califorina by mistake. It turned out to be somewhere people go to be, um, intimate with androids. They thought that was why Tang was with me. This geisha, is she . . . is it a similar thing, do you think?'

Kato raised his eyebrows, looking genuinely appalled – as Lizzie had said he would be. 'I do not believe so. It is an abomination to treat AI like that – they are unable to refuse.'

'But they are unable to refuse any order, aren't they? What makes one order cruel and another one acceptable?'

'You would never treat Tang that way, I think?'

'Definitely not. But I wouldn't give him any kind of orders, I hope. I don't expect him to do anything I say.'

'But you do, though. You expect him to go with you wherever you go, don't you?'

'I never thought about it like that. I like to think I *request*, rather than order, but I take your point. Besides, he's pretty obstinate – he gets his own way as much as I do, I promise you.'

Kato laughed. 'I believe it.'

The Cybergeisha had turned her attention from dancing to music. She'd seated herself on the floor and was playing a stringed instrument and singing. I'd never heard an android sing before; she was quite good.

'How do they make them sing?'

'They put a lot of energy into specific pieces of technology. That's what we do with our entertainment androids. You would find that this geisha has limited skills – she can sing and dance, and maybe serve tea to clients, but that will be all. No one has yet come up with an android who can do anything more. The closest I have seen is one who fulfils two functions – housekeeping and gardening, for example. There is only so much an android can do, as I think Bollinger discovered. And maybe humans do not want androids to be too diverse. How would we control them?'

I thought of Tang and his propensity for wandering off.

'You couldn't. The best you could do would be to plead with them or shut them down.'

'Exactly.'

As I made my way back to the hotel via the singing Metro system, I worried about Tang. The dinner conversation with Kato had left me uneasy. I'd promised Tang back in Texas that I wouldn't leave him behind again, and yet I had, although at least this time I had warned him. But it didn't stop my heart rate being a little too high as I rode the elevator in the hotel.

I was relieved to find him in the room, exactly where I'd left him, still watching television.

'I'm back, Tang.'

'Ben eats nice?'

'Thank you, the food was lovely.' I elected not to mention the geisha entertainment. 'What have you been up to while I've been out?'

'Up to?'

'What have you done? Did you watch telly all the time?'

'Yes, except for phone.'

I wasn't sure I'd heard properly.

'I use phone.'

'For what?'

'Rings telly. Man on telly says to ring. Holds up number. I rings.'

'You rang a live game show?'

'Yes.'

'Did you get through?'

'Yes.'

'Well?'

'Man speaks Japan-ese. Does not understand.'

16

The Last Resort

THE PLANE THAT BROUGHT US TO PALAU WAS A TINY THING that looked like it featured in disaster movies – ones where the plane gets struck by lightning and nosedives on to a sandy beach, and the passengers get eaten by wild boar. Besides which, I had good reason to fear flying: my parents had died in a plane crash. Be that as it may, I put on a brave face for Tang, who looked every bit as nervous as I felt.

'It'll be fine, Tang, I promise. My dad used to fly planes like this – well, sort of like this . . . a bit smaller, actually. It was one of his retirement fads. Light aircraft. He and my mum used to go up and fly on nice days. They took Bryony up too, once or twice, and the kids. They never took me, though. Ah well, I'm not sure I'd have liked it anyway. Maybe that was why, ha ha.'

I elected to tell Tang only the positive things I knew about small planes, but he still stared at me with an intensity that took me aback.

'Look, Tang, they do this journey all the time. Well, once a week anyway. There and back means they do it about a hundred times a year; I think they know what they're doing.'

Tang still didn't look convinced, and I couldn't blame him – I'd barely convinced myself. We'd been spoiled by Premium and Quality Fancy or whatever it was the last time. This plane wasn't used to carrying androids, let alone robots. I had to pay extra for the weight of Tang, even when he told them he was made of 'alu-minininium' and was therefore light. I don't think they believed him, but I appreciated the attempt.

The flight itself was uneventful: noisy, gin-free and five hours long. Tang couldn't squeeze himself into the window seat, so he spent the journey leaning across me to see the view, which resulted in a dead leg for me and a number of reprimands from the flight attendants for not sitting in our seats properly. We did, however, land in perfect safety on Koror's small runway, though I had to close my eyes when it looked like we were going to run off the end and land in the sea, and Tang covered his face. The other passengers laughed at us for being a pair of big girls.

Despite the plane journey, or perhaps because of it, our transition through the airport and into Palau itself couldn't have felt sweeter. Under a hot sun, there was some sort of traditional greeting going on, with dancers wiggling around, festooning the necks of arriving passengers with lei as we passed through to the arrivals hall. Tang received a very warm welcome, collecting no fewer than five garlands and as many kisses on the top of the head. I don't think I'd ever seen him so chuffed.

The flight attendant had recommended a hotel to us – a resort complex set a little way from Koror town. We took a bus from the tiny airport to the main street in the town, and as it looked so beautiful I decided we could walk from the centre to the hotel. I pushed up my sleeves and placed a panama hat on my sweaty head. As we made our way there, I noticed Tang getting slower and slower.

'Are you OK, Tang?'

'Hot.'

'I know it is, mate.'

'No, hot. Very hot.' The lei from the airport were still around him, and he pulled them off and threw them on the ground.

'I know, I'm sorry, Tang. What do you want me to do about it? I can't turn down the sun.'

Tang looked at me as though this was news to him. He took up his cause again, this time with more urgency.

'Hot!' He pointed to his head. 'Hot . . . hot . . . hot . . . hot . . . HOT!'

I felt the top of his head. It was very hot indeed. I grew concerned.

'Does it hurt?'

'Here.' He extended his grabber so it went over his head to the very top. 'Can't think. Confused.'

It then dawned on me what was happening, and I cursed myself for my neglect. Even five minutes out in the open in temperatures like this could be enough to fry his circuits.

'I'm so sorry, Tang. I've been so stupid.' I herded him to the shade of a palm tree while I considered what to do. I fanned him with my hat, and while he cooled down I glugged a bottle of water that I'd taken from the aeroplane. After a few minutes or so, he began to look a little more cheerful.

'How are you feeling now?'

'Better . . . er, more better . . .'

'Just "better",' I corrected him.

169

'Yes. Not confused now. Not so much.'

'Good.' I was relieved, but the problem still remained; we couldn't sit under the palm tree for ever. 'You need some sort of hat,' I told him.

'Yes. Hat.'

I thought for a moment. My own panama hat would not stay on him – it was the wrong shape entirely and would have slid over his eyes instantly. Then I had an idea. I pulled a white handkerchief from my pocket, the one I'd used to mop Tang up back home at Harley Wintnam, which had since been washed. That moment seemed like such a long time ago, though in fact it had been less than a month. I tied a knot in each corner of the hankie and placed it over Tang's head. With a bit of adjustment, it fitted nicely. 'Will that do, Tang, do you think?'

'Will it do . . . what?'

'I mean, will that work to help you in the sunshine?'

He shrugged. 'Maybe?'

'Well, I guess there's only one way to find out.' I hoisted my rucksack on to my back again and, offering my hand to Tang to hold, we set out once more into the equatorial afternoon heat.

Tang fared better with the knotted hankie, although when we made it to the hotel he still looked ill. The second we got to the reception desk, he plopped himself down on the floor. His flap popped open. He closed it and smoothed the gaffer tape shut, absently picking at it. I chose not to mention it.

Our room was on the ground floor, as I requested, and large with a wide shuttered window that led out on to a veranda. The veranda, in turn, led on to the garden with its infinity pool and a private beach beyond. It was warm in the room, so I opened the shutters to allow the light tropical breeze to blow through on to Tang's hot head, and he clanked over to one of the oversized twin beds to lie down. He flopped on it and his flap came open, but he didn't seem to care. I put my hand to his usually cool chest and found him very warm.

Through the rest of the day, he got worse and worse, and I began to panic uselessly. He lay on the bed with his head to one side, staring fixedly through the veranda shutters towards the beach, the sunlight flickering over his body.

'Ill,' he told me.

'I know you are, mate. I really want to help. What should I do?' I tried not to let my concern show.

'Don't know.'

His head still felt hot. Pacing the room in bare feet, I pondered how best to cool him. First, I turned the air conditioning up in the room. Then I moved the floor fan over and trained it on him. The breeze made his eyes flutter, and he closed them.

'Eyes cold.'

I angled the fan away slightly, but he kept his eyes closed.

After fifteen minutes, I checked him again. He was still hot, and a soft hissing noise was coming from somewhere I couldn't identify. I looked at his cylinder. The fluid level had gone from half full in Tokyo to only a quarter.

'Oh God. Tang, I'm going for help. Stay here; please don't go wandering off . . . You're in no fit state.'

There was no response.

'Tang?'

Still nothing. I bent down and touched his head. Then I shook him gently. He didn't move.

'Tang? Say something. Why aren't you moving?'

Nothing.

'Come on, say something. Please?' Tremors welled up inside me. I shook him harder. 'Tang? You have to be OK, you just have to be. I can't lose you. Tang, please say something!'

Tang opened one eye.

'Ben stop shaking now. Hurts.'

I ran as fast as I could down to the reception desk and dinged the bell assertively for attention. The attendant that had checked us in appeared.

'Can I help you, sir?'

'Yes, please . . . I hope so. It's an emergency,' I panted. 'Do you remember the little robot I came in with earlier?'

'The retro model? Yes, sir. Very sweet.'

'Well, he's really sick and I don't know what to do about it. I'm so afraid I'm going to lose him.' My voice broke slightly.

'He's sick? What happened to him?'

'He got hot on the way here . . . the sun . . . he's not used to it. Now he just wants to lie on his bed, and he's still hot. Do you know if there's anyone staying in the hotel who knows about robots that can come and see him? Please, I'm worried sick about him.'

'It's OK, sir, I can do better than that. We have several androids in the complex doing a number of jobs, and we have a specialist engineer who deals with them. He's not used to dealing with robots, as such, but I'm sure he'll be able to help. I'll give him a call and get him to come to you straight away.' He picked up the desk telephone.

I felt tears rising, despite myself. 'Thank you. Thank you so much.'

A tear slid down the side of my nose. I made a note to tip him when we left.

I'd not been back at the room five minutes before there was a knock at the door. A short, kindly-looking man with white hair and beard, wearing round spectacles and a pair of blue overalls, stood in the doorway, carrying what looked to be a large black-leather tool bag.

'You have a sick robot?'

'Yes, please, do come in. He's here.' I ushered him over to where Tang lay, still with his eyes closed and still facing the veranda and the fan.

He crossed the room rapidly over to Tang, placed his bag on the floor, hitched up his trousers and sat down. He felt Tang's head. 'Ooh, you're a classic model, aren't you? Oh, and you're a warm fellow, too, I see.'

Tang attempted to open an eye, but the effort seemed too much for him and he closed it again.

'Ill.'

'Oh dear, dear. It's OK, my little friend, I know you feel ill. You just lie there for a while.' The robot doctor picked up Tang's nearest grabber, then knocked on his body, then looked in the holes that passed for ears.

In a shaky voice, I explained about the cylinder, and he peeled back the gaffer tape to have a look. He got out a canister of something and sprayed it across Tang's head, then in specific places in short bursts under his flap. Then he stood up and beckoned to me. We drew away to the far end of the room, and he spoke quietly.

'He's not a well robot, and I must admit I'm very worried. There isn't a great deal to be done, I'm afraid. I could try to open his head up and see if there's any circuitry that's broken, but not while he's so warm. And I've never seen a robot like him before, so there's nothing to say I wouldn't

173

make it worse, anyway. Do you know who made him?'

I explained the story of Tang's cylinder, and that I was looking for Bollinger but that I hadn't had a chance to find him.

The doctor shook his head.

'His name sounds familiar, but I wouldn't know where he lives. I'll ask around and see if anyone else knows him. In the meantime, we'll just have to wait and hope he cools down. If he wakes up at all, then try not to stress him and try not to make him think too much; give his circuits a break. I'll pop back whenever I can to check on him.'

'Was it the sun?' I asked.

'It was, yes. I suppose you could say he has sunstroke.'

He looked over to Tang, who lay still and silent with his eyes closed and his arms flopped out flat and extended above his head. Then he continued, 'I just can't predict how he's going to respond. As I say, he's nothing like anything I've ever seen before. At a guess, I'd say the cylinder is part of his cooling mechanism. Every time he moves, speaks, does anything – even thinks – the coolant is deployed. While his cylinder was intact, he would have been fine. The crack in the glass is tiny, so the leakage has been small. But a tropical environment is just too much. The hissing noise you can hear is his body trying desperately to cool him down.'

I paused to take this in.

'I put a hankie on his head . . .' My words sounded pathetic, but the doctor held up a hand in reassurance.

'And you may have saved him by doing so.' He patted me on the arm. 'You shouldn't feel guilty, you should feel proud of yourself.'

I didn't feel proud. I'd taken him to numerous hot places

– California, Texas. I thought I was doing the right thing, trying to get him repaired, but all the time I'd been making it worse. I hadn't thought it through.

'You didn't know,' the doctor said, kindly, 'and it's true that you were lucky, but think: when it did happen, you reacted straight away.' He paused then said, 'I'll come back in a few hours and see how he is.'

I thanked him and showed him out. Then I sat down heavily on the bed, head in my hands.

The doctor came back two hours later, just as he said he would, then twice a day for what seemed like a lifetime, each time administering sprays from his magic canister, which he explained would help cool the robot but was no substitute for his own system. Each time he left, he patted me on the arm and smiled weakly, telling me to just 'sit tight'.

So, I sat with Tang all day and all night, hardly able to sleep, ordering room service once or twice a day but eating very little of it. Tang grew fitful sometimes, his head clonked from side to side and his arms flailed around. Each time he did so the hissing grew louder, and I had to intervene to calm him and conserve his remaining yellow coolant fluid.

After about four days, his eyes began to open occasionally, and I watched him stare out of the window from time to time, blinking slowly before closing them again and falling still.

On the sixth day, I awoke to the sound of the doctor knocking at the door. I answered it rubbing my neck, stiff from where I'd fallen asleep sitting in one of the plush hotel-room armchairs with my head on the bed, next to Tang.

The doctor carried out his checks, by now familiar to me, and as he did so I realized the hissing had stopped. Tang's eyes were open, but he wasn't moving. My stomach lurched.

'Why isn't he hissing?' I asked. 'Tang? Why isn't he moving?'

The doctor stood up and raised his hands to calm me.

'He isn't hissing because there is no need. His cooling system is returning to normal.' He smiled. 'I think he's going to make it.'

Before I knew what I was doing, I'd flung my arms around the man, who patted my back awkwardly and made soothing noises. Over the doctor's shoulder I saw Tang's eyes roll towards me and his CD-slot mouth appear to somehow widen into a small smile. I let go of the doctor and went to Tang, taking a grabber in one hand and resting the other on his head.

After the doctor left, I shuffled round the hotel room for a while, not really knowing whether to sit, stand, watch telly or just stare at the sea and the tropical plants outside our window. The doctor had said that although he was now confident it was not necessary to open Tang's head, it would still take some time for him to be fully recovered. He also said he would need a lot of rest, and sure enough by the time the doctor left us he was asleep. He awoke after twenty minutes or so, however, and called my name. The sound of his voice, absent for nearly a week, flooded me with relief. I darted over and kissed his familiar cool forehead.

'Can we dive?' asked Tang as I pawed over him, feeling his head and peering into his eyes.

Dive? I looked at him, puzzled.

'If I get not ill, can we dive? See fishes.' He pointed a grabber in the direction of the veranda. From his position on the bed he could see a group of people in snorkelling equipment, popping up and down again in and out of the water. Occasionally, one of them would stand up suddenly and whoop, explaining what they'd seen.

'I thought you hated water?'

'This water different. This water pretty.'

'Mate, I'm sorry, we can't go diving.'

'Why?'

'It might be pretty water, but it's still bad for you. You'll rust.'

He waved a grabber vaguely over his body. 'Aluminininium. Does not rust.'

'But you'll sink, won't you?'

'No. Tang floats.'

I didn't want to know how he knew these things, but nothing about him surprised me any more. It felt like I could know him for years and still not get to the bottom of his thoughts and feelings.

The fact remained he couldn't go diving.

'Well, all the same, I don't think it's a good idea to submerge yourself in sea water, Tang, I'm sorry.'

'Man said to relax. Man said not to stress. Dive?'

Eavesdropping little heap of scrap metal.

'Tang, that's called emotional blackmail.'

He paused to consider this.

'Listen, what kind of person would I be if I let you do something I thought would be dangerous? I almost lost you there, mate. I'm still in shock. I can't let anything else happen to you; besides, you're still broken, remember?'

Tang picked at his gaffer tape.

'I'll make it up to you, I promise. I'll think of something different, something better that we can do, OK?'

Tang sighed but eventually nodded his head.

'Look, you need to rest, and I need to eat. Are you going to be all right if I leave you here while I go out?'

Tang nodded.

'You're not going to try to come after me?'

'No.'

'Good bo . . . good robot. I'll try not to be long.' I believed him, but I closed the shutters on the pretence of keeping out the late-afternoon sun, which had bathed half the room in a saturating orange light. I decided to lock the door after me, too. I laid my hand on his head once more and left.

Over the next few days, I began to leave Tang on his own while I continued to search for Bollinger. The robot doctor's investigations had turned up nothing at all, and although the immediate danger to Tang was over, time was still running out for him.

As the days passed, he seemed to get used to his convalescence and even requested my departure to collect magazines, shells, seaweed, dead crabs, live eels and other things for him to look at while he was confined to the room. He even insisted I bring him a plank of driftwood from the beach that was as tall as him and covered in barnacles, just because he'd seen it through the window and wanted it.

I walked often into town, taking photographs of the things I saw to show Tang when I returned, like a street vendor selling grilled fish on skewers, or a grand domed building that someone told me was an aquarium but looked more like a cathedral. I chuckled to myself as I thought of showing my family the pictures – I couldn't deny it was a diverse and sometimes strange collection of things to photograph. I could just imagine Amy's eyebrow raising at one particularly random picture I'd taken – of a three-legged dachshund that I thought might remind Tang of Kyle. It would mean nothing to Amy, but then for all I knew I might not even get to show her the photos.

Tang had come round to the idea of a camera now and kept looking underneath my phone to see where the rest of the boat, or island view, or market stall was.

'It's flat, Tang.'

'Inside phone?'

'No, not inside, not quite.' I didn't really know how to explain a photograph to a robot, even one like Tang, so I just had to keep telling him – 'It's flat. It's what you're looking at when you get the picture, and it comes up flat on the phone.' Eventually he seemed to accept my explanation, and after a while, whenever I walked back through the door after an excursion he held his grabber out eagerly for the phone, though as it was a touchscreen I had to work it for him.

Tang was getting better every day, but he was still weak and confused at times. One day around two o'clock in the afternoon, he woke up suddenly and started screeching, and I had to spend a long while calming him down, stroking his shoulder and his head with my hand. As I sat with him, I felt a growing unease crawl up my spine and spread through my body. If this Bollinger person really was Tang's creator and could fix him, then by taking him back home with me I'd be risking his life. We'd got this far because the crack in Tang's cylinder was small; if a replacement one suffered worse damage, who knew if we'd ever make it here in time? It could mean the end for Tang.

The realization crystallized in my mind. I thought the situation over. Wouldn't the best thing for Tang in the end be to leave him with the man who had created him in the first place and who would be there to fix him if anything life-threatening ever occurred?

My heart contracted at the thought. It would be OK, I reasoned. Tang would be safer there than at home with me, and probably happier for it.

But now a weight had settled on my chest, seeming to press the air from my lungs and constrict my throat.

After three weeks of walking into town, one morning I decided to take a different route down to the harbour. I needed a change of scenery, because despite its staggering beauty, the island felt lonely without Tang and grew more so when every time I left him I realized I could be one step closer to finding Bollinger and saying goodbye.

On the other hand, my worry about what would happen to Tang if I couldn't find Bollinger was continuing to build. I'd imagined someone would tell us where he lived, he'd fix Tang, and we'd be on our way back home to Harley Wintnam within a few days. But things had shifted, and although Kato had pointed us here, he had not been able to give us any further information. Despite my asking around in stores and bars, I'd found not a single soul who knew of Bollinger.

I made my way to the beach and stepped up and over a slope in the sand dunes. What I saw made me smile. Below me, at a jetty on the beach, was a sightseeing boat. A crowd of tourists fluttered around it taking photographs, and nearby stood a man who looked to be the captain taking money from people and issuing tickets.

As I approached the jetty, a break in the throng of sightseers revealed a sign: 'Glass-bottomed boat trips. Swim with the fish without even getting wet!' Closer still and I could read a smaller paragraph below it: 'Afraid to dive? Forgot your swimsuit? Or just plain turned off by water? Join our Swimming with the Fishes trips – all the fun of scuba without setting foot in the sea!'

I placed my hands on the top of my head in disbelief. I might not have found Bollinger, but at least I had found something to cheer Tang up a bit. We could do something wonderful together before I had to leave him – something he could remember me by. It was perfect.

17

Fish

I DIDN'T TELL TANG ABOUT THE BOAT TRIP; I WANTED IT TO be a surprise. The next day, I simply told him I thought it would do him good to be out of doors. I promised Tang I would protect him from the sun and borrowed an umbrella from reception as we left.

Tang was nervous, understandably, picking at his gaffer tape and glancing at the sky as though the sun might laser-beam his head open. I took him the way I'd walked the previous day, over the sand dunes. At first he walked well, the sand underfoot being compacted and mixed in with long grass flattened by feet. But as we moved further down the beach, Tang began to struggle – his feet weren't wide enough to keep him from sinking. Nevertheless, he held his head up high, bless him.

When eventually we arrived at the jetty, it took no time at all for Tang to work out what we were doing. His eyes widened and he wrapped his grabbers around my leg, squealing with electronic delight at the prospect of fish.

'No diving, diving!'

'Yep, that was my thinking.'

'Ben . . . Ben . . . Ben! Fish! Ben! Thank Ben! Thank yooou.' And with that, he clanked off up the jetty.

The second Tang saw the glass bottom, with its array of starfish on show, he wobbled from foot to foot, clapped his grabbers together and let out an enormous 'wheeeeee'. He clanked up the steep gangplank as fast as he could, fell forward and crawled the remainder of the way. He tumbled into the vessel and lay on his front with his face pressed against the glass. It was not his most dignified entrance.

There were a few other passengers aboard, but not many. We were out of season – those who'd come for a Thanksgiving break had left a week ago, and it was too early for the Christmas parties to have arrived.

I sat on a bench that ran along one side of the boat, hanging my hand over the edge. My fingertips touched the sea, just about, and I felt its warmth rise into my insides, especially when the skipper cast off and the boat picked up some speed.

The boat itself was a charming mixture of rustic, flaking painted panels and high-tech instruments, which I could see arranged across the cockpit . . . dashboard . . . whatever, even from my vantage point, which was towards the back of the boat. The fierce sun in this part of the world had taken its toll on the outside of the boat, but there was nothing neglected about it.

Luckily, the boat was also covered by a large tarpaulin fixed to metal rods that stuck straight up from the edges of the craft. I'd fretted incessantly about Tang since I nearly lost him. He had on my makeshift hankie hat, which he seemed to love, and though the tarp provided him with ample shade, I kept reaching to place my hand on his back to check the temperature of his body and then his head. He waved me away a number of times.

'Tang fine, Ben. Tang not hot. Tang best happy.' Maybe it was all the television he watched while he was sick or the magazines I'd brought him, but from somewhere he'd learned superlatives and tried often to use them, with varying success.

'Look! Ben! Blue fish!' Then a bit later, 'Green fish! Ben . . . Ben! Look! Ben! Look! Ben! Orange fish!'

After we'd motored some way from the shore, the skipper left one of his assistants at the tiller and came down with a coolbox of drinks. He gave me a beer and took a seat next to me.

'Cute little robot you have there.' He had an American accent and looked the part – deeply tanned and stubbly, with shades, a baseball cap, white vest and denim shorts – but his voice was tinged with something else, which suggested he'd been on the island for a long time.

'He is, thank you. He's loving the fish.'

'Can't say I've ever had a robot on the boat before. AI ain't usually interested. In fact, you don't see too many of them out and about on the island in general. Too hot.'

I nodded gravely.

He nodded back. 'Don't get me wrong, there are androids on the island . . . it's just that they keep themselves to themselves. You know, get on with their work and stay out of trouble . . . and indoors. It's nice to see a robot, although he's a bit unusual, ain't he?'

'You can say that again. He may look like a tumble dryer, but he's pretty special inside.'

'You don't need to explain, dude, here we live and let live. It's all good.'

I told him I was glad to hear it. Then I complimented him on the ingenuity of his glass-bottomed boat and the beauty of his excursion route. He thanked me and pointed out a patch of bright-yellow coral and a school of red snapper moving as one as the boat passed by.

'Seems a strange place to come for a vacation with a robot, though, if you don't mind me saying.'

I smiled. 'Not at all. It's a long story, but the short version is he's broken and I'm looking for his owner.' I gave him the highlights of my dealings with Tang, right up to the point where Kato told us where he thought we could find Bollinger. Then I told him that even on the island no one seemed to know where I could find him, if they'd even heard of him at all.

The second I mentioned Bollinger's name, the skipper said, 'I think I know him! Crazy old man; always wears cut-offs and a straw hat. Goes barefoot. Comes here for supplies once in a while. I only see him when I'm on the boat. Always uses the same jetty over there.' He gestured back to the beach, to a set of small, unassuming planks of wood now in the distance. 'Keeps himself to himself. He lives on that island out there.' He pointed in the direction of a tiny pinprick on the horizon. 'I see boats going back and forth with containers and so on. Yeah, boats deliver what he needs straight to him, and boats take away his trash and other things he don't want.'

I didn't hear clearly the last of what the skipper said. My stomach suddenly felt like it had turned inside out. I stood up and gazed at the island. Then I looked over at Tang and placed my hand on his head and stroked his shoulder. We had arrived.

*

That evening I hung out with Tang in our room, ordering room service so I didn't have to leave him. We talked about the boat trip and what we'd seen, although I didn't tell him that I'd arranged with the skipper to take us to Bollinger's island the next day. By this point I wondered that Tang still hadn't asked what my plan was. I started to tell him a few times, but somehow couldn't bring myself to say it. In hindsight, I wonder whether he knew all along but pretended he didn't, hoping I would change my mind.

I read Tang the area guide in the hotel-room manual. One entry caught my eye.

'It says here that we get a good view of "Koror's famous sunset" from these rooms. How about it, Tang, you feel up to watching the sunset?'

Tang's eyes narrowed and he blinked at me a couple of times, obviously nervous.

'Tang not friends with sun.'

'Aw, Tang, I understand. But it's OK. The sun's not all bad. Can't you forgive it?'

'Forgive?'

'Yes, forgive. You know, like when someone does something to upset you or hurt you, and they say sorry and you're friends again? No?'

'Tang not . . . never forgiven. Don't understand.'

'I think you have,' I told him. 'I think you've forgiven me hundreds of times without even realizing it. Remember when I tried to put you in the hold on that first flight, and you got upset with me?'

'Yes.'

'Well, then you stopped being upset with me, didn't you?'

'Yes.'

'Then you must have forgiven me, otherwise we wouldn't still be friends. And we are friends, aren't we?'

'Yes. Ben is Tang's friend. Tang loves Ben.'

I felt a lump in my throat, then, and didn't know what to say. Here was a robot who didn't understand the concept of 'why', who struggled with the idea of motivations. He'd never been taught forgiveness, so he hadn't known whether he was doing it or not. But of all the complex human emotions he could have settled on, he seemed to understand love.

I bent down and put my arms around his small shoulders.

'Come on, Tang, let's watch this sunset.'

18

James

WE SAILED ON THE AFTERNOON TIDE. TANG WAS DELIGHTED when he realized we were going back on the boat.

'Glass boat! Glass boat! Glass boat!'

'It's a glass-*bottomed* boat, Tang. The rest of it's made of wood, mostly.'

'Glass bottom?'

He found the idea of something having a glass bottom hilarious.

'Glass bottom! Glass bottom! Glass bottom!' He lay down on the floor of the boat as he had done before.

I turned to the skipper. 'I'm sorry about this.'

'Not a problem, pal. He's not so very different from a child, if you ask me, and it looks like you're the perfect dad.'

My heart beat a little harder at this – that was the last thing I would expect to be described as.

The boat was fun, the island beautiful, the weather glorious, and what's more I'd been successful in my mission . . . I was on the verge of returning Tang to his rightful home, where he would be mended and he would be happy. But again there was a crushing sensation at the thought of going home without him. For the first time I asked myself: would *I* be happy without Tang? The answer hung in a gloomy mist, just out of range. I wouldn't know until I left him.

I watched the skipper as he turned to Tang every now and again to point out a reef or a dark shoal of fish he saw coming up. Tang took in every word the skipper said, kicking his legs and squealing whenever the promised sights came into view. The skipper was right: he was so like a child. I suppose I'd always known it, but as I'd spent my life trying to avoid my sister's offspring and had little experience of children, I hadn't really thought about it. All of this made it somehow more painful to imagine taking the boat back to Palau alone, without my little metal box beside me, perhaps in only a few hours' time.

I bent down, lay my sweaty body next to Tang on the cool floor and watched the fish with him.

The skipper dropped us off at a small beach jetty. Tang was reluctant to get out of the boat, casting his eyes around and frowning. I'd expected a bit more glee from him when he worked out where we were going. I thought he'd know that here, finally, was the place where his cylinder could be replaced. Where he could stop worrying about his fluid running out. Where *I* could stop worrying. As usual, I hadn't really thought it through – the big reveal. What did I think I was going to do when the penny dropped – go 'Ta da!'?

We'd shuffled as quickly as we could about fifty metres up the bright white beach, Tang with his knotted hankie and me with my panama, when I spotted a figure in the distance. Squinting in the sun, I saw the figure was getting closer, then it occurred to me that it was running and in fact the figure was a 'he'. I glanced at Tang. He was staring straight ahead, but he'd stopped walking. He shifted from foot to foot, but I couldn't tell why; given the terrain, he might just have been sinking.

'Tang, do you know who that is?'

'Yes.'

'Who?'

Tang made no answer. He just stared at the fast-approaching man, eyelids lowered and grabbers curled into fists.

'Tang, who is the man?'

There was another pause, then came the word – 'August.'

'Tang, we've been through this before . . .'

Tang gave me one of Amy's looks. But, as usual, I still didn't understand.

'Tang, who is the man?'

'August! August . . . August . . . August!'

'OK, fine, it's August! I'll just ask him directly when he gets here.'

The man was close now, close enough for me to discern that he was about six feet tall and, I guessed, about sixty. He wore a straw hat with broken ends that stuck out all over and was otherwise appropriately dressed for a tropical beach, with cut-off canvas shorts and a white cheesecloth shirt, and his feet were bare. Unsurprisingly, he was deeply tanned. He waved to us as he ran, and hollered something that I didn't catch on the first few occasions but turned out to be, 'James, oh my God, I can't believe it . . . James, I didn't think I would ever see you again!'

James?

Upon reaching us, the man fell to his knees and flung his arms around Tang, who stood stiffly with his arms down. Undeterred by the robot's cool response, he began to look him over, inspecting each and every scratch and dent. The ragged gaffer tape covering Tang's flap did not escape his notice.

'What in God's name have you done to yourself, James?' He tried to peel the tape off but Tang placed an arm across his flap and growled, a low noise I had not heard before. 'James, let me look at it; let me fix it.'

'No.'

'James, please . . .'

'No!' Tang's face set in a determined frown.

The scene was awkward. I didn't understand Tang's resistance to the man, since he was obviously concerned for him.

'Tang, your cylinder . . . You should let him look,' I said, but Tang's grabber stayed fast where it was.

My words diverted the man's attention, and he got to his feet and took hold of my hand in a vigorous shake.

'You found him. Thank you so much. I can't tell you how relieved I am. Who are you?'

'Ben,' I said simply, unsure what to make of this new acquaintance, who was still shaking my hand.

'I'm dreadfully sorry. I should have introduced myself first. August Bollinger at your service. People usually just call me Bollinger.'

August?

Tang had been telling me who owned him all along . . . I'd just not been listening. 'Tang, why didn't you say something?'

Tang shrugged and shook his head.

'Where did you think we were going all this time? You knew we were looking for someone who could fix you.'

Tang picked at the gaffer tape, his eyes downcast. He paused for a few seconds before replying, 'Holiday.'

I hung my head. It hadn't occurred to me to tell him where we were going. I'd just assumed he knew as much as I did. Neither had it ever occurred to me to ask *why* he'd left in the first place. I suddenly wondered if that's the way I'd been with Amy all the time we'd been together.

Throughout this exchange, Bollinger had been crawling on the warm sand around Tang, examining him even more closely. I'd been right about one thing: Tang's owner did seem to have missed him.

The 'August' revelation had distracted me from the urgency of the robot's broken state, but watching Bollinger inspect Tang's metal body I remembered what we'd come here to do.

'Please,' I said to Bollinger, anxiously, 'let's get out of the heat. It's not good for Tang . . . His coolant cylinder is broken and he's hardly any fluid left. He's already been really ill once . . .' I trailed off, not really wishing to relive the anxiety of the previous month.

'This way,' Bollinger said, nodding, then added, 'Come along,' which he directed at Tang. The robot remained totally still. Then, with one pointed look at me, he drew himself up and strode past Bollinger and off down the beach in the direction from which his master had come.

I made to follow Tang, but Bollinger laid a hand across my chest.

'It's best if you let him go when he's in this mood. It'll pass.'

It irritated me that Bollinger thought he could tell me how to handle Tang. On the other hand, it looked like Tang

192

was in no humour to talk to me, clanking along the beach as defiantly as if he were leading a revolution.

'Come,' Bollinger said, 'let's follow him at a safe distance, and we'll talk.'

I nodded, and we started to walk.

'First, can you tell me why you call him Tang?'

'That's his name, isn't it? Why do you call him James?'

'Because that *is* his name.'

'Why James?'

'I had to call him something. I believe it helps develop a personality. I picked James because I like it.'

'When he arrived in my garden, all he would say was "Acrid Tang" and "August". And he's been responding to Tang. He never told me his name was James.'

'It sounds like he didn't tell you a lot of things.'

It was true: there were a lot of things he hadn't told me. I knew that. But then, I hadn't thought to ask.

'I assumed "Acrid Tang" and "August" were clues as to who he was and where he'd come from, but it turns out that the one I ignored is the only one with any relevance.'

'I wouldn't say that . . . It's complicated, but I think I can explain. Might I offer you dinner and a bed for the night?' He held out his arm, his small eyes smiling.

It's the least you can do, I thought, but I held my tongue.

We found Tang shut in a cupboard near the entrance to Bollinger's impressive monochrome house that was somehow shielded from view from the beach. Bollinger shut the door behind us, then headed for the cupboard.

'He'll be in here,' Bollinger said.

'How do you know?'

'He always used to come here if he was cross with me.'

He knocked on the cupboard door. 'James? James? Open the door!'

There was a pause.

'Tang,' came a small metallic voice from inside.

'Your name is James, James. Don't you remember?'

'Yes.'

'Then I shall call you James.'

'No.'

'Yes.'

'No! Tang! Tang . . . Tang . . . Tang . . . Tang . . . Tang!'

I should have been more mature than to feel smug, but I wasn't.

'He gets like that when he's adamant, Bollinger. I suggest you just give him what he wants.'

Bollinger gave me a searching look, then he sighed.

'Very well, "Tang", if that's now your name.' He delivered the name with unnecessary emphasis, and I realized I wasn't the only one with maturity issues. He continued. 'Will you come out and talk to us?'

'No.'

'Come out!'

'No!'

'Yes!'

'No! No . . . no . . . no . . . no . . . no . . . no!'

'Fine. We'll see you later. Come on, Ben, I'll show you to your room.'

We left him. From behind us came a little click as Tang opened the door, but he didn't come out.

Bollinger led me through his large single-storey house, so shiny and so at odds with the natural beauty outside his window. It was certainly not made from local materials.

Here was a man who'd spent his working life in the company of solder and of steel, and it showed. I wondered why a recluse should feel the need to build a house so expansive, and the answer came almost immediately.

'You're probably wondering what I'm doing living with all this space? I suppose a man in my position doesn't need it, but I spent so long working in cramped offices and tiny labs that when I moved here I decided there was nothing stopping me from building the house of my dreams. So I did. It seemed like a good idea at the time, but now . . . recently, I have found it too big. That was while Tang was away. But he's here now, thanks to you.'

He led me down a corridor and stopped abruptly around a corner.

'Here,' he offered. 'I think this is the nicest guest room. I'll give you some time to rest. Where have you been staying? Do you have anything you would like laundering? I haven't a 'bot, I'm afraid – I never got round to making one – but I do have a washing machine . . . if you don't mind the wait while your things dry?'

I told him where we'd been staying, and explained that I'd checked out as I'd planned to head home as soon as I could. I thanked him for the offer of some help with my laundry and handed him a bundle of the clothes from my rucksack that I considered least fresh.

The guest room was more like a suite, with a large walk-in wardrobe and the largest freestanding mirror I had ever seen. To the right of the door sat a black-leather sofa with a footstool to match, from which one could take in a view through picture windows of a wall of green tropical foliage. It was easily the best hotel I'd ever stayed in.

It was the bed that really captured my attention: a four-poster steel affair with snow-white linen, which accepted my body graciously as I flopped upon it. As I lay on the bed, I felt confused. Both Kato and Tang were angry with Bollinger, and from what Cory had said back in California there was the possibility that he had deliberately given Tang an inferior build. On the other hand, he had been utterly charming and seemed to have been genuinely worried about the robot. It didn't make sense. I needed answers, but later – after some sleep.

19

Champagne

IT WAS DARK WHEN I AWOKE. THE SLEEP HAD BEEN GOOD FOR me, and although I felt sadder than I had done, I also felt lighter. I'd achieved something after all, for the first time in my life, and that achievement had saved Tang's life . . . just as soon as he let Bollinger replace his cylinder. But I felt a bit hollow. As far as I knew, Tang was still in the cupboard, and I wasn't sure whether to leave him to come out of his own accord or to go and plead with him. I wasn't even sure it was my place to do that any longer. Bollinger was Tang's owner again, and I was just a guest. I felt a knot in my stomach.

For something constructive to do, I began to re-pack the remainder of my clothes in my rucksack. As I packed, I realized I'd been taking clothes from only the top few layers for the entire journey. Suddenly I was curious to see what else I'd packed all those weeks ago. As I tipped the contents of my rucksack on to the bed, I saw I'd brought a range of entirely unsuitable garments. I shook my head in particular at the shiny-black dress shoes I never wore at home, let alone on a round-the-world backpacking trip. One, more sensible, item strayed into my hand: a pair of shorts that I'd packed even though I'd not worn them for years. I should have been wearing them now. I turned them over to check they were clean, and as I did so something fell out of a pocket. It was a champagne cork. I dropped the shorts and, frowning, picked up the cork. As I brought it to my nose to inhale its smell, Amy's younger self came into my mind.

I first met Amy at a dinner party at Bryony's. The country was experiencing its annual heatwave, the one that always happens but still catches everyone out; where hospitals are inundated with topless men bearing chilli-red torsos, drunken girls suffering from morbid dehydration and balding retirees with sunstroke. Bryony said she was having an 'al-fresco party', which I took to mean a barbecue. So I wore shorts . . . and the same white casual cotton shirt I'd been wearing on the road trip, incidentally. But the shorts are the main point. It wasn't until I arrived that I had any inkling of the faux pas I was about to commit.

Bryony opened the door to me with one hand, a glass of champagne in the other. She was dressed in a simple, sensible black dress and a string of our mother's pearls, but it didn't occur to me that there was a disparity in the smartness of our outfits.

'You're late.'

'I know. I'm fashionable,' I told her.

She raised an eyebrow.

'What are you wearing?'

'What do you mean? I'm wearing shorts.'

'Why are you wearing shorts?'

'Because it's hot. Why do you think I'm wearing shorts?'

'But it's a dinner party.'

'You said it was a barbecue.'

'No, I didn't, I said it was an al-fresco party.'

'Isn't that the same thing?'

'No, of course not. Oh, for goodness' sake, Ben, don't you ever listen? You'd be a reasonable-looking man if you smartened yourself up a bit.'

'Thank you,' I said. It wasn't the first time she'd told me that, and it probably wouldn't be the last. She sighed dramatically but nevertheless stepped aside to let me in. I was relieved – I thought for a minute she was going to make me go home and change, like a schoolboy who'd got the wrong non-uniform day.

'What am I going to say to the other guests?'

'Tell them there was a misunderstanding.'

Bryony screwed up her round nose and raised an eyebrow. This clearly wasn't good enough. She led me through into her expansive sitting room – the 'bringing-the-outside-in' area – drew a deep breath and announced me.

'Everyone, this is my baby brother, Ben. He got the wrong end of the stick about an outdoor party, apologies.' She laughed. Everyone else laughed, too. I remembered why I fucking hated Bryony's parties . . . and her entire world, for that matter.

But it wasn't all bad. By the open French windows there was a girl, shaded from my view by the sunlight streaming past her, but I could still see she wasn't laughing at me like the rest of them. I decided there and then that this was the person I was going to spend the evening with. If anyone made me talk to anyone else, I would jump in Bryony and Dave's outdoor heated pool and attempt to drown myself. As soon as Bryony had released me, I made a beeline for the girl.

'I'm Ben.' I held out my hand.

'I know.' She shook it. I felt a flicker of excitement.

'Ahh . . . how do you know?' I hoped I sounded flirtatious.

'Bryony just said.'

Oh.

'Who are you? I mean, what's your name?'

Just then Bryony dinged her champagne glass and the murmur of laughter and pleasant conversation fell away.

'Amy, come here.'

The girl next to me smiled and moved towards her. I could see her more clearly now. She was about a foot taller than Bryony and therefore slightly shorter than me, and of a slim to average build (I found out later she always thought she was on the big side, because she had been as a child). She was pretty, with carefully styled blonde hair with wispy bits that suggested she had to work hard to get it that way. Very different from the sleek, groomed professional who walked out on me years later.

'This is my brand-new very best friend, everyone,' began Bryony, obviously a bit tipsy already, otherwise she'd never have been so emotional in front of a whole room of people. 'She's our guest of honour here tonight, because she's just reached the Bar!' At this, there was a riot of applause, and Amy blushed. Qualifying to be a barrister still sounded to me like some sort of posh race to get the booze in, but I decided this should not be my chat-up line to Amy.

The Guest of Honour mumbled a 'thank-you' to the warmed-up crowd.

'Dave, pass me a bottle, please.'

Bryony's husband complied. If my sister had wanted to be slick, she'd have put a towel over the bottle before opening it. But on this occasion she didn't. She wanted a flourish. With a slight of hand that only the truly experienced champagne-drinker can muster, she popped the cork out of the bottle, and everyone squealed as the drink flowed over the top and into a tray of glasses Dave had efficiently provided in the nick of time. Against all expectations, I caught the cork.

When I say 'caught', what I think I really mean is I put my hands up to stop Bryony's crap – or possibly superb – shot from hitting me in the nipple. She was always more robust than I, and never understood what hurt and what didn't, even when we were children. She was like a rhino: no-nonsense, rectangular and muscular.

Amy accepted a glass from Dave's tray and, to my surprise, sidled back to where she'd been standing with me.

'That was embarrassing,' she said.

'My sister's like that. I'm sorry.'

'Don't be. It's sweet, really. If she wants to make a fuss, then I'm happy to let her. My parents don't really understand what a barrister does, so they aren't particularly bothered. It's nice to get some recognition.'

'Here,' I said. 'It's the cork from the bottle . . . You should save it. Then you'll always remember the occasion. When you got recognition, I mean.' I handed her the cork.

'You caught this?'

'Er . . . yeah.' *Why not?*

'You keep it. Save it for a time when I'm feeling low, then you can show it to me and it'll remind me of today.' She smiled. I smiled.

And that's how Amy and I met. Six months after my parents had died, when Bryony was emerging from her grief and I was still wondering why I felt none. Amy's career

201

was about to take off, and her confidence with it, whilst mine had shuddered to a halt not days before, when the supervisor in charge of my veterinary training told me to go and 'sort myself out' and then come back, neither of which I had done.

As I stood packing a rucksack on an English eccentric's remote island in the South Pacific, a depressing thought occurred to me. I still had the cork.

With no further thought, I pulled out my phone from my pocket and dialled Bryony's number. Annabel, my niece, answered.

'Annabel, hi, it's Ben.'

'Who's Ben?'

'Uncle Ben.'

'Ohhh, hi, Uncle Ben.'

I heard some commotion in the background and the stomp of feet that could have only been my sister. Then there was some muttering during which I heard 'Give it to me', and then Bryony was on the line.

'Where in God's name have you been all this time? You just left without a word to anyone; we thought you were dead, we thought you'd killed yourself . . . We thought the robot had killed you. Where are you? Are you OK? Are you at home?' And so on. I let her rant for a few minutes, not really minding the telling-off and in fact quite glad to learn she cared enough to worry.

'I'm fine, Bryony, really . . .'

'Are you in California?'

'No . . .'

'Then where are you?'

'If you let me get a word in, then I'll tell you.'

Silence.

'I'm in Micronesia.'

'Where's that?'

'The Pacific. I'm on an island. It's a long story. I'm with the robot and a man called Bollinger.' I realized as I said it that my explanation raised more questions than it answered, but I didn't have time to elaborate. 'Bryony, listen, I don't have much time to talk at the moment, but I'll be home soon and I'll come and see you, I promise. But for now . . .' I paused, almost dreading the answer to my question '. . . is Amy still there?'

'Yes, but . . .'

'Please, Bryony, can I talk to her?'

'I'm not sure it'll do either of you any good. It's not a good time, Ben.'

'Please.'

There was a pause. 'Hold on.'

I heard the telephone being set aside and footsteps retreating, before another pair, lighter this time – more graceful – came into hearing. Amy picked up the receiver.

'Ben?' She sounded uncharacteristically timid.

'Amy, it's good to hear your voice.'

'Ben, it's been ages . . . Why didn't you call before? Everyone's been so worried about you.'

'Everyone?'

'Yes, everyone. Where are you?'

'On a Pacific island, but, look, that's not why I called . . .'

'Will you be home for Christmas?' As she talked, she grew more confident. She sounded like Amy again – my Amy.

'I don't know. Yes. Probably. But listen . . . I've been thinking a lot about you while I've been away. I wanted to say I'm sorry for my part in the break-up. At the time I didn't know what I'd done wrong, but I understand now. I've been able to see myself through your eyes a bit, and I can understand how frustrating I must have been to live with. Can you forgive me? Please forgive me.'

I paused to give her a chance to respond, but there was silence. 'Amy? Are you still there?'

'Yes, Ben, I'm sorry, too. Of course I forgive you . . . I'm not the easiest person to be around either, and I didn't take your feelings into consideration as much as I should have.'

'Then it's OK? Might we be OK, Amy?'

Silence again. Then I knew what she was going to say.

'Ben . . . I've met someone.'

My stomach felt like it had dropped out as I heard these words, though they weren't the least bit surprising.

'Oh. Anyone I know?'

'One of Dave's friends. He knows him from Cambridge. Don't say it – how can a Cambridge/Oxford relationship ever work out, right?' She chuckled, but it was a delicate, nervous sound. 'He's a surgeon. He's here at the moment, actually.'

Of course he is, I thought.

'Well, I'm happy for you, Amy, truly.' And in a way I was. It sounded like she had the man she'd always wanted, as opposed to one who only fitted the bill on paper. He sounded like a go-getter.

'Thank you,' she said quietly. Then, 'Ben, I hope we can still be friends?'

I thought back to my monologue to Tang all those weeks ago, where I'd decided I never wanted to see any of them ever again. I'd been hurt and drunk, but hurt mostly, and I'd meant every word. Then I thought of all the time I'd spent with Tang and how I felt about him now, and how I felt about myself.

'Sure, Amy . . . Why not?' And I meant it. But it didn't stop the tears.

20

Fault

I STARED AT MY PHONE LONG AFTER I HAD ENDED THE CALL, and stayed sitting on the edge of the bed for even longer. I heard clanking in the hallway, and the next moment Tang appeared in the room.

'Not angry with Ben now.'

I wiped my eyes. 'Thank you, Tang, I'm glad.'

He clanked over and stared up at me.

'Ben has wet face.'

'Yes, Tang, I do.'

'Ben leaks like small dog. Ben is faulty? Ben is breaked?'

'I'm not broken, Tang, don't worry. Well, maybe I am, but I'll be OK.'

'Tang can fix?'

I smiled. 'No, I don't think it's anything anyone can fix, but thank you.'

'How is Ben breaked?'

'Broken. I just spoke to Amy on the phone. I thought maybe . . . Well, I thought maybe she might come back to live with me, but she loves someone else now. I'm too late.'

'Why does Amy not love Ben?'

I put my palm on his head. 'It's complicated, Tang. The simple explanation is that I wasn't the right man for her. I couldn't make her happy.'

Tang seemed worried, shifting from foot to foot and looking up at me from under his eyelids. 'Does not understand.'

'It's OK. You don't have to understand. The house is going to feel very empty when I get home, without Amy – and without you.' My eyes filled up again.

'Without . . . me?' Tang said, frowning up at me. Or at least he seemed to me to be frowning. Sometimes I think I projected expressions on to the robot, filling in the gaps in his physical capacity with what I assumed must be his feelings. Or perhaps they were just my own.

Bollinger knocked at the door.

'Ben? I'm sorry to disturb you, old boy, but I thought you'd like to know dinner will be ready in fifteen minutes.'

I rubbed the blurriness from my eyes. 'Er . . . thanks. I'll be along soon.'

Bollinger's bare feet padded back down the corridor.

'Tang can stay in here?' he asked.

'Yes, of course you can. I'm going to go and have some food and a chat with Bollinger now, but I'll be back later. We'll talk then.'

Despite my melancholy, the thought of a home-cooked meal cheered me, and I pulled myself together as I wound my way through Bollinger's cool block of hallways. There was door after door opening on to rooms filled with space and nothing else. Now and then I'd open a door and find a motorcycle engine in the centre of the room sitting on a tarpaulin, or what passed for a library with avant-garde bookshelves, nothing more than stacks of books supporting themselves. I passed one room where the door was ajar, so I peeked and instantly regretted it, since what came into view was a pair of disembodied metal legs, which gave me the creeps. They had obviously been intended for some sort of robotic individual, but they were never used. The room was full of dust.

Eventually, I reached the dining room, only identifiable because of the unnecessarily long dining-cum-conference table with incongruous glass candelabra set at each end. In fact, it looked more like an upmarket games room, and I wondered whether Bollinger could press a button and the whole table would rotate to reveal baize and a roulette wheel, whether he wasn't so much a recluse as the proprietor of an island gambling racket. But, no, Bollinger was just a man with a collection of disparate things, a man whose brain flitted from one fad to the next as he failed to concentrate. He didn't seem so very different from me, in fact. Be that as it may, Bollinger had upset two of my friends, so he had ground to make up.

The man himself appeared as I was surveying the table, carrying two large, delicate wine glasses and wearing a navy-blue Le Creuset apron, with a matching tea towel slung over his shoulder. He did a double-take when he saw me.

'Are you all right, my boy? You look quite downcast.'

I told him I was fine.

'It's chicken,' he said, changing the subject.

'Fine. I'm sure it'll be lovely.'

'I don't have much in my repertoire to accommodate more than one. Chicken in some sort of sauce is about the best I can do.'

He gestured me towards a seat and poured half a glass of

expensive-looking leggy red from a decanter already set on the table. Then he exited the room, returning with two pasta bowls of steaming food. Exactly as he had said: chicken in some sort of sauce, with some sort of green beans. Then he settled himself and motioned me to eat.

I think neither of us quite knew how to begin to say what we wanted to say, nor how to continue once we'd begun. It's not every day you ask a once-eminent engineer what they did to make a robot run away, and in turn have to tell him what the hell you're doing showing up unannounced on his island . . . I think the reasonably comfortable silence during which we ate was a credit to both of us. Bollinger finished before me, laying his heavy knife and fork down across his bowl and heaving a great sigh before he spoke.

'I suppose Kato told you what happened? You did come from Kato, I trust?'

'Yes, he told me some, but I'm guessing not all.'

'He shouldn't have told you anything.' There was a darkness to Bollinger's voice as he said this, and for the first time he put me on edge. I felt I should defend Kato, so I backtracked.

'It wasn't much. He told me that you and he worked together for the East Asia AI Corporation until there was an accident, then the project was shut down and everyone got made redundant with generous packages. That's all.'

Bollinger nodded. 'Good old Kato,' he replied ironically.

'I don't understand. Both Kato and Tang are angry with you. Why, Bollinger?'

'My dear boy, I'm not sure you really want to know. Take it from me – it's best if I don't tell you.'

'But I can't leave Tang here unless I know he'll be happy. Surely you must see that?'

209

He looked hard at me for a long time, but I stood my ground.

'Bollinger, in order to leave Tang here I'm going to need to know what happened.'

'As you wish,' he said, standing up. 'I'll get another decanter – it's going to be a long night.'

'I brought everything with me when I came to the island,' Bollinger began. 'I suppose in my situation you're meant to "downsize", but I wasn't going to part with anything – even my old notebooks. Over the years, I'd collected steel and aluminium sheets from various projects, titanium and Kevlar, too, when I could smuggle it out of the labs. It all came with me.

'I needed time to think. But running a house takes work, even a new house. I needed help. So I pulled together all my grifted steel and knocked a robot together. Almost literally, I think you'll agree.'

'Hmm.' I thought back to what both Cory and Kato had said about Tang being made in a hurry. Bollinger had confirmed it. 'The broken cylinder,' I asked, 'have you fixed it?'

He waved the question away with a somewhat limp hand.

'Don't concern yourself, Ben. He just needs a new cylinder and a refill. I imagine Tang himself could fix it if he knew where the parts were kept, which he probably does. Now, the robots I used to make . . .'

He treated the whole point of my lengthy mission as though it were nothing, like changing a battery or filling a kettle. I opened my mouth to say so, but he carried on speaking.

'He's not my finest work. You should have seen me in my

prime. The designs I came up with. Truly amazing, even though I say so myself . . .'

Then I had another question. 'Wait a minute. You said Tang's made of steel?'

'Yes, why?'

'The lying little wotsit. He told me he was made of aluminium.'

Bollinger laughed. 'So he's learned to lie, then?' There was a tinge of pride in his face and voice. He was right – Tang had been learning things, and learning them from me, which meant the bad stuff was coming from me as well as the good.

'I notice his voice has changed, too,' said Bollinger. 'I built him with a very basic vox mechanism, but somehow he's developed it. He must be listening to the qualities of the voices around him and incorporating them.'

It was true. When I met Tang, his voice was entirely electronic and contributed to the overall impression of a school project. But now . . . now there was nuance in his voice, light and shade, and he'd lost some of the metallic harshness of his original tones.

I was curious to know how all this evolution was possible.

'Bollinger, how is it that Tang is sentient? If he's just some old bits and pieces of steel, how come he's so . . . well, human?'

'He's not just some old bits and pieces of steel. Oh, he may look like that on the outside, because I was in a hurry and you can pull a shell like that together in a few hours, but on the inside he has all the faculties of the subjects I was building before . . . before the accident. Amongst the things I brought with me was the only surviving chip that makes my AI so special. It's what makes the technology coherent; what makes it work, if you like. Tang has that chip.'

I was right all along: Tang really was special. He was unique.

'So this is a different chip from the one he has that lets him go through airports?'

'Yes, my dear Ben – entirely different, I can assure you. And he doesn't have one of them anyway. It wasn't in my interest to put one in.'

'Hang on a minute, he told the clerk at the check-in desk in America that he did have a chip. The man scanned him and everything. How is that possible?'

Bollinger looked proud again. 'I honestly have no idea. He's learned to lie, maybe he's learned to fake whatever it is he needs to get the result he wants.'

'That seems unlikely.'

'Why, do you not think him clever enough?'

'No, Bollinger, it's not that. I just don't think he's that, well, calculating. He'd have to understand all sorts of human emotions before he could draw that conclusion: cause and effect, motivation. He still doesn't really understand the meaning of "why". He's like a child.'

'You haven't been around many children, have you?'

The question piqued guilt in me that I'd largely tried to ignore my niece and nephew since they were born, and I felt affronted. 'No, it's true, I haven't. Have you?'

'Touché. And the answer is no – I never had children of my own. But it doesn't take much to know that a child who fears the wrath of their parents over a broken vase will pretend it wasn't them who broke it.'

I remembered Tang breaking Lizzie's model at the museum in Houston. I hated to admit it, but Bollinger was

212

right: Tang was more than capable of getting what he wanted. Hell, he'd gone halfway across the world on his own, and I still didn't know how. I'd try to get the truth out of him before I left, but right now it was Bollinger's truth I was after.

'I've got sidetracked. Please continue with your story. You were telling me about your technology.'

'Yes. The technology we were working on used inorganic compounds to make living matter. The androids we see today, around the house and so forth, are nothing compared with what I could create. We were trying to make subjects that were robust on the outside, titanium exoskeleton, etc., etc., but with new learning tissue on the inside: alive and yet not alive. They would have something that more closely resembled a human brain. Of course it wouldn't be human, but it would learn. The subjects would have muscle memory, pain reflexes. They would know how to grow . . . how to change.'

'What would they do, these "subjects"?'

'Well, we built them, ultimately, to do everything from clearing land-mines to performing long medical surgery, or to be on the front line in a battle.'

'And you thought that making them feel pain would be good for that? August, that's . . .'

'I know what you're going to say, and you are wrong! You're going to witter on about ethics and so on, but you're missing the point.'

'Which is?'

'The closer they are to humans the better they are at human jobs. The fact that they're robots just means we don't have to care about them!'

I gaped at him.

'You were going to send out learning robots – androids – whatever, who were no more developed than children, to do adult jobs and expect them to be able to cope. What did you think they were going to learn? All you taught them was how to hurt and be hurt, and you wonder why it all went wrong? Did any of you stop to think what you were doing?'

'Yes, plenty of them did, I can assure you. But they were all under contract and all sworn to secrecy. They had no choice but to carry on. Until the accident, of course.'

'What happened, exactly?'

'One night, the subjects were supposed to be undertaking instruction in firearms . . .'

'Jesus Christ, Bollinger . . .'

'Don't interrupt. They were undertaking instruction in firearms, and one of them developed a fault and accidentally shot another one. The one that had been shot got angry and killed the first. Then all hell broke loose and they killed all of the engineers on the night shift. In the process, one of them shot a gas pipe and the whole place exploded. Burned to the ground.'

'Oh my God.'

'In case you were wondering, Kato was on the day shift. He was nowhere near, for which I am glad. He has great potential. Had, I suppose.'

'And how did you survive? You tell the story like you were there, so you got out somehow, right?'

Bollinger was quiet.

'I had orders to stop the subjects in the event of a malfunction. So I did.'

'How do you mean?'

'The best and quickest way to stop them was to contain

214

them. And the best way to contain them was to lock the doors.'

'You left them to burn, to die?'

'It was the best way.'

21

Going Nowhere?

IT WAS A FULL MINUTE BEFORE I COULD SPEAK.

'Kato was right,' I said eventually. 'What you did was cowardly . . . unforgivable.'

Bollinger's face clouded over as I delivered my verdict, and as I stood up to leave, a frown developed above his glowering eyes. It frightened me.

'Right,' I said, 'we're leaving.'

'I'm afraid that's something I cannot allow to happen.'

'Bollinger, it's not negotiable, you *have* to let us leave.'

'Sorry, Ben, I'm afraid I can't do that.'

The tremor in his voice scared me. But I ignored his words. With a thumping heart, I hurried out of the dining room and caught sight of Tang clanking down the corridor to find me. I took his grabber. He was cool to my touch, and there was a brightness to his eyes, both of which suggested to me that at least his cylinder was now repaired. I pulled him firmly back to the guest room and hastily stuffed my things into the rucksack. Half of my clothes were still in Bollinger's laundry.

'Ben? We are going?'

'Yes, Tang, we are. We're going right now. It's very important that you walk as fast as you can and don't let go of my hand.'

Tang's face spread into a wide smile, and he hopped from foot to foot.

We headed back through the winding corridors until we reached the hallway. Across the open space stood Bollinger.

I hoisted my rucksack and made for the front door. As I went to grasp the handle, there was a clunk of metal as three solid bolts slid home. We turned to look at Bollinger. He was smiling now, and in one outstretched hand he held a small box.

'Remote-control locking,' he told us. 'It's very useful if I'm feeling lazy; one push of this button and all the external doors in the house shut and lock; the windows, too. An excellent security measure for an old man living on his own, I'm sure you'll agree. Oh, and I wouldn't touch the door if I were you. You'll get something of a shock.'

I looked down at Tang – he was looking back up at me, and I could feel a quivering in his grabber that was now so tightly wound round my own hand that it began to hurt.

'Bollinger, don't be ridiculous. Unlock the door.'

'Neither of you are going anywhere,' he responded. 'So why don't you come back with me to the sitting room and make yourselves comfortable. You don't even have your washing, Ben.'

As we made our way back to the sitting room, I thought I'd try to keep the old man talking while I worked out what to do. I genuinely wanted to know why he was so afraid to let us leave. So I asked him.

His answer was simple.

'Because you know Tang's secret – my secret. You know

my technology. I can't have you telling anyone else, and I can't have anyone else getting their hands on Tang. The knowledge must stay with me, do you understand?'

I realized with horror that the old man had more to do with the laboratory massacre than he'd admitted.

'Oh God, Bollinger! It wasn't the androids that shot the gas pipe, was it? It was you. You didn't just let everyone die, you actually wilfully killed them. You should be in prison!'

Bollinger laughed loudly. 'The authorities wouldn't dare put me through a trial – they wouldn't dare cross me! They're scared of what I can do, and sooner or later they'll realize they *want* what I can do.'

As my eyes bored into this old man, with his pale hairy arms and furrowed white brow, I was almost unable to believe what I was hearing.

I tried to keep him on side.

'Bollinger, I don't give a shit what Tang is made of, or any of your technology. I just want to take my friend home with me, that's all.'

The old man shook his head vigorously.

'I can't take the risk. Besides, I need the chip. Without it, I can't make any more. Tang was supposed to stay here until he'd reached a satisfactory level of sentience. Now, thanks to his growing relationship with you, he has achieved a proper level that I can work with. So now I can retrieve the chip and use it to make others like him. Only better. Just as I planned.'

'But that would kill him, wouldn't it?'

'Ben, it's a robot. You really ought to be less sentimental.'

'You're joking. You must be.'

Tang tugged at my hand. 'No joke.'

I looked down at my little friend. He seemed to be panicking. 'Ben and Tang locked in house. Ben must not touch electric door. Please.'

'Listen to the robot, Ben. He knows all about it, don't you, Tang? This is what happens when my technology tries to leave me.'

'Yes,' the robot replied. 'Tang knows. Tang tries to leave because August needs Tang to make androids. Tang does not want to. Androids dangerous. August dangerous. Tang wants life. Tang knows August needs him. So Tang leaves.'

'You have life, you stupid box. I made you that way.'

'Don't talk to him like that,' I shouted at Bollinger, furious now. I felt I might punch him, but I was afraid what technology might leap out at me if I did. 'He means he wants *a* life, a life of his own.'

I wondered if there were any windows open, and as I started to pace the room to look, Bollinger made a rush at me. He grabbed me from behind, but I twisted round and pushed him away. I was surprised at my aggression. Then Bollinger ran at me like a raging bull; I think he meant to deliver a punch. Without thinking I stepped aside, and Bollinger tottered over, falling against the sitting-room door, which it seemed had locked automatically along with the outside doors. There was a sudden flash, like sheet lightning, a huge bang, and suddenly the air conditioning and lights went out.

For a moment I was too scared and too confused to move, then there was the sound of a generator starting up, and the lights came flickering back on.

Bollinger lay on the floor in front of us, perfectly still. The remote control lay next to him, smashed into small, useless pieces. I nudged Bollinger's foot with mine. He didn't move. So I knelt down and poked him. 'Oh my God. Tang . . . I think he might be dead.'

Tang started to clank off towards the front door.

'Tang, come back! We need to call the police. Oh God, I'm going to rot in a desert-island jail, I just know it. Tang, we have to get help.'

'No.'

'What do you mean, "No"?'

'Leave him.'

'Tang, we can't just leave him.' I pulled my phone out of my pocket.

Tang clanked back over to me and rested a grabber on my wrist.

'No phone. Is OK. Not dead.'

'What?'

He pointed his grabber at Bollinger. 'Sleeps. Wakes up. Confused. Then fine. Electricals not so dangerous. Just hurts a bit.'

'How do you know?'

Tang shrugged. 'Happens before. August forgets he locks doors. Tries to go out. Bang.'

I looked closely at the old man's chest and, sure enough, he was breathing. 'He really is quite insane, isn't he?'

'Yes,' said Tang. He lifted a grabber to the side of his head and made a circular motion with it. 'Craaazy.'

'We still have a problem, though, Tang.'

'What?'

'We can't get out.'

'Ben does not worry.'

'I do worry, Tang.' I sat down again, my head in my hands. I felt so bad that I had ever brought Tang here. 'I'm so sorry, Tang.'

'Forgive Ben. Ben did not know. Ben sees only good coming.'

'I was wrong, though, wasn't I? You didn't want to come.'

'No, but Ben was not wrong. Ben was right. If Ben had not brought here, coolings would be broken still. Would have stopped. Now I go with Ben *and* I does not stop. I am happy.'

I crouched down and folded my arms around him, but then I remembered the decision I'd made while he was ill.

'Oh God, Tang, supposing your cylinder breaks again? What would I do? How can I take you with me knowing I can't make you better?'

'No, Ben, don't leave me. We go together!' He sounded panic-stricken and crushed my arms with his grabbers. I looked into his wide eyes.

'But you'd be risking your life to be away from here.'

'Yes. Would be free and with Ben, not shut in house with August. Also . . .'

He gave me a wide boxy smile and peeled open his flap (still stuck down with gaffer tape). Inside, tucked on a ledge, were two empty cylinders.

'August did not fix,' he told me, 'I fix. When I sit in cupboard. Easy – takes breaked one out, pours flu-id in not-breaked one, puts in. Shuts flap.

'Flu-id is oil for kitchen. Yellow oil,' he added, when I looked blank.

'You mean to tell me that all this time you've been cooling yourself with *cooking oil*?' I stared at him. 'How does that even work?'

He lifted his metal shoulders in a shrug.

'So you knew it was coolant?' I said, but he shook his head.

221

'Knows important, knows what is. Does not know what for. Hears man say in ho-tel. When sick. Did not know before.'

I shut his flap and hugged him to me. My relief came out as an overflow of tears, and as they plink-plinked on to Tang's body I felt him place a grabber on my back.

I wiped my hand across my face to dry it, then smiled grimly. 'It might be academic, though, Tang – we're stuck here.'

'No.'

'Yes, Tang, we are.'

'Tang says Ben must not worry. Tang leaves before; Tang *and* Ben can leave again.'

I looked down at Tang, whose face was a picture of calm.

'Tang has plan.'

'But the doors and windows . . .'

Tang shook his head. 'Not doors and windows. Flap.'

'Flap?'

'Flap.'

'Tang, was this how you got off the island before?' I asked, as he led me by the hand to the cupboard by the door.

'Yes. Bin boat. You'll see.'

'I don't understand.'

'August does not think about bin boat. August puts rubbish into bins and it goes – magic. He does not think how. But Tang knows.'

'You mean to say that all Bollinger's refuse sits in the basement until a boat comes along and picks it up?'

'Yes. Not nice smell. But way out is good.'

'So we sit in a large bin until a boat comes to rescue us?' I meant to sound more encouraging than I felt, but it didn't come out that way.

'Yes. Boat comes when sun comes up. Not so many hours to wait. Ben and Tang lucky.'

He opened the cupboard, pointed to a panel with a handle on it and grinned.

'Flap.'

'It really does smell in here, Tang,' I said as we waited for the boat, my bottom on a pile of banana skins, old English-language newspapers, chicken bones and the odd rusty metal screw.

'Acrid smell. Acrid tang.'

'*Acrid tang?*'

'Yes.' He smiled at me.

'You named yourself after a bad experience?'

'No, I names Acrid Tang after escape. After I free.'

I had no words with which to reply to that, so I put my arm around him and gave his small metal shoulder the biggest squeeze I could manage.

'You know Bollinger's going to be furious when he wakes up and finds we're gone?'

'Yes,' he said.

'Do you think he'll come after us?'

'No.'

'How do you know?'

'Doesn't know. But does not come for Tang before, so will not again.'

It was logical, and I think I chose to believe him because the idea of the old – but sturdy – Bollinger trekking across the globe to hunt me down to Harley Wintnam wasn't something I wanted to dwell on.

'You're right. Still, you don't think we should have called for help?'

'No.'

We sat in silence in the darkness for a while, then I remembered something.

'Tang, why did you say you had a chip at the airport when you don't?'

'Tang does have chip.'

'Bollinger said you didn't.'

'Yes.'

'Yes, what?'

'Does not know Tang has chip. Found chip in ship on broken android on way to Ben. Borrowed.'

'You chipped *yourself*?'

'Yes. Can reach round. Pushed in.' He demonstrated by pointing to the place where the check-in clerk had scanned him. Sure enough, a little metal object the size of a grain of rice was wedged in underneath one of his more wobbly rivets. In amongst the general battered air of the robot, it had gone quite unnoticed.

'Did you know it was broken?'

'Maybe. Thinks maybe useful, maybe not. Borrows anyway.'

'How did you know what it was?'

'Sees and-roid has chip.' He shrugged, like it was obvious.

'Good work,' I said, for want of a more intelligent reply. 'So then, tell me, how did you end up in my garden? What happened after you got in the bin boat?'

'Moved to place with big lots of broken things. Dirty. More acrid tang.'

'And then?'

'Hid in box. Big metal box. Dark a long time. Box got

opened. Hid behind other boxes. Men moving boxes, walked away. Got on train.'

'Did you know where you were?'

'Got off train. Was at plane place. Where we were.' He looked at me.

'Heathrow?'

'Yes. Got on bus. Saw nice house. No androids. Got off bus. Gate open. Looked through gate. Saw horses, a tree. Sat under tree. Ben falls me over.'

I laughed, remembering how I made him jump the first time I tried to speak to him. 'So what you're saying is you managed to get on a container ship from Koror to the UK, via God-knows-where, and stayed there the whole time until it docked? Weren't you bored?'

'Standby. Set to active by light.'

'Do you mean you slept all the way but programmed yourself to wake up when they opened the container or something? That's very clever, Tang.'

'Yes.'

'And you chose my house because you saw it from the bus stop and it looked nice and you couldn't see any other androids?'

'Yes.'

'Well, bugger me.'

Tang shrugged again, like it happened to him all the time. To me, it was yet another way in which Tang was extraordinary, but he was still a robot, albeit a sentient one, and to him the journey was merely a sequence of logical events. If Amy and I had been away for the week when he arrived, he might easily have moved on.

'And horses,' Tang said, interrupting my thoughts.

'Horses?'

'Yes. Sees horses from Ben's garden.'

'I don't understand – what's so special about the horses behind my house?'

Tang shrugged again. 'Horses new to Tang. Horses run. Look free. Look happy. Makes happy to see.'

We sat in silence for a while. Then I asked him, 'Tang? Did I do the right thing in talking to you in the first place? In bringing you into our home?'

'Yes.'

'Would you have moved on?'

'Maybe. But I found Ben. I love Ben.'

22

Homecoming

THE BOAT CAME TO COLLECT THE RUBBISH LATER THAT
night, just as Tang said. On his previous escape, Tang had
managed to stow away without being seen, somehow, but
there was no hiding the two of us together. I decided the
best thing for it was to throw ourselves at the mercy of
the rubbish collectors. The idea that Bollinger was some
sort of madman came as no surprise at all to the men on
the boat, and for a handful of large-denomination notes
they saw us safely back to the airport. They also said they'd
check on Bollinger next time they came over, just to make
sure he was alive.

We boarded the very same plane out as we'd come in on.
At the end of what seemed like a very long journey, we were
homeward bound.

The trip back to Harley Wintnam was plain sailing,
or flying, rather. As a reward for all Tang and I had been
through, I bought us Premium seats.

We arrived back at home in time for Christmas, just as I'd
told Amy we would. I didn't even manage to open the front

door before Tang, full of joy, went straight through the side gate and out to the back garden to look at the horses. I, on the other hand, felt unsettled. The house seemed somehow different. I half expected to see my father in the kitchen making us bacon sandwiches while my mother shouted at Bryony for leaving her schoolbooks all over the sitting room, and chased our old cat outside for clawing the sofa.

I'd also expected the doormat to be covered with post, but it was stacked on the hall table in neat piles. A parcel containing the presents I'd bought in Japan was balanced on the top.

'Bryony must have been in,' I said to myself.

On the top of one of the piles there was a postcard. On the front it showed Lizzie Katz's space museum. On the back:

Ben, I think you should know I'm very angry with you. You had no right to talk to Kato about me. He says I should set my new android on you. Love, Lizzie. xxx

P.S. Don't be a stranger, come visit us sometime.

P.P.S. Kato says when you went for dinner you mentioned the vet thing to him, too. Get off your butt, Chambers.

'Give me a chance,' I said to the postcard, 'I've been halfway round the world.' But I appreciated the nudge, the kind of nudge Amy had been giving me all our married life, the kind of nudge I had always ignored. In the New Year, perhaps I would begin to build a new life.

Applauding Kato's fast work, I went into the kitchen and stuck the postcard on the fridge, under a papier-mâché Tower of London magnet made by my nephew. I felt giddy – and a bit smug – that I had been the one to bring them together. The feeling was bittersweet, though, since it seemed unlikely that I was going to be reunited with Amy. Not now, when she had the man of her dreams.

'Maybe I'll try Internet dating,' I said to myself. I made a cup of tea using some milk I'd picked up at Heathrow (an Englishman has his priorities). As I reached into the cutlery drawer for a teaspoon, I spotted my wedding ring. My hand hovered over it for a moment, before I picked it up and went to put it in the same box as I keep my passport and birth certificate. Though I had no reason to think I'd need the ring again, somehow it didn't seem right to get rid of it.

I couldn't help feeling melancholy as I drank my tea, so I phoned my sister.

'I'm back,' I announced, mustering a light tone of voice.

'You're back where?' Bryony asked.

I'd be lying if I said I wasn't a little deflated by her response.

'Home . . . Harley Wintnam, of course. Where did you think I meant?'

'Oh good, finally.'

'Thank you for picking up the post.'

'I didn't. Amy's been looking in on the house while you've been away. She was worried.'

'She was?'

'Of course, we all were. You just disappeared. Don't do it again.'

'I won't.'

'In the meantime, if you're back then you can come for Christmas.'

'Oh . . . OK . . . Will Amy be there?'

'Yes, of course. With . . .' she checked herself.

'Do you think it'll be awkward?'

'Not if you behave like a grown-up. You can do that, can't you?'

'I think I can manage it.'

'Good. Look, I have to go; I have a million things to do, but I'll see you at Christmas, OK? Come at one.'

'Oka—' I went to say, but she'd rung off. After a few seconds, I called her back.

'I just thought of something. Can I bring Tang?'

'The robot?'

'Yes . . . the robot.'

'He came back with you?'

'Yes, he's fixed now. Can I bring him?'

There was silence while Bryony considered my question.

'Well, I guess . . . but why does he need to come? Won't he be fine at home?'

'Not really, Bryony. He's . . . well, he's not like other robots. He won't be a nuisance, I promise.' This promise was entirely meaningless, as I didn't have the faintest clue whether Tang would be a nuisance or not, but it felt like the right thing to say.

'OK then, if you're sure. I guess he must be special, otherwise you wouldn't be asking.'

'Indeed.'

'I hope you're going to tell us where you've been all this time?'

'I will, Bryony, I'll tell you all about it. I can't guarantee you'll believe me.'

'Oh, I don't know, give me enough champagne and I'll believe you, you know what I'm like.'

I chuckled.

'Ben,' she said, 'I'm glad you called back. I've missed you. I should've told you. It's not been the same without you being just down the road. Despite what you might think, I really am proud of you. It might not have been the way I would have done things, but you picked yourself up after Amy left. You could've curled up into a ball and hid, but you didn't. You went on a journey. That took some courage.'

'Bryony, have you been at the Christmas booze already?'

'A little bit, maybe,' she said, and laughed. 'But it doesn't change anything. I'm still proud of you.'

'Thank you, Bryony. That means a lot.'

A few days after we got home, the first snow of the English winter fell, and Harley Wintnam awoke to a clear-blue sky and a sparkling brightness outside. I got dressed and hurried downstairs, found my welly boots in the understairs cupboard, and after checking them for spiders I pulled them on and called for Tang.

'Tang, come here, you have to see this!'

He was way ahead of me. I found him with his face and his grabbers pressed against the French windows, staring out at the garden and paddock beyond, both of which had vanished under a thick blanket of white.

'Horses are . . . where?'

I looked to the paddock and, sure enough, they weren't there.

'They're probably inside, Tang. It's really cold outside, even for horses.'

'Cold?' He pondered. 'Do I like cold?'

I thought for a moment. 'You'll probably like it more than hot, but we do need to make sure you don't get *too* cold.' It seemed weird to consider dressing Tang when he usually walked around, well, naked, I suppose. But I couldn't let him get the robot equivalent of hypothermia, and I worried about his potential to rust. He at least needed a hat. And boots of some kind.

'Stay there,' I told him, and went up to the spare room. I pulled the duvet off the bed, rooted around in my bedroom for the roll of gaffer tape, trying to remember where I'd put it when I'd unpacked my backpack, eventually finding it wrapped up with some socks in my underwear drawer. As an afterthought, I returned to the spare room and picked up the pillows from the bed too, then I brought the whole lot downstairs, collecting two plastic bags from the kitchen as I went.

'Right, let's see . . .' I wrapped the duvet around Tang and wound a length of gaffer tape around several times.

Tang blinked at me and tried to move.

'Ben . . . arms . . . can't move.'

I paused, then went to the bureau and found some scissors. Hesitating just for a moment, I began to cut my way through the duvet and its cover until there was enough room for Tang to put his grabbers through. 'Fuck it, I never have guests, anyway.'

I did a similar thing with the pillows, cutting holes deep enough and wide enough for Tang to get his feet in.

'Tang, lift your foot up, please, will you?'

He did so, though it was clear from the look on his face that he wasn't sure he trusted me in this instance. I put a pillow over each foot in turn and a plastic bag over the top, and when I'd finished he looked like a cross between a sheep and a metallic sausage roll.

'Looks bad?' Tang asked.

'Nah, it's fine, mate, don't worry about it. Anyway, better to be warm and look a bit funny than freeze and get sick.'

There was still a problem, though: his head. I dug out

a tea cosy from the 'misc. crap' drawer in the kitchen and brought it back to Tang. When my parents were alive, we were the only household that still used a tea cosy, I'm sure of it. My grandmother had made it for my parents because my mother complained she could never find a cosy to fit our enormous teapot. It made me happy to be putting it to good use again.

With a bit of stretching, the tea cosy just about fitted over Tang's square head. The two spout and handle holes defeated the object a little, but I arranged the cosy so that they were over his ear grates, and it almost looked like I'd done it on purpose. I stood up and looked at him. He looked a little ridiculous. I didn't tell him that, though.

'Come on, Tang, we're going out to play in the snow.'

'Why?'

'Because it's fun.'

'Why?'

'Look, you'll see, OK? Trust me.'

I slid the windows open and stepped outside, nearly slipping head over heels on the decking where the warmth of the house had made the snow unstable. 'Careful, Tang, it's slippery.'

'Slippery?'

'Erm . . . slidey. It'll make you fall over unless you hold on and are very careful how you walk.' I took his grabber in my hand and helped him over the window threshold.

'Why is fun?'

'Well, this bit's not all that fun, I guess, but it gets fun.'

'When?'

'Look, soon, OK?'

It was harder work than I thought it would be. In my head I had imagined Tang flinging the windows open and taking a flying leap out into the snow, landing belly down and immediately making snow angels. But if that ever did happen, it wasn't going to be today.

We made our way across the decking and down on to the grass. Tang felt the cold piercing through his pillows instantly.

'Oooh . . . brrr . . .' He looked at me with a face that told me he still wasn't getting it.

'Yes, brrr . . . definitely.'

I decided to create the fun myself, so I let go of his grabber, made a snowball and threw it at him. It thudded into his duvet and he squealed, his arms flailing around.

'Ben, why?'

I laughed. 'Because it's FUN, that's why!'

'Not fun!'

'OK, how about this?' I scooped some snow together a few feet from him and began to make a cube. 'Help me pile the snow up, Tang. Like this.'

As his grabber touched the snow he withdrew it, looking confused.

'It's OK, Tang, it's cold, but that's just what it feels like. It won't hurt you, I promise.'

He looked dubious but joined in anyway. I think he'd decided to humour me.

We built the cube up until it was the same height as Tang, then I turned aside and made another, smaller cube, which I placed on top of the first. I looked around to find some rocks and pushed two into the front of the top cube. Then I drew a smallish rectangle in the front of the bottom cube, packed two bulges of snow on either side and then two to match on the ground at the front. I stood back and waited. Tang stood perfectly still for a second or two, then he looked at me, then back at the snowbot, then back at me. He squealed and clapped his hands.

'Ben . . . Ben . . . Ben . . . Ben . . . Ben . . . It's me! Me! Ben . . . Ben . . . !'

'Yes, Tang, that's right – it's you! See, I said snow was fun, didn't I?'

He grinned and poked at the snowbot's face. Then he hopped from foot to foot.

'Do you like it?' I asked.

'Yes. But . . .' he hesitated, 'we can go in now? Brrr.'

I smiled. 'Sure. Of course we can, Tang. Let's put a film on.'

23

Christmas

ON CHRISTMAS EVE, I WOKE SUDDENLY TO THE SOUND OF AN altercation coming from the front of the house. I flung my old dressing gown on and threw myself downstairs in time to see Tang standing in the front porch trying to wrestle a cardboard box from what looked to be a type of miniature helicopter. Tang was shouting in a high pitch.

'No! No! Give! Off! Off! Off! No! Off! Give!'

'Tang, what's going on?' I shouted over his noise.

'Box is for Ben. Flying machine will not give. I try to take for Ben. Can-not. Ben make flying machine give box!'

'Tang, it's OK, it's just a drone delivering the kids' Christmas presents that I ordered. They're programmed not to give them to anyone except the original customer. Here, let me.' He let go of the box, and the drone span back a few feet, righted itself and flew back to us. It peered at me for a few seconds then dropped the box into my outstretched hands. Then a signature panel came out of its front, along with a stylus, and I signed for the package. The drone glared at Tang, its eyeball headlamps spinning around in disgust, then turned and flew away.

The next morning, I gathered my robot and my Christmas offerings all together in the hallway and went with trepidation to the garage to check out the state of the Honda. I'd ordered a grocery delivery and some presents online, enjoying my time at home with Tang and not feeling the slightest bit inclined to venture out into the pre-Christmas chaos. But it did mean I hadn't turned the car over since before we went away, which in turn meant it was more than two months since it had last worked.

I squeezed in between the garage wall and the car door and into the driver's seat, and part of me felt a little frisson of excitement to see if it still worked. It didn't. I was worried – if I couldn't get the car working, then we wouldn't be able to go to Bryony's. Then I realized how much I *wanted* to go to Bryony's. I wanted to see them all. I had a lot to tell them. I had to get the car working.

I knew nothing about cars, but a bell jangling in the back of my mind told me the battery was dead and that if I could find some jump leads from somewhere then I could get it started. I went back into the house and collected Tang.

'Mate, can you help me push the car out on to the driveway, please? Are you strong enough?'

'Yes,' he said, but looked confused.

'It won't start. I need to get it outside so I can hook it up to someone else's car and . . . I don't know why I'm explaining any of this.'

'No.'

I opened the garage door and took the handbrake off the car, and between us we managed to relocate it to the end of the drive. Then I went next door. Mr Parkes answered, wearing a paper hat (at eleven in the morning) and

237

a red-and-green zig-zagged pullover that could have only been home-made by his wife and intended for the season.

'Ah, Mr Parkes, Merry Christmas to you. Do you happen to have any jump leads I can borrow, please?'

Mr Parkes looked over my shoulder at Tang, who was waiting patiently next to my car, and frowned.

'The car won't start,' I explained, which I'd have thought should have been obvious, but from the look on his face it wasn't.

'I think it's the battery. My sister's expecting us over there, and I haven't checked the car since we got back and . . . well, you know what Bryony's like. She'll be furious if we don't make it.'

It wasn't the battery. No combination of myself, Tang, Mr Parkes and Mr Parkes's jump leads were going to get the damn thing going. I had no choice. I had to phone Bryony. The conversation started pretty much how I expected.

'Bryony, it's Ben.'

'Merry Christmas. Are you on your way, yet?'

'Er . . . Merry Christmas to you, too. That's just it. The car won't start.'

Bryony took a deep breath, like bellows filling up.

'I bloody knew this was going to happen! I knew you'd phone with some excuse. And I told you to get rid of that car ages ago. I don't know why you couldn't . . .'

'Bryony, listen,' I interrupted her. 'I'm not calling to tell you we can't come, I'm calling to ask if someone can come and get us, please?'

'Oh.'

'We can get a taxi back or something, later. But right now we've got presents to bring and some bottles, and it'd

238

just be a lot easier if someone could get us.'

Bryony's tone changed. 'Yes, yes, of course we can come over. Sorry. I . . .'

'It's OK, Bryony, not so long ago that's exactly what I'd have been ringing to say. But not now. I really want to be there.'

'Hang on,' she said, and I heard Dave's voice in the background.

'Dave says he'll see if he can get Roger to send his driver over and take you home again later. Then you don't need to worry about finding a taxi later.'

'Who's Roger?'

'Erm . . . he's a friend of Dave's.'

'He's not Amy's boyfriend, is he?'

Bryony hesitated. 'Yes. But please don't let that stop you taking the lift.'

'No, OK. It won't.' I paused. 'He's got a driver? And one that's prepared to work Christmas Day? Wow, he must be doing really well.'

'Moderately, but it's a Cyberdriver, so it's not a problem.'

'A what?'

'A Cyberdriver. They're made by the same company that makes Cybervalets. It's a new thing. The car's adapted for it, but apparently they're going to purpose-build them soon. They reckon they're safer than automated cars. Roger swears by it.'

'Ah, that's very kind. It'll be a new experience for us.'

My first impression of the Cyberdriver, if I'm honest, was that he was a bit creepy. He looked like a pimped-up crash-test dummy and was absolutely accurate in his driving as he pulled up outside the house.

'Why can we not have human drive?' Tang asked petulantly.

'Because the car's broken down, Tang. Dave's friend has very kindly sent us his driver. I know it's weird and it's an android, and I'm nervous, too. But we're going to get in the car and not worry, and before we know it we'll be at Bryony's. If you're good and don't make a fuss, you can have some diesel later.'

Tang grinned.

'We get in car now, Ben, come along.'

The Cyberdriver got out of the large black vehicle to open the doors for us, but Tang bundled himself into the back seat without waiting. Undeterred, the driver opened the front passenger door for me, then took the parcels and wine from my arms and stacked them neatly in the boot. He shut my door and Tang's, got back in the driver's seat and we skidded off down our drive.

Bryony and Dave only lived in the next village, so the journey wasn't long, but I wouldn't have minded if it had gone on for miles, because I've never had a comfier ride. The Cyberdriver drove with the most care and respect I've ever seen for car, passengers and other road users. It was like being in a hearse that drove at the speed limit. Even Tang conceded it wasn't as bad as it could have been.

It was the giant force of my sister who answered the door. She threw her arms around me, threatening to crush the presents and make me drop the bottles.

'My baby brother, thank GOD you're back! Don't ever go away again without telling me, will you? That was very bad of you. Don't just stand there, come in and get some mulled

240

wine. Ooh, presents, how sweet. Annabel and Georgie are dying to see you.'

I doubted that, but I let her lead me through into the sitting room. My niece and nephew fell upon the wrapped parcels as soon as they saw me, looking for the ones with their names on. I'd bought some sort of music-playing thing for each of them . . . matching, which I'd hoped would be fine, even though they differed in ages.

'I'm sorry,' I said, 'I don't know what kids like. I don't really know anything about kids, actually. I'll work it out in time for next year, I promise.'

They stared at the boxes in their hands, then at each other.

Bryony prompted, 'Say thank you.'

'Thank you, Uncle Ben,' they mumbled in unison.

In the corner, sitting with the ankle of one leg resting on his other knee was a man I guessed was Roger. He was sharply attired and looked like the kind of guy who played golf and squash. He was sitting on the sofa talking to Dave like there was no problem.

Bryony pressed a huge mug of mulled wine into my hands. I was grateful for both the warmth and the alcohol, since it wouldn't do to dwell on what might have been. Not on Christmas Day.

'Where's Amy?' I asked my sister, needing to address her glaring absence. Bryony gave a cursory look around.

'Oh, she's probably in the bathroom. She'll be back soon.'

'Too much wine already?' I joked, although Bryony didn't seem to get it.

'Er . . . maybe. Anyway, your robot . . .'

'What?' I said. 'You said it was OK to bring him.'

'Yes, I know. It's not that. I was just wondering whether

I should be offering wine or anything to it . . . I mean him. Amy said you're very clear that it's a He.'

I nodded. 'Thanks for the thought, Bryony, but he's fine, really. The only thing he drinks is diesel, and I promised him he could have some later. I brought some with me, but it's best if he doesn't start on it yet, trust me.'

'Diesel?'

'It's a long story.'

'Everything in your life is at the moment.'

'I'll tell you about it over dinner, when I have a captive audience.' I laughed, and she joined in.

Bryony excused herself to go and check on our dinner just as Amy was coming back from the bathroom. When she saw me, she smiled shyly and gave me a rigid hug.

'Welcome back,' she said.

'Thanks.'

'You look different.'

'Different, how?'

'I don't know, just different.'

A blank interlude followed, where Tang looked back and forth at Amy and myself, and I looked at Amy, and she looked at me and then at Tang, and then I looked at Tang, too, and then to break the awful tension I asked her how she was.

'I'm . . . well, thank you. The usual festive texts from my family, of course, but I'm used to it. I won't let it spoil my day.'

I nodded, then to change the subject I told her about her present.

'There's a gift for you here somewhere. I got it in Tokyo . . .'

Amy looked pensive and seemed not to have heard me.

242

'Listen, Ben,' she began, but was interrupted by Roger, who when standing up appeared to be very tall. He strode over and put his long arm round her shoulders.

'There you are. Are you feeling OK?'

Amy glanced at me. 'I'm fine. Of course I am. Why wouldn't I be? It's Christmas. I was just welcoming Ben back. I should introduce you.'

Then she introduced us. We shook hands.

'I'm sorry,' I said to Roger. 'I didn't bring a gift for you. I didn't know if . . .' I trailed off.

'Don't worry about it, I didn't get you one either,' he said, then he laughed loudly. Amy forced out a fake chuckle.

'Thanks for sending the driver, by the way.'

'No probs, pal. The girls wouldn't have shut up about it if you couldn't be here.' He gave another loud laugh.

Pal? The girls? I wasn't yet sure I could bear this man's company, even for Amy's sake.

'Listen, pal, how about you and I go golfing one day soon, when the snow's gone? I'll buy you lunch after. It's the least I can do.'

I didn't really want to go into what he meant by the last statement, so I said, 'Why not? Sounds good.'

'Excellent.'

Amy puffed out her cheeks. It seemed she'd been holding her breath. Roger clapped me on the shoulder.

'I'm going to get us a drink,' he said, then sidled away.

Amy gave me a strange look.

'That was very mature of you.'

'You sound surprised.'

'I am . . . a bit.'

'Well, it wasn't the most comfortable conversation I've ever had.'

243

'You don't have to go golfing with him, you know.'

'It's fine, maybe I should.'

There was a tug at my shirt sleeve. Tang was standing behind me, peering round at Amy. Then his eyes widened, and he smiled at her.

'You still have the robot, I notice,' Amy said, with a degree of annoyance. 'What's with the gaffer tape? I'm guessing you didn't manage to get him fixed?'

'He is fixed, actually. You're good as new now, aren't you, mate? He just likes the gaffer tape.'

'Yes,' replied Tang.

Amy and I stared at each other for a long time.

'Well, I guess you have your reasons for still wanting him around,' she said eventually.

'I do.'

'Ben . . . Ben . . . Ben . . . Ben . . . Ben . . .'

'Yes, Tang, what is it?'

'Amy is special.'

I didn't really know what to say to that. I looked at Amy, who seemed taken aback. She blushed.

'Er . . . yes, she is. Remember what we talked about when we were away, though. Amy lives here now. No?' I added, as I saw Amy shake her head.

'Oh, well, Amy used to live here and now she lives somewhere else. She lives with some*one* else?' I asked, hoping to be contradicted.

'Yes,' persisted Tang, 'but . . . Amy is special.'

'I know, Tang, but you must stop saying that now. Sorry,' I said to Amy, 'I haven't managed to teach him subtlety yet.'

*

Over dinner, I relayed the story of my trip with Tang, who interjected whenever I said something inaccurate or missed out a vital detail. Though he didn't eat, and didn't seem to understand what Christmas was all about, Bryony had been very kind and set a place for him so he could sit at the table with the rest of us. He had his own cracker, which frightened him, and his own paper hat, which he loved and insisted on wearing for the rest of the day (and overnight, too). Naturally, the episode featuring the Hotel California had the adults in the room in stitches. It was clear Tang and the children didn't understand why, but they laughed anyway for the sake of joining in.

'So, what was the French maid expecting you to do?' asked Bryony, giving a hearty laugh and clutching her chest.

'I have no idea, but I bet it featured the WD-40 and the twelve-volt under the bed.'

'Sounds absolutely terrifying,' said Dave, 'but then, we've all been on dates like that.'

That made us all laugh, Roger especially, whose guffaws must have carried along the entire street to the post office.

I told them how I'd nearly lost Tang to sunstroke, and then almost lost him again when I had to consider leaving him behind. I also explained how he fixed his cylinder all by himself, which earned him several pats on the shoulder and admiring smiles and shakes of heads. Tang clapped his grabbers together and kicked his legs up and down in response to the praise.

I decided to gloss over much of the interlude with Lizzie, although I did tell them that we went for dinner at her place, and about the diesel, the pumpkin and the lipstick. Amy's face looked cloudy, but she said nothing. When I told them about the postcard waiting for me when I got home, there were cries of 'Ahhhh' and 'Oh, that's lovely'. It was good to know other people thought I'd done the right thing by Lizzie and Kato.

An unusual moment of silence followed as I reached the end of my tale, before Amy said, 'That's an astonishing story, Ben. You should write it down before you forget it.'

'No,' said Tang, 'Ben does not forget. Tang keeps in head. Tang remembers.'

'He really is an amazing robot,' Dave chipped in. 'I'm not surprised you wanted to keep him. I wish our android understood things the way he does.'

'That's a point,' I said, looking around. 'Where is your droid?'

Bryony blushed. 'I thought it would be nice to give him the day off. You know, because it's Christmas.'

I couldn't quite believe what I'd heard.

'I don't know what you've done to your sister, Ben,' said Dave, 'but she's really changed the way she talks to the android. You should hear her.'

'I was thinking about you bringing Tang,' Bryony attempted to clarify, 'and it started me thinking about our android. Then I found myself feeling sorry for him. That's all.' I think it's the first time I've seen my sister look embarrassed.

'I don't understand it myself,' Roger chimed in. 'I didn't even think of giving my driver the day off. Whoever heard of such a thing? And it's a good job I didn't, otherwise Ben and his little friend wouldn't be here.'

It was true, but Roger's statement had stopped the free flow of conversation we'd been enjoying. Bryony fixed things in the way Bryony does best.

'More wine, anyone?'

*

After dinner, I helped Bryony clear the table and stack the dishwasher. Every now and then she took a peek into the sitting room to make sure everyone was happy. Then she smiled and waved me over. We saw Tang sitting on the sofa apparently in conversation with Amy, then I realized she'd found her Tokyo present and he was helping her to open it. I say 'helping', but I think it was more that he was amusing her rather than being of any practical benefit. He was stuck all over with bits of sticky tape and wrapping paper, and was trying to shake some off his grabber. Amy was clearly finding it hilarious. Then we saw Roger make his way over to them and Amy stopped laughing, like her sense of humour had been switched off all of a sudden. I'd seen enough and retreated back into the kitchen.

'Roger's a charmer,' I said.

Bryony paused for a moment.

'I'm sorry about what he said about the Cyberdriver at dinner. He's not usually like that – well, not as bad, anyway. Maybe he's more uncomfortable around you than he thought he would be.'

'I don't see why. He won after all. I get that Amy's with him now, and I understand why. I don't have a problem with him, and it's not like she's going to come back to me now, is it?'

Bryony closed the dishwasher door and headed for the sitting room.

'Let's check my unruly children aren't abusing your robot,' she said.

It turned out that not only were Annabel and Georgie not abusing Tang, they were also playing on their games console with him, taking it in turns to challenge one another on a split screen shoot-em-up game. I say 'taking it in turns', but the transition from one to the other seemed more like a debate in a courtroom than a simple swapping of the controller. I suppose with Bryony as their mother and Amy their aunt that shouldn't have been too much of a surprise.

Tang's eyes began to cross in bafflement at the arguments between the pair, but I think he felt equally relieved they were not directed at him. The children seemed almost to be showing off to Tang, something I don't think anyone could have predicted.

In the end, Bryony separated them and suggested they change the game to one we could all play, so Annabel picked a dance game that made her brother grumble and the adults want to reach for a crack pipe, but it saw Tang in his element.

'Ben can buy game?'

'We'd need a console first, and all the stuff that goes with it.'

'Can buy?'

I looked down at him and saw a wide-eyed Tang blinking up at me, trying his best to look cute.

'We'll see.'

After the children had gone to bed, Bryony opened another bottle of champagne and ordered a toast. Bryony was very particular about the glass she offered Amy.

'I'd like to take the opportunity to toast A—' she began, but Amy cut her off.

'To toast Ben. For his safe arrival home and for his amazing round-the-world achievement.' She glared at Bryony, who seemed – unusually – cowed and fell silent. I wondered what had happened between them, but it didn't seem the moment to ask. I was flattered by Amy's toast and wanted to ride the wave of near-adulation that followed it. I leaned back in my father's old armchair, which Bryony had inherited and which now resided in the corner of her sitting room, and watched my family. And Roger. All things considered, it was probably the most fun I'd had on Christmas Day for many years, and though I couldn't understand why that should be the case, I let the feeling bed down in my chest. Towards the end of my glass of champagne, I glanced around for Tang and found him slumped in a corner with Bryony, both giggling their heads off. She'd found him some diesel, then. I considered going to take it from him but decided against it. Instead, I went to Amy to thank her for the toast.

'You're . . . you're welcome,' she said. 'I didn't want the moment to pass. You deserve some credit – the trip must have been a logistical nightmare.'

I shrugged. 'I guess so, at times. I'm glad I did it, though.' I thought for a minute, then pulled the well-travelled champagne cork out of my pocket and gave it to her.

'What's this?' she asked, though I could see in her face that she knew.

'I took it round the world with me. I didn't mean to; I found it in a pair of shorts.' I realized at once I shouldn't have added the last bit and tried to recover myself. 'But if I'd found it before I went, then I still would have taken it with me.' I shook my head, then told her about being at Bollinger's when I found it and how I'd phoned her straight away. I thought it best not to remind her that that was when she told me about Roger. 'I figured you should have it now because . . . Well, because although we're not together I'd like you to have something to remember me by.'

Amy kissed me on the cheek. She looked like she was going to cry.

'I don't need this to remember you, Ben. But thank you.'

24

Civic Duty

ONE MORNING BETWEEN CHRISTMAS AND NEW YEAR, I FOUND Tang sleeping on the spare bed. He was diagonally across it with his head at an angle and looked generally uncomfortable. I waited until he'd woken up and come downstairs before I made an announcement.

'Tang, we're going on an excursion today. A trip.'

'Where?' he asked suspiciously.

'To buy some furniture for you.'

'Why?'

'Because if you're going to stay with me, then it's only right you have your own room with your own things in.'

'My own things?'

'Yes.'

'I have not "things". Only socks Ben gets in Tokeeoo.'

'I know, and it's about time that changed. You're your own person, so you should get to own things.'

I tried to bundle Tang into the passenger-side door of the Honda, standing dusty in the garage after my failed attempt to start it on Christmas Day, but he couldn't fit between the car and the wall, so I had to leave him until I was on the drive.

'Come on, you bloody thing, you'd better start,' I pleaded. When Amy and I were still together, we always used her car. It was at her insistence, and although she claimed it was just because hers was always on the drive and therefore easier, I knew it was really because it was a smart, expensive Audi and she looked better in it than she did in a Civic. She never let me drive the Audi, either. I'd say I'm an averagely good driver, but it didn't make a difference to Amy. I don't think she trusted me with it. Either that or she liked to retain control in a situation. Or both.

Anyway, I ground the door of the garage up from the inside and prepared to cajole the Honda outside, leaving Tang with instructions to follow me out, which he managed to do without incident. By some miracle, the car crawled out of the garage. It creaked and complained with every turn of the wheel, but it was at least running. Maybe it hadn't liked the snow at Christmas.

'I probably need a new car,' I said to myself, though part of me was very fond of the old banger. I remember my parents buying it, and it didn't seem so very long ago that it was brand new and the 'latest thing' in small family cars. Well, maybe not the latest thing but certainly serviceable for my parents' needs. They'd told Bryony and me that they wanted to downsize, since they were retired, and it was either going to be the house or the car. They chose the car, much to the relief of both of us.

'Do you need to downsize?' I'd asked them. They'd looked at me like I was quite stupid, though I thought it a perfectly reasonable question.

'Yes, of course,' my mother said.

'Why?'

'Well . . . because. We're retired, it's what you do, Ben.'

'Yes, but if you don't need to . . .'

'Look, don't question your mother,' my dad took up the battle. 'You'll understand when you get to our age.'

This was their explanation for everything they didn't feel like justifying – 'You'll understand when you get to our age' – it always had been. Most of the time it was a source of amusement for Bryony and me.

As I got out to close the garage door, Tang heaved himself into the passenger side of the car. I returned to find him struggling with the seatbelt, which hadn't been a problem in the Dodge, but in the Honda seemed to utterly fox him. I fastened it for him and he frowned.

'I know, Tang, I know. I need a new car . . . one that you're comfortable in.'

'Too small.'

'Yes, I know. It can't be any smaller inside than the Dodge, though, can it?'

As I backed out of the driveway, he considered this for a few seconds, coming to the conclusion that, yes, it was smaller. I gave him a look, suspecting a lie, but said nothing. It didn't change the fact that I needed to replace the Honda. I'd heard from friends that it was time to get a new car when your current one started costing you money, but I'd never understood it before – surely all cars cost money? However, as we trundled along, it became clear what they meant: it obviously needed more work than Mr Parkes's jump leads could help with.

'OK, look, we'll go and get a new car tomorrow, Tang.'

'Why not today?'

'Because we're going to get you a bed today. And it'll probably need putting together, so then there won't be time.'

'Putting together?'

'Things from the shop we're going to come in pieces so you can put them in the car. But it means you have to make the furniture when you get home. With screwdrivers and stuff.'

'Screwdr—'

I cut him off. 'You'll see what I mean when we get home.'

He was quiet for a minute after that, and I could tell he was formulating an argument.

'Ben . . .'

'Yes, Tang.'

'Are the pieces fit in the car?'

'You mean *will* the pieces fit in the car?'

'Yes.'

'Of course they will . . . probably. I'm sure it'll be fine.'

'Ben is not sure, is he? Tang knows. Would be better to get new big car today. Get furniture other day. Pieces fit.'

Tang's logic never seemed to fail to show up the flaws in my plans, but since the only reason for insisting upon getting the furniture that day and the car the next was to get my own way I decided to give in and agree with Tang. Obstinacy was not a character trait I wanted to show in front of the robot, who had enough natural talent at it without my help. So, after a brief return to the house to dig out all the relevant documents for the car, then finding them in the glove compartment, where they'd been all along, we set out again, this time in the direction of an industrial park where the local car dealerships could be found.

Tang, of course, wanted to sit in absolutely every car in every showroom, but as the dealerships were mostly unwelcoming to a robot like Tang we ended up at the only one where no one seemed to bat an eyelid. We narrowed the selection down to one we liked, Tang testing every seat in the car. He also made the showroom staff demonstrate the radio, especially the volume, which seemed to go higher than I felt necessary.

The thing Tang liked best about the car, though, was that it had an automated cup holder, which popped out and folded itself away with the touch of a button. I have no idea why this pleased him so much, but whatever the reason he seemed completely absorbed by it for the entire time it took me to wrap up the paperwork.

The night before the car was due to arrive Tang found me sitting in the garage in the Honda, staring into space. There was a tap on the window next to me.

'Ben is o-kay?'

I rolled the window down and mustered a smile. I nodded.

'I'm just a bit sad, that's all.'

'Why?'

'Because this car belonged to my parents. It feels like I'm getting rid of them.'

He looked around the garage, confused. 'But Ben's parents are not here?'

'No, they aren't. That's the point. They passed away, don't you remember me saying?'

Tang frowned, and I realized I probably hadn't ever told him. 'I guess we never talked about it, did we?'

'No,' he said, then, 'Ben . . . what is "passed away"?'

'It means someone's died. Like when I thought Bollinger was dead on the island?'

Tang nodded. 'But why does it make Ben sad?'

'Well, because it means someone goes away for ever, and you'll never see them again.'

'Like Ben was going away from island and Tang was not?'

'No, no, not like that. It means they've gone away from the world – their body has stopped working.'

'Cannot be fixed?'

'Exactly.'

Tang looked down at his feet. 'Ben's parents could not be fixed?'

'No.'

'Why?'

'Well, they were flying a small plane and a bird flew into the propeller and made them crash. It's hard to explain, but sometimes if people are hurt badly enough they are too broken to ever be fixed. Sometimes doctors can fix people, but if you hurt your head too much or lose too much blood or something, then your body can't repair itself. That's what happened to my parents.'

The hows and whys of my parents' accident didn't interest Tang. His eyes widened at the idea of a human body getting better all on its own. 'Human bodies repair selves?'

'Often, yes. If I get a cut on my finger, for example, my body has a way of fixing it by itself. It's called healing.'

'And Ben's parents could not healing?'

'Couldn't heal, no,' I said, then my throat tightened, and I was afraid I was going to weep. 'I was so angry with Mum and Dad for the way they behaved – they were always going off and doing stupid things, dangerous things. We saw photos of them rock climbing and doing stuff like that before we were born, but then they stopped when they had kids. I always thought they'd just, I don't know, grown out of it or something, but it's like when they retired they remembered what they had been missing and went back to it. They didn't seem to care how it would affect Bryony and me if something happened to them. And then they died, and I was angry that I never got to show them that I could be a worthwhile human being. At the time I'd been failing at my vet school, had no girlfriend and no interests. I was afraid to take risks. Then they were gone, and I was still the second child who'd not accomplished anything. And now . . . now it can never be different. Now I can never make them proud like Bryony did. And I can never tell them how much I've missed them . . .'

After a while, I felt Tang's sharp grabber on my head.

'I'm sorry, Tang, I'm leaking again, I know.' A tear slid down the side of my nose.

'No,' he said, 'Ben is not leaking. Ben is healing.'

The next day, Tang waited all morning for the car to arrive. He stood with his face pressed to the front window in the sitting room, occasionally calling for me.

'Ben – when?'

'I don't know, mate, sometime this morning. That's all they told me.'

'When car is here we can go out?'

'Yes, absolutely. We'll test it out by going to get some furniture for you.'

'Two things for Tang to enjoy!'

'Yes, hopefully.' He seemed to be developing a taste for posh cars, films and now shopping.

When the car did turn up, in his haste to get out of the front door Tang fell over. Halfway up the drive, he stopped suddenly, looking back at me with concern.

'What's the matter, Tang?'

'Ben is o-kay today?'

I smiled. 'Yes, thank you, Tang, I'm fine today.'

He frowned.

'Really, Tang, I'm OK. Go on – go and look at the car.'

Tang scrambled past the delivery driver and up to the car. The man looked confused, even more so when the robot laid his head on the bonnet.

'Don't ask,' I said.

I signed for the car and for the man to take away the rusty vehicle that seemed to represent my old life, watching as he drove it up on to the back of the truck where the new one had been. But any melancholy I'd felt about the loss of the Honda faded as I watched Tang tug at the door handle trying to get into the new car. He was my life now, or at least the start of it, and that meant making way for new things. My parents were gone, Amy was gone, and it was time to stop pretending they'd all left no hole in my life. More than that: it was time to fill the hole with a life of my own. A real life, not an existence of hiding in the house and ignoring the world and my wife . . . soon-to-be-ex-wife. Enough was enough.

I sauntered up to the car and heard the locks click back as it registered my key card. The doors opened wide. Tang seemed to have forgotten the concept of remote control. To him, it was magic. He looked at me, and his mouth opened wide.

'Car is alive! Ben . . . Ben . . . Ben – car is a-LIVE!'

'I'm sure that's true, Tang. But you know it's just remote control. Come on, shall we have a ride?'

He got into the passenger seat with no trouble at all, as he had at the showroom. He shut the door easily and kicked his legs up and down when he heard the seat belt go 'swish' across his body.

'Happy?' I asked him.

258

'Yes.'

'Good. Me, too.'

The escalator up to the furniture showroom was Tang's new playground. He'd been on an escalator before, but not like this one, which was flat for shopping trolleys and rose at a shallow angle. It confused Tang and he didn't adjust his posture to suit it, meaning that he was at a backward-slanting angle to the world as he rode along.

'Lean forward, Tang, you'll be upright then.'

'Yes,' he told me, but continued just as he was.

I stepped off the escalator and was just starting to look around to see where we should go first when I noticed Tang wasn't with me. A quick glance back revealed that he'd got off the upward escalator and got straight back on the downward one, leaving me at the top. Now he was angled diagonally towards the floor as the escalator moved, with one grabber on each handrail.

'Tang, what are you doing?' I called, and though I know he heard he pretended not to. 'Come back.'

He swivelled his head and looked over his shoulder at me, then turned and tried to walk up the down escalator. After a few fruitless steps, he got annoyed and stamped his foot, looking at me like it was my fault.

'Carry on down that one and come up the other one,' I called, gesturing as I did so, like it would help. He turned his back on me and rode the remainder of the journey down, then got on the upward one as I'd told him. Turning my back on the escalator while he rode it, I started to look around the showroom in front of me, filled with sofa upon sofa. Then I realized Tang still wasn't with me. He'd got back on the down escalator again, but this time was riding with his back to the direction of travel, looking up at me with a big grin on his face.

'Tang, stop it, will you? I told you to come back!'

But the game was clearly too much of a draw for Tang, who rode a full sequence of up then down then up again a further three times before I successfully took hold of his grabber and pulled him away. 'Come on now, Tang, you're being silly. We've got stuff to buy.'

He looked at me, then frowned and picked at his gaffer tape.

As I hauled a petulant robot away from the delights of the escalators, it occurred to me that I hadn't made a list of what I thought Tang might want, or rather need, which in this shop was dangerous. It possessed some sort of magic that made all but the very strongest of mind, or those with a list, buy things they didn't need or even know existed, only to get home to find they had no room for them and weren't sure what they were anyway.

Regardless, Tang needed a bed, that was for sure, so if nothing else we had to come away with one of those.

We followed a series of arrows around the showroom, Tang looking even more overawed than he had in Tokyo. He insisted on stopping every few metres to sit on a sofa, or climb on a stool, and once I caught him trying to hide in a wardrobe.

'Look, Ben! Witch cupboard!'

'It's a wardrobe, Tang; it's for clothes, not hiding.'

'But protects from witch.'

'I don't think you need protecting, mate. There aren't any witches around here.' I hoped by next Halloween he'd have forgotten all about the motel incident.

'Tang must hide from witch! Must have ward-roobe.'

'But you don't wear clothes, Tang; there are more import-ant things we need to buy you.'

'Must have ward-roobe . . . Must have ward-roobe . . . MUST HAVE . . .'

'OK, fine! We'll get the bloody wardrobe. Keep quiet now.'

'Yay!'

'Yay? When did you start saying "yay"?'

'Bryneebel says.'

'Who?'

'Bryneebel. Christmas. I plays.'

'You mean my niece?'

'Yes.'

'She's called Annabel, Tang. Bryony is her mum, my sister.'

'Bryneebel.'

'No, Annabel.'

'Ben sister. Brynee niece. Bryneebel.'

'No, look . . . you know what? Never mind. Let's look for a bed for you.'

'Yay!'

As we wandered around the store, I seemed to collect a variety of items I hadn't intended to buy: plates, a chalk-board, a swivel chair, some cushions and a spatula. Some of it was my doing, but it seemed every time the robot strayed from my side he returned with a small lamp or a packet of batteries, until I started to wonder where he'd learned to be such an accomplished shopper. I wasn't sure the items in my trolley would fit in the boot of the new car as it was, before we even collected the flat-pack stuff.

In the bed section, I looked around for Tang, doubt-less fetching me a throw or an under-bed storage bag. As

I looked for him my eye fell on the different families in the showroom. I saw a young boy arguing with his father, who wouldn't allow him to play with a salad spinner, and another parent was wrestling a candle-holder away from a wailing toddler. It didn't seem so very different from looking after Tang. Maybe one day I could handle being a father. Not yet, though. It was the one advantage to being a single man again – I had time now, time to do my own growing up without the risk of inflicting my half-finished self on a baby.

Tang returned to my side grinning and carrying what looked like a bendy brown tube.

'What have you got there, Tang?'

He held it out in front of him, pride written all over his face.

'Kyle!'

He'd found a draught excluder in the shape of a sausage dog.

'Also, I find bed! Come, Ben, come see bed.'

I let him drag me across to a futon. He flopped down across it with his arms and legs stuck out.

'This bed,' he announced.

'For once, I think we agree. It's nice and low so you can get on to it. Well done, Tang, that's a very grown-up choice.'

'Yes,' he said, 'I grows up. Ben grows up, too. Ben and Tang grows up.'

I smiled. 'I guess you're right, Tang. We are growing up together.' A moment passed. 'So anyway, this bed then, is it comfortable?'

'Comf . . . ?'

'Comfortable.' I cast around for another way of explaining it. 'Do you feel like it's the right size, and it's not too hard and not too soft?'

'Yes.'

'Then it's comfortable. When you're not comfortable, it means you feel like something's not quite right.'

'Like Amy not living at Ben.'

I gave him a half-smile. 'You mean "with" Ben, but that's not really what it means. You'll see what I mean sometime, I'm sure.'

I had a tough job convincing Tang to leave the futon.

'Fine, I'll go without you.'

My threat panicked him, and he clanked after me immediately and clung on to my leg.

'NO! BEN! NOT LEAVE TANG. NO, NO, NO, NO, NO!'

People started to stare, so I detached him from my leg and bent down to talk to him.

'It's OK, Tang, I don't mean I'll leave you here for ever. I just meant you could wait while I paid is all.'

'Ben wants to leave Tang on island. Ben leaves Tang in shop.'

'Oh no, look – I didn't want to leave you on the island. I just thought it was the right thing to do at the time. I won't even think about leaving you again.'

'Ben promise?'

'Yes. I promise. Of course I do. It's you and me now, Tang. You know that.' I put my arms around his small metal back. He returned my embrace.

'Ben buy bed now . . . please?'

'Where's the bloody Allen key?' I said, to no one in particular, as I sat in Tang's bedroom surrounded by flat-pack furniture.

263

'Al-len?'

'It's a sort of screwdr . . . Well, it's a . . . Look, I don't know what you'd call it. It's just a thing that you use to build stuff like this.'

'Why is Ben angry?'

'I'm not angry; I'm just frustrated. I don't see why these things need to be so complicated. It's like it's written in bloody hieroglyphics or something. Look at this picture – what the hell is he supposed to be doing? I'm not even sure which piece that's supposed to be.'

'Why does Ben not understand?'

'Because I'm not very good at this sort of thing, that's why.'

'Ben can learn?'

'Yes, thank you, Tang. That's precisely what I'm trying to do. I'm trying to learn how to care for you, but it's going to take a bit of time, OK?'

'If Ben learns, does Amy come back?'

I was silent for a moment, taken aback by Tang's attachment to Amy – the very person who had first ordered me to put him in a skip.

'No, Tang, I don't think so. I've told you before – it's too late. Look, do me a favour, will you, please? Go and watch telly while I do this. I'd rather be frustrated on my own.'

'O-kay,' he said, though he looked disappointed.

'I'll come and find you as soon as I'm done. I promise.'

It was the end of the day.

'Ben . . . Ben . . . Ben . . . Ben . . . Ben . . .'

'What?' I called down the stairs to him.

'Has Ben ready?'

'No, Tang. I told you I'd get you as soon as I was finished. Don't rush me.'

I heard him clank off back to the sitting room. We had the same exchange another three times before I did eventually finish, by which time Tang was properly fed up.

He forgot all about his boredom, though, when I showed him his new bedroom. I'd decided to use a bigger spare room than the one he'd been squeezed into previously. I'd put the bed and the wardrobe together, and covered a duvet and pillow that we'd bought at the same time as the furniture with a green set of linen that Tang had picked out himself (I never figured out why he was so keen on the green). I also bought him a bedside table and a clock to go on it, and a framed map of the world to put on his wall. On to the map I drew the route he'd taken from Palau to Harley Wintnam.

He gripped my leg and stared wide-eyed at the new possessions around him, all lit up by the late-afternoon winter sunset.

'These are my things?'

'Yes, Tang, they're all for you.'

'Thank. You.'

'You're welcome, Tang. Do you like your room?'

'Yes. I can sit on bed?'

'Of course you can, mate. You can do what you like.'

25

Scramble

'BEN . . . BEN . . . BEN . . . BEN . . . BEN . . . BEN . . .'

'What, Tang? I'm in the bathroom.'

Tang was calling me from the foot of the stairs as I stood over the loo on the morning of New Year's Eve, not quite awake.

'Ben . . . Ben . . . Ben . . .'

'What?' I called back.

'Breakfast.'

'What is?'

'Me.'

'You're breakfast?'

'No. I am . . . I has . . .' I heard him stamp his foot in frustration as he tried to remember the right words.

'You made breakfast, do you mean?'

'Yes. I creates. I creates breakfast.'

I smiled, washed my hands and face and went downstairs. Tang, wide eyed and blinking, was at the bottom of the stairs holding a tea tray out to me. On the tray sat a side plate, and on the side plate wobbled a pile of congealed eggs. I say 'pile'; it was more of a blob, flowing over the sides

266

of the plate and making its way to the edges of the tray. I took the tray from the robot.

'Thank you, Tang, that's . . . that's very kind.'

He beamed at me.

'How did you make this?'

He illustrated the action, stirring the air above him. 'I reach.'

'You reached up over the edge of the cooker to stir the eggs?'

'Yes. Hard to see. Had to guess.'

'I bet.' I looked from the tray down at the robot. 'Why did you make me breakfast?'

'Tang is useful, like and-roid. I shows.'

My heart melted. He was too short to stand at the cooker, or at least too short to see what he was doing. It reminded me of the androids in the shop in Tokyo, and of the argument I'd had with Amy all those months ago. She'd been right about him cooking, of course, but no android would ever have gone to these lengths to demonstrate their worth.

'Tang, mate, you *are* useful – you don't need to prove anything to me, or to anyone else. You're brilliant as you are. But if you want to cook again, then maybe we can find you a box or something to stand on . . . make it easier.'

He beamed again.

Tang watched while I ate the breakfast . . . every single mouthful of it. He followed my hand from plate to face, grinning every time I swallowed. For Tang it was a foray into a new world, and I was proud.

That evening, I decided to make a fire in the sitting room, using my best Boy Scout skills, and to sit down with Tang and a glass of warming Scotch to welcome in the new year.

But after a few minutes, Tang discovered that the fire was heating his metal too much and moved away to sit at the dining table. This meant that either I had to sit on my own by the fire, like a plum, or go and join him. I chose the latter. We could play a game. It might not have been the coolest way to spend New Year's Eve, but I was determined it should be fun.

I opted to teach him 'Scramble'. My game was a knock-off, not-so-famous version of the famous word board game. Some ancient and probably senile aunt had given it to my mother years ago for Christmas. It was a misguided gift that didn't interest any of us, and apart from a cursory attempt at a game on the day of its receipt Mum had put it in the cupboard where all family board games went to die, and we hadn't touched it since.

But now, with Tang, I saw there might just be some value in it – trying to teach him to speak properly and all.

'S-cram-bel?' Tang seemed unsure as I set up the game. 'What is . . . ?'

'It's a game, Tang. A board game.'

'Bored?' He frowned. 'Then do something else?'

'No, not bored, Tang, b-o-a-r-d. It's different. The game's to do with words.'

'Oh. What is s-cram-bel?'

'It's a game, Tang, I just said that.'

'No, word . . . s-cram-bel.'

'Well, it means . . . There are lots of different meanings, but in this case it means to mix something up. You see, we pick out letters and make words with them, like this.' I showed him. 'See there, I've spelt "gate".'

'Gate?' He pointed in the direction of the garden.

'Yes, exactly, like that gate.'

268

'Broken.'

'Don't you start, you sound like Amy.'

'Broken . . .'

'Yeah, OK, I'm going to fix it. Now play your word. It has to be at least two letters long and be attached to my word.'

Tang looked at my word, then at his letters. He seemed to understand the premise of the game with no trouble at all, but the nuances of the English language were somewhat lost on him.

'SQATCH.'

'I don't think you can have that, Tang.'

'Why?'

'Because you have to have a "u" after the "q".'

'Why?'

'Because you do. That's how it is in English.'

'Tang word. Tanglish.'

I muffled a chortle. I couldn't deny that – such perfect logic he had. 'OK, well, what does it mean?'

'Don't know.'

'You can't have it if it doesn't have a meaning.'

'Why?'

'What do you mean, "why"? Because it's the game . . . that's the whole point of the game.'

'Tang doesn't understand.'

'Tang, it's "*I* don't understand", remember?'

'Tang I don't understand.'

At that moment, we were interrupted by a ring of the doorbell.

'Stay here, Tang, we'll talk about it when I come back. One minute.'

*

On the other side of the door stood a snow-covered Amy bundled up in layers of wool but still looking chilly. A fine mist intermittently blocked her face as she breathed.

'Amy,' I said, unnecessarily. 'Hi.'

'Hi, Ben.'

'Hi.'

'Can I come in?'

'Yes, yes, of course. Sorry.' I stood aside to let her in, as the heat from the house rushed past her and out of the door.

'Whose car is that?' Amy asked. She gave me a kiss on the cheek and stepped into the house.

'Mine.'

'Ha, ha, very funny. But seriously, you have a Civic. Who does that one belong to?'

'I told you, it's mine. I part-exchanged the Honda for it.'

This stumped her.

'Wow, you really have changed. What on earth did you want a BMW for?'

'Why shouldn't I have a BMW?' It came out sounding more petulant than I meant it to, so I tried to impress her with everything I knew about it. 'It's got a multi-functional instrument display, a sporty chassis and accessible comfort driver . . . thingy, and it does an extra sixty-seven urban miles.' I glanced at Tang, who had followed me into the hall-way and who stood behind me clutching my leg, peering out at her as he had done on Christmas Day. He raised his eyes, then shook his head.

'I see,' said Amy. 'Do you know what any of that means?'

I shifted from foot to foot. 'Yes, of course I do,' I replied, then buckled under her hammer drill of a stare. 'No, not really. But it's comfy. And most importantly it's got a large boot.'

'For the robot?' Amy asked, looking unsure.

'For flat-pack furniture mostly. Tang goes in the passenger seat.'

Amy smiled. 'Of course.'

'Also top comes off,' added Tang.

'What?'

'The top,' I said, to clarify things, 'it comes off.'

'*You* buying a convertible? I wouldn't believe it if I hadn't seen it with my own eyes.'

'Yes, convertible. That's the word.'

'Why?'

'Why not?'

'You live in Berkshire, not the French Riviera.'

'I might take it to Tuscany or somewhere.'

She didn't seem convinced.

'Look, the old one was unreliable and it was starting to cost me money. So I bought a new one, that's all.'

'Fair enough,' Amy said.

I offered to take her outdoor clothes, and as she peeled off the snowy articles Tang stretched out his grabbers and took Amy's coat, hat, gloves and scarf, all the while watching her intently. Then he turned and draped them over the nearest radiator.

'Dry for Amy. No snow,' he informed us.

Amy looked at me, then addressed Tang.

'That's really thoughtful of you.'

'Must care for Amy,' he said, then took hold of her sleeve and tried to escort her to the sitting room. They exchanged a long look, then, to my surprise, she allowed him to lead her.

'Can I get you a drink, Amy?' I called after them. I headed for the kitchen, adding, 'Red or white?'

'Could I just have a cup of tea, please?'

'Wow, you've changed, too. I don't think I've ever heard you turn down wine.'

'Yeah, well, I'm . . . driving.'

I made a cup of tea for Amy and brought it to her. She was sitting on the sofa, and I'd arrived in time to see Tang pushing a footstool underneath her legs. She smiled and thanked him. Next, he disappeared and returned with a blanket, which he draped over her. Then he climbed up on the seat next to her.

'Would you like to share my blanket, Tang?' Amy asked.

'No. Amy must have warm.'

'Tang, it's OK, mate, I think she's warm enough now.'

Tang stared me down, making me feel like I was quite stupid.

'Care for Amy now.'

There was a pause while I tried to understand what was going on between Tang and Amy. I cleared my throat.

'So, Amy, I don't want to sound rude, but why are you here? Not that it isn't nice to see you, because it is.' Amy looked down at her tea, seeming to assess the best way to reply.

'I . . . I wanted to talk to you at Christmas, but there didn't seem to be a good moment.'

There followed an awkward silence, which Tang decided to fill.

'Amy must have food. I shall create eggs?'

'Tang, that's very kind, but I'm not sure Amy's that hungry at the moment . . .'

'I am. I feel like I'm always hungry these days.'

'In that case, can I offer you some supper?'

Tang smiled at me, looking pleased with himself.

'Can he really cook?' asked Amy.

I wanted to say 'not really', but Tang's wide eyes made it impossible to be so accurate.

'He's learning.'

Tang piped up. 'Yes, Ben and Tang learn together. I helps.'

Amy looked impressed. She turned to Tang. 'I don't think I'd like eggs, Tang, but if you could make me a sandwich, that would be lovely.'

I was about to speak, but Tang cut me off.

'I sandwiches for Amy. Care for Amy now. Amy is special. I goes.' And off he went to the kitchen, Amy watching after him.

I shook my head. 'I'm sorry. The sandwich will be horrible, just so you know.'

Amy said she didn't mind. Then I said, 'Amy, I have to ask: before you left you wanted me to chuck Tang in a skip. I don't understand why your feelings towards him have changed.'

She looked down at her tea again.

'We've been apart since October, Ben, and you've changed, I can see it.'

I nodded.

'Well, so have I . . . Everything's different now.' She paused. 'You said on the phone when you were away that you'd thought about me. Well, I've thought about you, too.'

'You did?'

'Of course. And part of that was thinking about Tang and trying to work out why you wanted to do what you did. Take him home, I mean, and then bring him back again.'

'Go on.'

'Well, I started to think maybe you must have seen something in him that I didn't. Maybe the trip wasn't all about

273

you. Then you told us all about it. On Christmas Day, I think we all realized that he must be pretty special. And you've been like a father to him, even though you always say you don't understand children. Just then he put my coat on the radiator to dry and get warm, and I knew.'

'Knew what?'

'There's more to him than a metal box.'

Before I could answer, Tang returned with a bowl containing a lump of bread between two cheese slices. He lowered it on to Amy's lap with great solemnity. She took his grabber in her thin hand and squeezed it. 'Thank you, Tang. It's perfect.'

And then Tang asked a question: 'How long does Amy have two heartbeats?'

Amy gave him a smile. Then she looked at me.

'Just over three months.'

26

Ultrasound

'SORRY FOR LIE TO BEN,' TANG SAID, AS WE SAT SHIVERING ON the terrace outside. He'd come to find me once I'd been out there on my own for a while. I suspect Amy sent him.

'It's OK, Tang, you didn't lie really.'

'But I did not tell Ben.'

'Never mind. But tell me, how did you know?'

'Can hear.'

'You can hear the heartbeat?'

'Yes.'

'You have supersonic hearing? Why didn't I know that?'

He shook his head. 'No. Not super. Can hear some things. Can hear Amy baby heart.'

'Maybe you have some sort of built-in sonar that even Bollinger didn't understand.'

Tang blinked questioningly at me.

'Don't worry, I'm thinking out loud.' I had a thought. 'God, does that mean you can hear everyone's heartbeats all the time?'

'No. Can choose. Tang hears all things when wakes up, turns down things no good.'

'Do you mean you can adjust your hearing and tune out whenever you please? That's clever. I wish I could do that.'

Tang's graphic-equalizer auditory system shouldn't have surprised me – by then nothing should have surprised me about Tang – but it still did. I'd never seen him adjust anything on his head, so it must all be internal – some sort of automatic calibration.

Whether by accident or as a survival technique, my mind had wandered off the point. Amy came out to join us.

'Ben? Are you OK?'

'I don't know.'

'Come inside, please, it's freezing out here.'

I let her coax me back through the garden door and accepted the mug of tea she had made me 'for the shock'. Tang took himself off to bed.

'Why didn't you tell me? While I was away, I mean.'

'I didn't know for a while. With everything that was going on it didn't occur to me that I'd missed a period until well after I'd missed a second one, and I didn't feel sick at all. I'd only known a couple of weeks when you called me at Bryony's, and I couldn't summon up the courage to tell you over the phone. It didn't seem right.'

'I would have come home if you'd told me.'

'Would you?'

I was silent, because I didn't know the honest answer to that myself.

'Besides,' she continued, 'I knew I needed to tell you about Roger, because of the things you were saying. What was I supposed to say? "Hi, Ben, listen, I'm with another man now but you should also know that I'm pregnant. It might be his or it might be yours. Soz."'

'When you put it like that . . .'

276

'I wanted to tell you at Christmas,' Amy said, 'but Roger interrupted me, then after that it never seemed like the right time. Then Tang worked it out and I realized that if I wasn't careful, one of Tang, Roger or Bryony was going to tell you before I did. I had to plead with them all to keep their mouths shut. I didn't want anyone to have to lie to you, least of all Tang. It was quite a stressful day, really.'

'I bet.'

'Don't be mad at Tang for keeping silent.'

'I'm not. It wasn't his place to tell me. It's just unfortunate that he worked it out – for him, I mean. He's good at keeping secrets, though. He kept plenty from me while we were away. He only ever tells me anything when he's good and ready. If you hadn't told me soon he probably would have, but if you swore him to secrecy then he'd have tried his best to keep his word.' I slouched back in the sofa and was quiet for a few moments, staring at the ceiling.

'I don't know what's more of a shock – you being pregnant or the fact that you don't know if it's mine or Roger's.'

'I understand.'

'I'm not sure you do, Amy. How could you understand? And how is it that you don't know, anyway?'

'Well, there was . . . there was some overlap.'

'Brilliant.'

'Please. I've said I'm sorry. I didn't come here expecting anything from you, I really didn't. I just thought you ought to know.'

I nodded.

'If it's any consolation, I want it to be yours. In my heart I feel like it is.'

'That's a bit soppy for you, isn't it?'

She smiled. 'I suppose it is. Being pregnant has made me softer, I think.'

Well, it helped explain her change in attitude towards Tang, at any rate.

'I was hoping for a chance to grow up, to get my shit together before becoming a father. I'm nothing like the person I'd need to be in order to raise a child. Not without emotionally damaging it at least.'

'Ben, you've been looking after a child since September, you just haven't realized it.'

I paused for thought.

'So, let me get this straight, you think I might be able to cope as a dad because I've been looking after a robot?'

'I only saw Tang as something you could use as an excuse to be more distant and self-absorbed. I didn't realize how much he would help you.'

'That makes two of us. How does Roger feel about it, anyway?'

She puffed out her cheeks. 'Much the same as you, I think.'

'Did you tell him you thought it was his, too?'

'Ben, that's not fair.'

'But you must see why I would say that.'

'I do. I think you're handling it better than he is, actually. Maybe it's because he doesn't think it's his.'

'What would happen if you found out? Would you pick the man whose baby it is?'

'I don't know, Ben. It's not that simple, is it?'

'Guess not. Anyway, why do you say you hope it's mine?'

'Because I think you'd make a better father.'

'Ha ha, very funny.'

'No, I'm serious.'

'But I haven't got a job and I can barely take care of myself. I didn't manage to take care of you, did I?'

'There are other important things in life besides having a job.'

Amy seemed to come over to see me and Tang quite a lot throughout her pregnancy. She never brought Roger, although she talked about him occasionally.

I was looking through the window, watching the March winds tug at the willow branches and pondering whether to go and bring the bins in before they blew over, when she said, 'I can't get him to have any input into the nursery. He just doesn't seem interested. I keep telling him that time's running out before the baby comes, but it's as though he doesn't care. I don't know why he asked me to move into his place; I might as well be living on my own.'

'I'm sure he does care. He's probably a bit nervous is all. I'm nervous, too – we're all nervous.'

'Yes, I know, but you do practical things like make me cups of tea and help with my breathing exercises. I'm only asking him to tell me whether he wants a plain wood cot or a white one – how stressful can that be?'

'Look, would it be useful if I came over and helped with the nursery?'

Two days later, she called in a panic in the middle of the night, Roger, again, not at home.

'The baby isn't moving!'

'Calm down, Amy. How long since it last moved?'

'I don't know, I've been asleep.'

'Well, maybe the baby's asleep, too.'

'But supposing it isn't! And Roger's not here.'

'Do you want to come over here?'

There was a pause.

'Yes,' she said. She sounded like Tang.

When Amy arrived, I was still in my dressing gown, being as it was four in the morning, but I had managed to put the kettle on. The doorbell woke Tang, and he clanked downstairs to see what was going on.

'What happens?'

'Amy's come over because she's a bit worried about the baby, that's all. Go back to bed, Tang.'

'Why worry for baby?'

'I haven't felt it move for a while, Tang. They say you should go to hospital if it's not moved for a few hours, so they can check the heartbeat and stuff.'

Tang shuffled up to her and put his grabber on Amy's bare hand.

'Baby is well. Hears heartbeat. Strong. Baby sleeps. Growing is tiring – needs sleeps. Amy needs sleeps, too.' He smiled and paused. 'Ooh. But baby wakes up now.'

Then as if to prove Tang right, Amy felt the baby turn over.

After that Amy hardly wanted to be apart from Tang. She tried hard to pretend she wasn't worried, but just knowing Tang could tell if the baby was OK reassured her.

When Amy eventually went on maternity leave Tang went with her to antenatal classes, too. He revelled in his new role as mum-to-be calm-downer, going round each of the expectant mothers in turn and telling them how fast their baby's heartbeat was. He even diagnosed twins, a fact that had somehow escaped both the mother and the medical team caring for her.

'Ben?' he asked, after a coffee morning just two weeks later.

'Yes, Tang?'

'I can be mid-wife when Tang I grow up?'

No idea how to answer that.

27

Playing Ball

'HOW ABOUT GOLF ON SUNDAY?' ROGER PHONED OUT OF THE blue, making good on his 'promise' to take me for a game and then dinner. I had hoped he would forget.

'Erm, yes, I think Sunday will be fine. I have an interview on Monday morning, but it's not like it's going to be a late one, is it?'

'An interview? You've decided to get yourself a job then, finally?'

I took a deep breath and didn't rise to the bait.

'I'm thinking of going back to vet school. Amy seemed to have needed me this year,' I countered, 'but I'm hoping to go back in September, if they'll have me.'

'Well, good luck. Hope they aren't bothered about you being out for so long.'

'Thank you. I'm sure it'll be fine,' I said.

Arse.

'What about this golf, then?' he said, returning to the matter in hand.

'Sunday will be fine.'

'Superb.'

We'd had a relatively mild winter since Christmas, but the snow made an unseasonal return at Easter and confused a lot of people. For some reason, Roger decided this was an ideal time to play golf.

'Won't the snow be a problem?'

'Oh no, it'll be gone by then – it is April, after all. Anyway, the whole course is heated under the turf so members can play all year round.'

'The *whole course* is heated? Wow, it must be a very classy establishment.'

'It is. Very exclusive. Do you have clubs?'

Hmm. Did I have clubs? My parents had taken it up as another retirement fad, but when my father realized his handicap was worse than my mother's and the gap was getting wider he decided it was a 'stupid game anyway' and gave up. If he'd kept the clubs, then they'd be in the loft, alongside his tennis racket and fishing rods.

'I'm not sure. Can I let you know?'

'Sure, pal, no probs. I have a spare set. Tell you what, I'll sling them in the car anyway; the boot's big enough.'

I gritted my teeth. *Do it for Amy,* I told myself. *It'll make her happy.*

'How about a caddy?' Roger continued.

'Do I need one?'

'Well, you don't *need* one, but my Cyberdriver also caddies, so I'll be using one.'

'Wait a second,' I said, then moved the phone from my ear. 'Tang, where are you?'

'Here,' he said, from somewhere in the house.

'Where's here?'

'Here.'

'OK, well, can you hear me?'

283

'No.'

'Tang, don't be difficult.'

I heard a clanking sound coming nearer, and Tang appeared.

'Can hear more Ben now.'

'Do you want to go out on Sunday morning?'

'Where?'

'To play golf with Roger.'

'What is golf?'

'It's a game . . . I'll tell you later. Do you want to go or not?'

'With . . . Roj-urgh?'

'Tang, you have to stop saying it like that.'

'Ben says that.'

'Yes, but that's not the point. Please come with me. Don't make me spend the day with him on my own.'

Tang pouted. 'O-kay.'

I lifted the phone back to my ear. 'Yep, I have a caddy.'

'Superb. I'll pick you up at nine, unless you've sorted your car issue out.'

He rang off. Tang tilted his head.

'What is cad-dee?'

Roger didn't have a good day. His Cyberdriver/caddy combo threw a wobbly and trashed both the course and the clubhouse. It had to be wrestled to the ground and taken away by Roger's insurers. Neither of us wanted to be the one to tell Amy.

'Do you want a lift back home?' I asked him (we'd driven separately), as we made our way – banned for life – out of the club.

I shouldn't have enjoyed giving him a lift quite as much

as I did. I know it's not a good thing to take delight in someone else's pain, but there are exceptions. The man who stole my wife being one of them. That said, I did feel a bit sorry for him – it was exactly the kind of thing that would usually have happened to me. Tang sat humming to himself in the back of the car like he'd just had the Best Day Ever.

As we pulled up, Amy opened the door, folded her arms across her bump and leaned against the door jamb. Roger didn't seem to know what to do with himself, so he stayed sitting in the car for longer than he perhaps should have. He apologized and said he would make it up to me some-how.

'Oh, it's no bother, really,' I said helpfully. In the rear-view mirror, I saw Tang grinning.

Roger picked awkwardly at lint balls on his trousers.

'Look,' I said, 'you'll have to go in sooner or later.'

He nodded and got out of the car. I saw him say some-thing to Amy then try to kiss her, whereupon she turned her head and walked quickly over to speak to me. She leaned into the window.

'Thanks for bringing him home. I'm so cross – this is going to cost a bloody fortune. I told him not to use the driver for anything other than driving, but he wouldn't listen.'

'It's no bother,' I said, 'Tang likes the ride anyway.'

She gave me a big smile. 'Shall I see you soon? Perhaps we can go for lunch?'

'Sure, Amy, that sounds lovely.'

'I'll call you,' she said.

I pushed the button and waited for the window to close up.

'I wouldn't want to be Roger right now,' I told Tang in the back seat, and I really meant it. Amy might have changed, but she could still be exceedingly scary . . . especially when pregnant apparently.

I didn't see Roger much after that.

Although the golf day had not gone to plan, it had made me think about how I should spend time with Tang. He loved electronic games, films and especially TV programmes about pets, and he loved watching the horses, but I felt I needed to do something else with him. Something active.

I took him to the park to play ball the next day, but it was beyond him in the way that word games and snow were. He just didn't seem to understand the concept of 'fun'.

I threw the ball to him, but it bounced off his head and landed two feet diagonally from him. He looked at me indignantly.

'You're supposed to catch it, Tang.'

'Why?'

'Because it's fun, that's why.'

'I don't understand.'

I paused to consider why it wasn't going in and what I could do about it. 'Remember when we went on the glass-bottomed boat? The one with the fish. You liked that, right?'

'Yes.'

'Remember how it made you feel?'

'Yes.'

'It's the same sort of thing. We're doing this because it's meant to make you feel the same as the boat trip did.'

The memory of the boat did nothing to clarify the ball

situation. The robot looked even more confused. 'Ball is fish? I pretend ball is . . . fish?' He plopped himself down on the grass and his flap popped open.

'I wish you'd let me get that fixed, Tang.'

'No.'

I sat down next to him on the damp grass. 'Catching the ball is like playing a game . . . Like Scramble. You remember Scramble?'

'Yes.'

'Well, board games make people feel happy.'

'Why?'

I put my hand on his little boxy head and sighed. I realized there was no way I was going to be able to explain the fun-ness of Scramble when I hated the bloody thing myself.

'How about this? The computer game you played on the way to Tokyo . . . with the people kicking each other.'

Tang's eyes lit up.

'You enjoyed it, remember? That is how some people feel when they play catch with a ball, or play Scramble. Do you understand now?'

'Which people?'

'What do you mean, "which people"?'

'Which people enjoy ball and Scram-bel?'

'I don't know specifically, just some people. That's not the point.'

'What is point?'

'The point is that not everybody likes the same things. And some people like ball games. Some people don't . . .'

'But which people?'

'I don't know, Tang. Can't you just accept that it's some people that I probably don't know?'

'How does Ben know they like?'

'What do you mean, "how do I know"?'

'If Ben doesn't know people, then maybe no one likes. Maybe Ben is wrong, maybe is not fun?'

He had me there.

'Shall we go home and watch a film, Tang?'

'Yes.'

The Terminator was a bad choice of film. I'd thought it might interest Tang, but instead he just looked alarmed. Within minutes, I decided we'd watch something else.

'Why does Ben stop film?'

'Because it's scary, Tang, I don't think you'll like it.'

'I can watch it another time?'

'Honestly, Tang, there are plenty of other films you'll like better, I promise.'

'Does we not watch film now?'

'Yes, of course we does . . . we do, just a different film is all.'

'Which film?'

'*Star Wars*.'

'*Star Horse*?'

'*Star Wars*.'

He repeated it correctly this time.

'There are a lot, though, so it might take a few days to get through them.'

'Many films?'

'Yes.'

'How many?'

'I don't know; twelve, I think. I can't really keep up.'

'Why does Tang like?'

'Because it has robots. Just watch it, you'll see what I mean.'

'O-kay.'

Tang was transfixed for a minute or two, then cried out, 'Look at golden and-roid! He he he he he he he! He he he he he! He he he!'

'I don't think it's supposed to be funny, Tang,' I said. Then, seeing it from Tang's point of view, I decided it was.

As he became more involved with the film, he stopped laughing and began to develop a 'bot-crush on R2-D2, getting very angry when any harm came to him. At the end of the first film he was nearly beside himself at the thought that his screen hero was broken for ever, so I had to convince him it was going to be OK before he'd stop watching from behind his grabbers. As we watched through the third and fourth episodes, I went online secretly and bought him an R2 poster for his bedroom wall.

In the middle of the night, I was woken by a series of bangs, rumbles and screams coming from the sitting room. The metallic screams suggested that Tang was involved, but I still armed myself with a half-empty mug of hot chocolate from the bedside table before going downstairs.

I found the robot cowering behind the sofa, the unmistakable image of the Terminator being crushed by his opponent on the screen. Tang was screaming and stamping from foot to foot until I switched the television off.

'Tang, what the hell are you doing? I told you not to watch this.'

I sat on the sofa and tried to persuade him to come out.

'It's OK, mate. Look – it's gone now.'

He peered over the top of the sofa at the black screen and clanked around to sit beside me.

'Why did you watch it?'

He said nothing but looked glum, casting his eyes downward.

'I wasn't trying to be mean to you, Tang, I thought it might upset you, which is why I turned it off.'

'It does upset.'

'Well, there you go, then.'

'Why do the humans fight the robots?'

'Well, because they're bad robots that have come to hurt the humans, that's why. They're trying to stop it happening.'

'No good robots . . . not fair. Not how it is.'

'I know that. But can't you think of it as cyborgs and humans rather than robots and humans?'

He picked at his gaffer tape. 'Maybe.'

I knew this wasn't an entirely ethical way to solve the problem. But it was two in the morning, and I wanted to get back to bed.

'So you're OK, then? You can sleep now?'

'Yes.'

'Good.' I stood up from the sofa and looked around for my slippers.

'Wait, Ben. No sleep. Tang no sleep.'

Damn. So close.

'But you said you were OK.'

'Still frightened.'

'Of what?'

'Human comes and crushes Tang.'

I sat back down again. 'No one's going to come and crush you, Tang. I promise. I won't let them.'

'Tang sleep with Ben?'

'Oh look, no, Tang, you need to be able to sleep in your own room.'

290

He gripped the hem of my dressing gown with his grabbers. 'No, please, please, Ben, please . . . please!'

'Oh, OK, just for tonight.' I slid my slippers back on to my feet. 'Come on, then.'

28

Messy

BONNIE EMILIA WAS BORN AT 7.29 A.M. ON 1 JULY, WEIGHING a healthy seven pounds and two ounces. Mum and baby doing fine. That's the short version – the one that got messaged to Bryony, Roger, Amy's boss and Amy's family. The long version is a lot more dramatic.

That evening I'd been attempting to create a nursery in one of the spare rooms, just in case Amy needed to put the baby down for a sleep when she came over to the house. Over a few days, I'd painted the room in neutral colours – Amy having decided she didn't want to know the sex – and I relieved the local baby shop of a number of its priciest items, chiefly because I didn't know what I was doing, so bought everything. Tang had helped where he could, but his paintwork was impressionistic and didn't suit the theme of the nursery, so I got him to ferry me cups of tea back and forth instead. He'd improved a great deal at kitchen tasks, especially since we'd got him a box to stand on. Finishing the nursery at just before midnight, I'd been looking forward to a good night's sleep.

At two in the morning, my phone rang.

'My waters have broken.'

'Where's Roger?'

'Away on business. He's not answering his phone.'

'Helpful.'

'Isn't it?'

'How far apart are your contractions?'

'I haven't had any yet.'

'Let me have a quick shower, then I'll come over.'

'A what?'

'A shower. I can't come over if I'm not clean.'

'Ben, there's a baby coming. I don't think it cares if you're clean or not.'

'OK then, I'll get dressed and come over.' I went to end the call but heard Amy still speaking.

'Ben.'

'Yes?'

'Bring Tang.'

'Er . . . OK, if that's what you want.'

'It is.'

I stumbled round the house trying to wake up properly, making a coffee in the kitchen and then going to wake Tang. He grumbled and pushed his grabber into my stomach.

'Ben leaves Tang alone.'

'I can't, mate. Amy's having the baby. She needs you.'

'Why?'

'I don't know – so you can reassure her, I suppose.'

'But hospital will be there.'

'I know that, but she wants you, OK? I know it's the middle of the night, but she's asked for you. I think it's more important that you're there than me, actually.'

'Where is Roj-urgh?'

'He's away.'

'Away where?'

'It doesn't matter where Roger is, OK? We're here and we're going to go and help Amy, because we love her. Don't we?'

'Yes,' he said, then rolled off the futon on to the floor. He fell with an alarming clonk and hauled himself to his feet.

'I comes now.'

'Right, I'm just going to iron a shirt.'

Tang blinked at me.

'I need to iron a shirt. I'm not dressed.'

'Why Ben need shirt? Any clothes fine, no?'

'But it's an important day, I need to be smart.'

'Tang thinks no.' He stared unblinkingly at me, then I came to my senses.

'What was I thinking? Amy's not going to care what I'm wearing, is she?'

Just then my phone rang again.

'Have you left yet?'

'No, we'll be leaving shortly, though.'

'Why haven't you left yet? You said you weren't going to have a shower!'

'I'm not. I had to wake Tang up.'

'He is coming, isn't he?'

'Yes, yes, he is.'

'Are you sure? Ben, I need him, I can't do it without him.' She started to cry.

Charming! Neither of the possible fathers were needed, and she hadn't yet mentioned Bryony, but it seemed absolutely essential to Amy that an outmoded robot was there. In nine months, we'd come a very long way indeed.

'Amy, listen to me, Tang is coming. We're both coming, we'll be with you very soon.'

'What should I do?'

'Um . . . what did they tell you to do at the birth classes?'

'They said to stay upright, breathe deeply and not panic.'

'Well, do that.'

'I'll try.'

'Sit on that ball thing you've got.'

'Good idea.'

Amy messaged while we were en route to say she'd left the door unlocked for us, so when we arrived we walked straight in.

'Amy, where are you?'

'In here.'

'Where's here?'

Tang pointed upstairs.

'Can you hear the baby, Tang? Is it OK?' I asked as we climbed the stairs.

'Yes,' he said, and I dashed ahead to get to Amy's bedroom, leaving Tang to follow in his own time.

I found Amy lying on her back on a sheepskin rug in the newly decorated nursery. She was looking at her phone.

'Amy, are you OK? What are you doing? Why are you on your back?'

'I'm playing a game.'

'You're *what*?'

'You said to stay calm, so I thought I'd play a game to take my mind off it. I just got my highest score ever.'

'I'm not sure that . . .' I started to say, but Amy glared at me. At that moment I realized that for the duration of the labour anything I did or said would be wrong, so I should just roll with the punches and do the best I could.

'I was sitting on the ball for a while, but it was boring.'

'Fair enough.'

'By the way, I've started contracting.'

'What?'

She explained about a small contraction she'd had a few minutes before.

'You're very calm about it.'

'I'm playing a game. Besides, I knew you were on your way.'

I thought it unlikely that I was going to keep up with Amy's mood changes throughout the labour, so I said nothing.

'Still haven't got hold of Roger, though.'

'We'll keep trying,' I said, but at that moment she rolled on to her side and dropped her phone, her face screwing up in pain.

'Are you OK?'

'Of course I'm not bloody OK, idiot, I'm in fucking labour!'

I went to rub her back.

'Don't fucking touch me.'

I held my hands up instantly, like I was in a bank robbery. Then Tang was by her side.

'Amy is well. Baby is well. Amy must breathe.'

Two minutes later, the contraction was gone.

'Sorry,' she said when it was over, 'I didn't offer you a coffee or anything. I'll make one.'

She tried to get up, and although I helped her into a sitting position there was no way I was going to let her deal with boiling water.

'Really, Amy, I think you've got more important things to think about right now. Don't worry about the coffee.'

She nodded.

'I do think we might need to get you to the hospital, though.' I felt like I was taking my life in my hands making the suggestion, not knowing which version of Amy was going to respond.

She agreed but said we should phone in first.

'I'll do it,' I offered, but Amy shook her head.

'They like the mother to phone so they can gauge how bad the contractions are and how close together.'

I nodded but picked up her phone to find the number for her.

'Careful, I've paused the game – I don't want to lose my score.'

On the phone to the hospital, Amy gave them a rundown of who she was, how many weeks she was pregnant (almost thirty-nine), and how she thought the labour was progressing. A minute later she hung up.

'Well?'

'They said it doesn't sound like the contractions are strong enough or close together enough to come in yet. They suggest a bath.'

'Really?'

'It's very good for pain relief.'

'OK, I'll run you one.'

I paused in thought. 'Do you want me to stay in the bathroom with you?'

She frowned. 'Of course I do. What kind of question is that?'

'It's just that, because we're not together any more . . . I thought maybe you might not want me to see you naked.'

'Ben, listen to me, you are going to be there for the birth of this child. You're going to see a baby coming out of my vagina. You seeing me naked in a bath is really not an issue.'

As I stood up from my crouching position on the floor, another contraction came. I wasn't sure what to do, but Amy offered some advice.

'Why're you just standing there? Get me some paracetamol. And go and put the fucking bath on!'

Amy spent hours in the bath. Four hours, to be precise. Tang and I sat with her, topping her up with warm water and moving the specially selected aromatherapy candles out of her reach whenever she felt a contraction coming. I wasn't allowed to touch her during the contractions, but Tang spent the time pushing her hair out of her face with his grabber (without poking her in the eye) and dabbing her forehead with a cold flannel.

When she wasn't contracting, I told her she looked good. She smiled, weakly, but I could see the compliment made her happy. I left Tang with her to go and make a coffee, at her insistence, and brought a range of food items back with me.

'I read that you should try to eat when you're in labour.'

'I don't feel like it.'

'Please try. Have a banana.'

'Ben is right,' said Tang. 'Amy bananas.'

She forced down the fruit, then another contraction came.

'Tang thinks hospital now,' the robot said.

'I'm OK, Tang,' replied Amy. 'I'm happy in the bath.'

'Amy, Tang's right, the contractions are quite close now. I really think we should just go to hospital.'

'If you think so, Tang.' She hauled herself up, and I helped her step out of the bath.

'Let me get your robe for you,' I said, disappearing out of the bathroom.

'Ben,' she called.

'Yeah?'

'I can feel the head.'

I was so proud of her in the car. She handled the contractions well, showing the controlled Amy I knew she could be. In between contractions, I told her so.

'I'm trying to hold the baby in,' she informed me, and I felt the blood drain from my face.

When we made it into the hospital, despite my protestations we were guided to triage. The midwife on duty gave us a pleasant smile and asked if I was the father.

'Yes, of course he is,' said Amy, and I glowed a bit. The midwife then looked down at Tang.

'Is this with you?'

'Yes,' I told her.

'I'm not sure a robot should be in here. Perhaps it can wait outside?'

I was about to argue, but Amy had it covered. 'NO,' she said, dangerously, then held out her hand for Tang to take.

The midwife dropped her bid to get rid of Tang and asked if Amy could try giving a urine sample, at which point she grabbed the bottle from the midwife's hand and tossed it over a tall cabinet in the corner of the room.

'I can feel the head of my baby,' she said. Without raising her voice or swearing, the menace in her tone was enough to galvanize the midwife. That tone is how she manages to win so many legal battles at work, I'm sure of it.

'OK, just hop up on to the trolley for me and we'll take a look,' the midwife said, pulling the curtain across in the little bay to one side of the room. Amy ripped off her clothes.

The midwife took one look at the naked Amy.

'Quick!' she called out. 'We're having a baby in here – get me a birthing pack!'

I peered down to see what was going on, and sure enough – there was a baby's head.

'The baby's head's sticking out, Amy!' I said. Tang stood by Amy's head, smoothing her hair. He gave me a Look.

'Can you give her anything for the pain?' I asked the midwife.

'It's far too late for that, I'm afraid. Don't worry, it'll be over in a few minutes – you'll see.'

Tang and I each held one of Amy's hands, him faring better with the crushing sensation than I did, though – all things considered – I tried hard not to show the pain.

Within minutes, there was the baby. A little girl. I knew straight away she was mine.

Roger turned up at the hospital an hour before visiting time ended – nearly twelve hours after Bonnie was born. Amy asked if Tang and I might leave her alone with him, so they could talk.

'Where was his business trip?' I said to Tang, as we went to get a coffee for me. 'Tuvalu?'

'No, Plimmooth.'

'Plymouth? How the hell do you know that?'

'Amy says. She says, "What so special about Plimmooth that Roj-urgh can't be here?"'

'Ouch. It doesn't sound like he's in her good books.'

'No.' He smiled at me.

'Tang, I know we don't like Roger, but it's not nice to wish things to go badly for people.'

He picked at his gaffer tape, so I added, 'But I can't help

feeling a bit pleased that I'm not the only one to fail Amy. At least I never did anything *this* bad.'

After half an hour, Amy messaged me to say Roger had gone and that she wanted us to come back before the hospital threw us out for the night.

'Amy, what happened with Roger?'

She shifted uncomfortably and cuddled Bonnie tightly to her. 'He's gone.'

I must have looked confused, because Amy continued.

'No, I mean properly gone. He never wanted to be a father. I don't think he ever wanted anything serious at all. I think he just thought I was a trophy that was on the same career level as him or something.'

I offered to deck him for her.

'That's really sweet, Ben, but I don't think it'll help,' she said tearily. 'Thanks, though.'

'What does that mean for you and Bonnie, though? Has he kicked you out of his house?'

'Not yet. He says I can have a few weeks to work out what to do.'

'That's big of him.'

'Isn't it?'

'I'm going to have a word with Dave about his choice of friends.'

'You'll have to get in line – I'm pretty sure Bryony's going to be first up.'

'Amy, I don't want you to think I mean anything by this . . . but would you and Bonnie like to move back to Harley Wintnam?'

'But . . . but I walked out on you. Why would you want me back in your house?' There were tears on her cheeks.

'A lot's happened since then, Amy. I'm not suggesting we

get back together. It's just . . . well, it'd be nice to have you both there. I have supplies and stuff – for a baby, I mean. I made a nursery for her . . . just in case you ever needed somewhere to go. I can get your stuff from Roger's so, you know, you don't have to see him . . .' I trailed off.

'You made a nursery?'

I nodded. Amy took my hand and pressed it to her lips.

'That's the best offer I've ever had. We'd be delighted to move in.'

Over the next twenty-four hours, I bustled about the house, cleaning. Tang clanked around with a feather duster, so by the time I went to collect Amy and Bonnie from the hospital the bottom half of both floors in the house was spotless.

'I stay here,' he told me as I was about to leave. 'I sandwiches for Amy and Bonnneee.'

'Bonnie just drinks milk for now, Tang, but thanks.'

He smiled and clanked off to the kitchen.

The moment we left the hospital, Amy said, 'I'm so looking forward to a glass of champagne.'

'Remember, Amy, motherhood is a *gift*,' I said, in my best Advice voice, and she punched me on the arm.

'I'm sure you can have a small glass,' I added. 'I'll get you one as soon as we get home – you deserve it. I've even got some brie and smoked salmon for you, if you'd like that.'

'Oh, I know, we could have that champagne Bryony and Dave gave us for our anniversary!'

'Erm . . .'

The first time Tang saw Amy breastfeed was quite something. To Amy's credit, she was very patient, but although she and Tang were fast friends by then it didn't stop her looking discomfited by the robot's fixated stare at her cleavage.

'What does Bonnie do?'

'She's feeding, Tang,' I explained.

'Feeding?'

'Yes. Milk comes out of Amy and Bonnie drinks it.' I probably could have found a better way of saying it.

Tang frowned. 'Milk comes out of Amy?'

'Yes.'

'Amy is broken?'

'No, why would you ask that?'

'Because Amy is leaking.'

'Oh no, Tang,' Amy explained, placing a small hand on his face, 'I'm not leaking. There's nothing wrong – quite the opposite. This is good for Bonnie.'

His eyes blinked in surprise.

'Though perhaps,' she said, 'you might see if you can find my breast pump from upstairs? It's in the nursery.'

'Pump?'

Amy explained what a pump looked like, and he took himself off upstairs.

He came back about ten minutes later with the breast pump stuck to the side of his head. He'd managed to switch it on, too, so there was a strange grinding and sucking noise coming from the robot as the pump tried to extract milk that wasn't there.

'Ow,' he said.

'Tang, what the hell are you doing?' Amy and I shouted at the same time, waking Bonnie.

Tang blinked at us and dropped the electronic unit, leaving the pump hanging off him, still pulsing away. I went over, switched it off and removed it from him.

'What made you put the pump on your head?'

'Wanted to see what would happen.'

'But why?'

Tang shrugged.

'Why not?'

One Sunday, my niece and nephew insisted Bryony drive them over to play with Tang. They entered the house like a pair of dervishes, dashing about the place until they found Tang, who was upstairs in his room climbing in and out of his wardrobe, which seemed to be one of his favourite hobbies (now entirely unrelated to fear of witches). Bryony went to chat with Amy while I made coffees.

'Where's my darling niece?' I heard, coming loudly from the sitting room, followed by the sounds of air kissing.

Just as soon as she could, Bryony grabbed me conspiratorially and led me to the corner of the sitting room, where we could talk. 'So what's going on with you and Amy?' she hissed. 'I've asked her but she won't tell me.'

'What do you mean?'

'Come on, Ben, she splits up with Roger the day Bonnie is born and then almost straight away moves back here. What am I supposed to think?'

'There's nothing to tell, Bryony. She split up with Roger because he didn't want to be a father and didn't want to try.'

'You didn't want to be a father, either.'

'But I do now.'

'So are you back together?'

'No, we aren't. Amy and Bonnie are here because it made sense for them to be. Roger didn't want them at his place any more and I was hardly going to leave them homeless. Besides, I want them here.'

'So you do want Amy back?'

'Look, I'd be lying if I said I wasn't thrilled when it didn't work out with Roger, but it's a delicate situation. I don't want to be a disappointment to Amy again, or to myself. Maybe one day, but not now.'

Bryony hugged me. 'Mum and Dad would have been proud of you, you know that?'

'I hope so. I didn't manage to do anything to make them proud while they were alive. It'd be nice if they thought I had a handle on things now.'

'They would have loved to hear about your trip.'

I smiled. 'I know, it's just the kind of thing they'd have done.'

'You take after them more than you think.'

'I guess so.'

'Do you remember that time they were talking about going into space?'

'Maybe we should do it on their behalf. Take Tang with us.' I paused. Then, 'I wish Mum and Dad had been able to meet Amy. And Bonnie,' I said, taking a conversational diversion.

'I do, too. But, you know what? I wish they'd been able to meet Tang, too. They'd have been totally all over him.'

'You think so?'

'Definitely. They'd have thought he was charming. Everyone thinks he's charming. The kids adore him. You were right about him.'

I didn't know what to say to this.

'Of course, it means we're all going to have to change the way we feel about other AI. I thought it was a nice idea giving our house android the day off at Christmas, but he just panicked. He spent Boxing Day following me around asking if there was anything he could do. I had to get him to paint a fence in the snow in the end, just to keep him busy.'

'Don't worry, Bryony, one step at a time, eh? You don't need to form an equal rights for AI movement yet. Just be kind to them, give them some respect.'

'Do you think that's why Roger's Cyberdriver malfunctioned?'

'Probably. But, then, I'd malfunction if I had to drive Roger around.'

'Bravo, Ben – glad to see that the old Ben hasn't been completely replaced by this new, upgraded one.'

'No, not all. Just the bits I needed to be happy is all.'

'You know, you didn't need to go halfway across the globe to make yourself happy.'

'Maybe I did.'

'Did it work? Are you happy?'

'There are still things I need to do, but, yes, I am.'

'Then that's all I can ask for.'

29

Déjà Vu

WHEN THE FAMILY WHIRLWIND HAD DEPARTED AND WHEN Amy was installed on the sofa, rocking the baby to sleep in her crib, I asked how she knew for sure Bonnie was mine.

'I got them to test . . . just so I knew for certain. I told Roger at the hospital. He was never in it for the long term, I realize, but he still wasn't happy to find out Bonnie was yours. I think it confirmed what he already knew.'

'Which was?'

'He was never going to be the right man for me. On paper I thought he fitted the bill, but in practice he didn't.'

'That's funny,' I said, 'that's exactly what I thought you reckoned about me.'

'Never.'

She let that hang in the air for a few seconds. The silence grew awkward, so I returned to talking about Bonnie.

'I knew from the second she was born. I mean, look at her – how could she have hair that ridiculous and not be mine?'

Amy smiled.

'I'm glad you got what you wanted,' I said. 'A baby, I mean.'

'I never wanted just any baby, Ben. I always wanted yours.'

'I wish I'd been able to see that.'

'I wish I'd been clearer.'

'We just never quite understood each other, did we?'

'No.'

'I didn't understand what you needed, and you didn't understand why I spent my time sitting around doing nothing.'

She nodded. 'I realize now that you were still grieving.' She was silent for a few seconds, then changed the subject. 'So does this mean you'll go back to training?'

I looked at her, a bit confused. 'Roger didn't tell you?'

'Tell me what?'

'I got a letter yesterday morning.' I opened a drawer in the bureau and brought out a large brown envelope that I gave to Amy.

'Dear Mr Chambers,' she read, 'we are pleased to confirm the renewal of your place at the college. You will once more be under the supervision of Dr Geoff Hamilton . . .'

She stopped reading and placed a soft hand on my cheek.

'Ben, this is wonderful news.'

I felt I needed to get some things off my chest, so I sat forward on my sofa and began.

'While I was away, I thought I needed to change in order to win you back. But then you said you were with Roger, and I knew I was too late. Then I realized that I wasn't sorting myself out for your benefit at all. It was for myself. Hearing that you were with someone else made me see that there was nothing I could do to be the man you wanted, so then it became a matter of deciding the kind of life I wanted, and how I was going to make it happen. I didn't expect it to include a baby just yet, but now I wouldn't have it any other way. I just hope my course at vet school in September means I can still be here for you and Bonnie.'

Amy looked at me for a long time. Her light-green eyes bored into mine. Then she broke into another smile, leaned over and kissed me near the mouth, but not quite on it. She smelled of tea and new baby.

Then, summoning up all my willpower, I slowly unwound her arm from my shoulder and sat back.

'Amy, this is not the right time.'

She looked worried.

'We hurt each other before. I don't want to risk any more pain, for either of us. Or for Bonnie.'

'What makes you think we'll hurt each other again?'

'Because you don't know if I'm the right man for you yet. I don't even know what kind of man I am, so how are we to know whether it could work between us a second time?'

Her worried frown turned to a fearful one, and she bit her lip.

I took her hand. 'I love you, and I'll do anything for you and the baby. But we both need time to adjust. I'm not about to go anywhere . . . Not this time,' I added.

Two tears rolled down Amy's cheeks. She wiped them away with the heel of her hand. Then she nodded.

'Would you like to go and have a sleep?' I said. 'I can look after Bonnie.'

'Can I?' she said, brightening.

'Of course. You can do anything you want.' And I meant it.

'Come on, Tang,' I said when she'd gone upstairs, 'let's go and show Bonnie the horses.'

Author's Note

So where did it all start?

It started with the name: *Acrid Tang*. My husband and I were discussing smells one night (we had a newborn baby in the house), and he was describing one such olfactory delight. I said 'acrid tang' sounded like a robot. We both laughed.

Regardless, I knew instantly what the robot looked like – one metal box plonked on top of the other, thrown together in haste by a mad-scientist character. I also knew Tang would have a broken friend called Ben, who would take the robot around the world, looking for his creator. By morning, I knew Ben would meet the robot in his back garden, and that this is where the story would begin. I started writing.

Having a baby – then a toddler – in the house provided a limitless supply of material for comedy, and I would be lying if I said I hadn't lifted elements of my son's behaviour and applied them to my robot, if not directly then stylistically.

It would be almost impossible to write a robot novel without considering technology. But despite being a technophile I found that the mechanics of Tang – how he was powered, whether he ate or slept – did not interest me as much as his personality. Early on, I made the decision to develop the characters of Ben and Tang and their relationship and deal with practical considerations later, except when these things led to humour. In fact, I found that they often did, so as Ben learned more and more about Tang, I did too, and robotics in general, although I knew I could never do justice to the field if I walked the path of making my robot technologically accurate.

I opted to give Tang the ability to be empathic, instinctive, stubborn and sometimes manipulative, and knew that these traits were going to be developed to a far more sophisticated level than his creator Bollinger ever intended, or in fact was even aware he could engineer. In a way, Tang's emotional sensitivity demonstrates Bollinger's lack of it. The villain's problem is the assumption that his creation would be a reflection of himself.

Tang's facial expressions have been somewhat of a headscratcher. I have always felt that Tang expresses himself largely through body language, stamping from foot to foot in excitement, for example, or that sometimes Ben sees the expressions he's expecting to see on the robot. I have sometimes likened Tang to Gromit, whose expressions and emotions come from eyes, ears and body language, since there is no mouth or indeed any language with which to convey feeling. Tang has a greater range of options available to him, but I think the principle is the same.

I imagine some readers will be disappointed never to learn the nuts and bolts of how Tang works, especially how he is powered. To them I offer the chance to decide for themselves – perhaps Tang has a solar panel that Ben never discovers? Perhaps Bollinger's chip that he is so determined to steal back holds the key to perpetual motion? Perhaps Tang simply runs off a very efficient battery whose charge has lasted longer than the scope of the novel?

Perhaps that is a different story . . .

Acknowledgements

First and foremost, my love and thanks must go to my husband, Stefan. His encouragement to pursue my lifelong dream of publication came in the face of financial insecurity, but his faith that I could make it work is the reason this book exists. Similarly, I thank Mum, Phil, Jane and the rest of my family and friends for their support, childcare and never once suggesting in the past two years that I give up my ambition and go and get a 'proper job', as writers hear so many times. I must also thank my son, Toby, for his superlative napping prowess that allowed me to write, and his unerring ability to make me laugh every single day.

Next, my thanks must go to my writing group, the Solihull Writers' Workshop, and in particular my beloved Pub Club, whose encouragement, friendship and criticism helped me write the book. Pete, Liz, Den, Sarah, Ray and Carla, I'm especially looking at you. I also consider it a massive privilege that I get to hear your work regularly.

Sincerest thanks go to my agent, Jenny Savill, who saw the potential in a beaten-up first draft of a robot and helped me to make him shine. I extend the thanks to the rest of my wonderful agency, Andrew Nurnberg Associates, who have all been working incredibly hard to sell Tang around the world.

I thank my editor, Jane Lawson, who has turned me into and made me feel every bit the professional novelist I'd always dreamed I'd be, even when I felt like I didn't have a clue what I was doing. By extension the lovely folk at Transworld, whose ability to get a book from computer to readers is a talent I'm so completely impressed by.

I would also like to throw in a thanks to the great hive-mind that is Twitter. Over the last year or so, I have made the acquaintance of many readers and writers who have reminded me that, although a lot of the time a writer works on their own, they are never really alone.

Finally, I would like to thank The Writers' Workshop, without whom I would not have the honour of writing these acknowledgements. I met Jenny at their Festival of Writing conference in York in September 2013, as a direct result of them giving me the opportunity to read my work out to a room full of people. Like others, the confidence they have given me has made Tang come alive.

Deborah Install has worked as a website copywriter. Her debut novel, *A Robot in the Garden,* is inspired by her own young son, and is backed up by copious technological research. She lives in Birmingham with her family.

Wake
Anna Hope

REMEMBRANCE DAY, 1920. A tragic secret connects three women: Hettie, whose wounded brother has been struck dumb; Evelyn, who still grieves for her lost lover; and Ada, who has never received an official letter about her son's death, and is still hoping he will come home. As the mystery that binds them begins to unravel, far away, in the fields of France, the Unknown Soldier embarks on his journey home. The mood of the nation is turning towards the future – but can these three women ever let go of the past?

'A moving novel about the aftermath of the 1914–1918 conflict . . . Unlikely that many will prove better than Anna Hope's *WAKE*'
SUNDAY TIMES

'Superb. Beautifully crafted'
IRISH TIMES

Fever At Dawn
A novel
Peter Gardos

IN JULY 1945, MIKLOS, a Hungarian survivor of Belsen, ends up in a refugee camp in Sweden. He's skin and bone, with very few teeth. The doctor gives him six months to live. But Miklos, a wilful young man, has other plans.

He whistles up a list of 117 Hungarian women in another camp. In his beautiful handwriting he writes to each of them.

One of these young women, Miklos is convinced, will become his wife . . .

The Truth According To Us
Annie Barrows

SUMMER, 1938: the small town of Macedonia, West Virginia, is celebrating its 150th anniversary, to be commemorated with parades, picnics and, most importantly, a book recounting its history. Its reluctant author, the debutante Miss Layla Beck, recently disinherited by her father, arrives in town with one goal – to get out of it as quickly as possible.

Macedonia's history seems simple enough – brief and un-eventful. Then Layla meets the Romeyns: Jottie, Willa, Felix, Emmett, a family at once entertaining, eccentric, seductive, and inextricably bound up in Macedonia's most well-kept historical secret – a secret yet to be told.